PRAISE FOR

BEST KIND OF
BROKEN

"By turns humorous and heartbreaking, BEST KIND OF BROKEN has become one of my favorites!"

—Cora Carmack, *New York Times* bestselling author of *Losing It*

"You'll fall for Pixie and Levi, just like I did!"

—Jennifer L. Armentrout (J. Lynn), #1 *New York Times* bestselling author of *Wait for You*

"Tangled with friendship, history, and heartbreak—not to mention a huge dose of humor—Chelsea Fine's New Adult novel is not to be missed! Beyond an incredibly HOT read, Pixie and Levi's longing for each other will have you rooting for them till the very end."

—Jay Crownover, *New York Times* bestselling author of *Rule*

"This book destroyed me. Tore me into little tiny pieces. But somehow with lots of laughs and some very steamy times, Chelsea put me back together again! Chelsea Fine's style is witty, visceral, and fresh. All I wanted to do was crawl inside this book and live with the characters. And now all I want is MORE."

—Chelsea M. Cameron, *New York Times* bestselling author of *My Favorite Mistake*

"Sandwiched between laugh-out-loud moments and some serious heat, BEST KIND OF BROKEN is an unforgettable story of loss and forgiveness that will leave your heart aching."

—Lisa Desrochers, *USA Today* bestselling author of *A Little Too Far*

WITHDRAWN

ALSO BY CHELSEA FINE

Perfect Kind of Trouble

Right Kind of Wrong

BEST *kind of* BROKEN

A *Finding Fate* Novel

Book One

CHELSEA FINE

FOREVER

NEW YORK   BOSTON

This book is a work of fiction. Names, characters, places, and incidents are the product of the author's imagination or are used fictitiously. Any resemblance to actual events, locales, or persons, living or dead, is coincidental.

Copyright © 2014 by Chelsea Lauterbach
Excerpt from *Perfect Kind of Trouble* copyright © 2014 by Chelsea Lauterbach
Excerpt from *Right Kind of Wrong* copyright © 2014 by Chelsea Lauterbach

All rights reserved. In accordance with the U.S. Copyright Act of 1976, the scanning, uploading, and electronic sharing of any part of this book without the permission of the publisher constitute unlawful piracy and theft of the author's intellectual property. If you would like to use material from the book (other than for review purposes), prior written permission must be obtained by contacting the publisher at permissions@hbgusa.com. Thank you for your support of the author's rights.

Forever
Hachette Book Group
1290 Avenue of the Americas
New York, NY 10104

www.HachetteBookGroup.com

Printed in the United States of America

RRD-C

Originally published as an ebook

First trade paperback edition: January 2015
10 9 8 7 6 5 4 3 2 1

Forever is an imprint of Grand Central Publishing.
The Forever name and logo are trademarks of Hachette Book Group, Inc.

The Hachette Speakers Bureau provides a wide range of authors for speaking events. To find out more, go to www.hachettespeakersbureau.com or call (866) 376-6591.

The publisher is not responsible for websites (or their content) that are not owned by the publisher.

Library of Congress Cataloging-in-Publication Data

Fine, Chelsea, 1982–
   Best kind of broken / Chelsea Fine. — First trade paperback edition.
      pages ; cm. — (Finding fate)
   "Originally published as an ebook."
   ISBN 978-1-4555-8311-9 (softcover)
  1. Young women—Fiction. 2. Man-woman relationships—Fiction. I. Title.
   PS3606.I5335B47 2015
   813'.6—dc23
                                        2014036041

To Suzie, for believing in me from the beginning.
Here's to all the endings that have yet to come.

ACKNOWLEDGMENTS

First and foremost, thank you to my beautiful readers, for believing in my stories and giving me the very best job in the whole world! I couldn't do this without you—and I wouldn't want to. Thank you for being a part of my storytelling journey.

Thank you to Lynsey Newton, for reading this story before anyone else and telling me it was worth finishing. You are more valuable than you know.

Thank you to my girls in Room 718, Heather Hildenbrand, Angeline Kace, Kate Copsey, and Heather Self, for sharing laughter and tears with me every year at UtopYA. You make this thing we call "work" ridiculously fun.

Thank you to Janet Wallace, for creating UtopYA and giving me a place to become great—and cry, of course. You always make me cry, woman! You are amazing, and I hope to someday change the world like you. One cup at a time...

Thank you to my amazing agent, Suzie Townsend (to whom this book is dedicated), for...well, everything. You make my dreams come true, and then you make them come true again. You're kind of like a genie. A really rad New York genie.

Thank you to my editor, Megha Parekh, for making this book what it is. You are brilliant, and I'd be lost without you.

Thank you to my good pal Kristen, for the many years of friendship. I would be a crazy person without you. I mean, sure. I'm a crazy person *with* you, but that's beside the point. PRIME RIB!

Thank you to my siblings, Kiele, Heath, and Jorden, for constantly showing me what unconditional love is capable of. We are winners.

Thank you to Cameron, my very first friend. You keep me together, which isn't easy, and you do it with honesty and humor. I love you, I love you, I love your guts.

Thank you to my wonderful mom, for being the best mother in the universe. You have always been there for me, no matter what, and because of you my life has been beyond blessed. Oh! And thanks for reading this book and crying in all the right places. You get me, Mama. You totally get me.

Thank you to my grandparents Johnny and Milly, for a lifetime of love and encouragement. Thank you for letting me run through the sheets on your clothesline and dream out loud on your porch swing. Your home is where my heart learned how to fly, and I love you both more than words could ever say.

Thank you to my incredible children, Kiana and Caleb, who inspire me to believe in everything—including myself. Dream big, my littles. The stars are yours.

And finally, thank you to the man who is the other half of my soul. Brett, you never cease to amaze me with your patience and wisdom, and I could not do any of this without you. Thanks for sharing the human experience with me and for encouraging me to find more than what I see. Here's to all the adventures ahead!

BEST *kind of* BROKEN

I

PIXIE

*I*f my bastard neighbor uses all the hot water again, I will
    suffocate him in his sleep.

I listen as the shower finally goes off and huff my way around
my room, gathering my shower supplies. I don't politely wait for
him to leave the bathroom, oh no. I stand outside the bathroom
door—which has steam escaping from the crack at the bottom—
with a carefully applied scowl and wait.

Still waiting.

The door swings open to a perfect male body emerging from a
billow of hot fog. His dark hair is loose and wet and frames his face
in a haphazard way that manages to look sexy despite the fact that
he probably shook it out like a dog before opening the door, and of
course he's wearing nothing but a towel.

Kill me now.

I peek into the bathroom, totally pissed, and block his exit with
my body. "A thirty-minute shower, Levi? What the hell?"

A smile pulls at the corners of his mouth. "I was dirty."

Oh, I bet.

"I swear to God," I say, "if I have to take another cold shower—"

"You shouldn't swear to God, Pix." He brings his face close to mine and the steam from his skin dampens my nose and cheeks. "It's not nice."

This close up, I can see the tiny silver flecks in his otherwise bright blue eyes and almost feel the three-day scruff that shadows his jaw. Not that I want to feel his scruff. Ever.

I curl my lip. "I want a hot shower."

"Then shower at night."

"I'm not kidding, Levi."

"Neither am I." His eyes slide to my mouth for a moment—a split second—and there it is. The electricity. The humming vibration that never used to exist between us.

He snaps his eyes away and pulls back. The damp heat from his body pulls away as well, and some stupid, primal part of me whines in protest.

"Now, if you'll excuse me…" He waits for me to move out of his way. I don't.

I jab my finger at his chest. "I haven't had a hot shower for three days—"

Cupping my upper arms, he lifts me off the floor and moves me out of his way like I'm light as a feather. Then he walks the ten paces down the hall to his room and disappears inside without a look back.

Jackass.

With a muttered curse, I stomp into the small bathroom and try not to enjoy the smell of spearmint wafting into my nose and settling on my skin. Damn Levi and his hot-smelling soap.

My freshman year of college ended two weeks ago, and since Arizona State dorms don't allow students to stay during the summer, I had to find a new place to live and, consequently, a job. So I started working for my aunt Ellen at Willow Inn because one of the job perks—and I use that term loosely—is free room and board.

And my free room shares a hallway and a bathroom with the only person I was hoping to avoid for the rest of my life.

Levi Andrews.

Hot guy. Handyman. My long-lost…something.

Ellen conveniently forgot to tell me that Levi lived at the inn, so the day I moved in was chock-full of surprises.

Surprise! Levi lives here too.

Surprise! You'll be sleeping next door to him.

Surprise! You'll be sharing a sink, a shower, and a daily dose of weird sexual tension with him.

Ellen is lucky I love her.

Had I known that Levi lived and worked here, I never would have taken the job, let alone moved in. But Aunt Ellen is one conniving innkeeper and, honestly, my only other option was far less appealing. So here I am, living and working right alongside a walking piece of my past.

Since we're the only two resident employees, Levi and I are the only people who sleep in the east wing—a setup that might be ideal were it not for the giant elephant we keep sidestepping during these epic encounters of ours.

Memories start creeping up the back of my neck, and a hot prickle forms behind my eyes. I quickly blink it back and turn on the shower, scanning the bathroom for safer things to focus on.

Little blue dots on the wallpaper.

Purple flowers on my bottle of shampoo.

Dots. Flowers. Shampoo.

With the threat of tears now under control, I thrust my hand into the shower and relax a tinge when hot water hits my fingers.

Stripping off my pajamas, I step into the spray with high hopes, but water has just hit the right side of my neck when it goes from warm to ice-cold.

Sonofabitch.

There will be suffocation tonight. There will be misery and pain and a big fat pillow over Levi's big fat scruffy face.

Biting back a howl of frustration, I turn off the water and wrap a towel around my half-wet body. No way am I taking another cold shower. I'll just have to be unclean today. I hastily grab my stuff and yank the bathroom door open just as Levi leans into the hallway.

He's traded in his towel for a pair of low-slung jeans but hasn't gotten around to throwing on a shirt, so I have to watch his chest muscles flex as he grips his bedroom doorframe.

He looks me over with a smirk. "Done so soon?"

I flip him off and enter my room, slamming the door behind me like a fourth grader.

I throw on some clothes, pull my hair into a messy ponytail, and step into my paint-stained sneakers before looking myself over in the mirror. Ugh.

I tug at the V-neck collar of my shirt for a good twenty seconds before giving up and changing into a crew-neck shirt instead. Much better.

My phone chirps on the dresser, and I knock over a jar of paint-brushes as I reach for it. As I pick up my phone, paintbrushes go rolling off the dresser and onto the floor, where they join piles of discarded clothing and crumpled college applications. I glance at the text message and frown.

Miss you.

It's from Matt.

Miss you too, I text back. I do miss him. Sort of.

Call me. I have news.

I start to call Matt but pause when I hear Levi's footsteps in the hallway, making their way back to the bathroom. I hear him plug something in, and the sound of his electric razor meets my ears. I set my phone back on the dresser as a wicked smile spreads across my face.

Levi should know better by now. He really should.

Casually moving around my room, I plug in every electric item I own and wait until he's halfway through shaving. Then I turn everything on at once. The electricity immediately goes out and I hear the buzz of his razor die.

"Dammit, Pixie!"

Ah, the sweet sound of male irritation.

Plastering on an innocent look, I open my door and peer across the hall to the bathroom. Levi looks ridiculous standing in the doorway in just his jeans—still no shirt—glowering at me with half of his face shaved.

He stiffens his jaw. "Seriously?"

I mock a look of sympathy. "You really should charge your razor every once in a while." I exit my room and move down the hall, singing out, "Have fun rocking a half-beard all day."

As I head down the stairs, the wet side of my ponytail slaps against my neck with each step. Another smile pulls at my lips.

If Levi wants to play, it's on.

2

LEVI

*T*welve days.

Pixie's been living here for only twelve days and I already want to stab myself with a spoon. Not because she keeps blowing the fuse, though that reoccurring shenanigan of hers is certainly stab-worthy, but because I can't do normal around Pixie.

But fighting? That I can do.

After pulling a shirt on, I march downstairs and out the back door. The large lavender field behind the inn sways in the morning breeze, and thousands of purple flowers throw their scent into the wind, reminding me of things better left forgotten. Things I used to have locked down. So much for all that.

I blame Ellen. Maybe if she'd given me a heads-up about Pixie moving in, I could have prepared better.

Another breeze blows by and shoves more lavender up my nose.

Or maybe not.

The sky hangs above me, bright blue and free of clouds, and the early sun slants across the earth, casting a long shadow behind me as I walk the length of the building. I squint up at the white siding and notice one of the panels is cracked, which is nothing new.

Willow Inn is nearly one hundred years old, and parts of it are just as broken as they are picturesque. It's a quaint place, with white cladding and a wraparound porch beneath a blue-shingled roof, and it sits on ten acres of lavender fields and swaying willow trees. It has two wings of upstairs rooms and a main floor with the usual lobby, kitchen, and dining space.

The newly remodeled west wing has seven bedrooms, each with its own bathroom. That's where all the guests stay.

The east wing has yet to be remodeled, which is why Ellen allows Pixie and me to stay there and why I'm a live-in employee. Along with my other handyman duties, I'm also helping Ellen gut the old east wing so she can have the area remodeled to accommodate private bathrooms in every room.

I reach the fuse box at the edge of the inn and, flipping a breaker I'm far too familiar with, restore electricity to the east wing.

Fortunately, all the gutting and redesigning requires the east wing to run on its own electricity and water supply, so guests are never affected by my hot water usage or Pixie's electricity tantrums, but damn. We really need to find a less immature way to be around each other.

I turn and follow my shadow back to the door, holding my breath as I pass the purple field. The wooden floors of the lobby are extra shiny as I walk inside, which means Eva, the girl who cleans the main house, probably came in early and left before anyone saw her. She's tends to work stealthily like that, finishing her work before anyone wakes. Sometimes I envy Eva that. The solitude. The invisibility.

Back inside, I see a figure up ahead, and a string of curse words line themselves up on my tongue.

Daren Ackwood.

I hate this douche bag and he's headed right for me.

"What's happening, Andrews?" He gives me the chin nod like we go way back. We went to the same high school and I think we had a class together senior year, but we're not pals. He looks over my partially shaved face. "What the hell happened to you?"

"Pixie," I say.

He nods and looks around. "Is Sarah here?"

Sarah is Pixie's real name. The only people who've ever called her Pixie are me and Ellen and . . .

"Why?" I cross my arms and eye the case of water he's carrying. "Did she order water?"

Daren is the inn gofer, delivering groceries and linens and anything else the place needs, so unfortunately he's here twice a week with his preppy-boy jeans and nine coats of cologne. And he's always looking for Pixie.

"No, but you never know." He lifts a cocky brow. "She might be thirsty."

"She's not thirsty."

He looks over my facial hair again. "Oh, I think she's thirsty."

And I think Daren's throat needs to be stepped on.

"Morning, Levi." Ellen walks up with a smile and hands me my To Do list for the day. Her long dark hair slips over her shoulder as she turns and throws a courteous smile to the gofer. "Hey, Daren."

"Hey, Miss Marshall."

As Ellen starts talking to me about the fire alarm, I watch Daren's eyes cruise down her body and linger in places they have no business lingering in.

More than his throat needs to be stepped on.

Ellen Marshall is a very attractive forty-year-old who's used to guys checking her out. Not me, of course—Ellen's like family to me and I respect her—but pretty much any other guy who sees her instantly fantasizes about her, which pisses me off.

"...because the system is outdated," Ellen says.

"Routine check on the fire alarms," I say, my eyes fixed on Daren, who is still ogling her. "Got it."

"Can I help you with something?" Ellen smiles sharply at him. "Looks like your eyes are lost."

He readjusts his gaze. "Uh, no, ma'am. I was just wondering where Sarah was."

"Sarah is working. And so are you." Her hazel eyes drop to the case of water. "Why don't you take that to the dining room? I think Angelo is stocking the bar this morning."

He gives a single nod and walks off.

Ellen turns back to me and looks over my face. "Nice beard," she says. "Pixie?"

I rub a hand down the smooth side of my jaw. "Yeah."

She lets out an exasperated sigh. "Levi—"

"I'll check out the fire alarms after I finish shaving," I say, quickly cutting her off. Because I don't have the time, or the balls, to undergo the conversation she wants to have with me. "Later." I don't give her a chance to respond as I turn and head for the stairs.

Back in the bathroom, I stare at my reflection in the mirror and shake my head. Pixie timed it perfectly, I'll give her that. My facial hair is literally half-gone. I look like a before and after razor ad.

I think back to the irritated expression on her face and a small smile tugs at my lips. She was so frustrated, waiting outside the bathroom door with her flushed cheeks and full lips and indignant green eyes...

Why does she have to be so goddamn pretty?

I turn on the razor and run the blades down my jaw, thinking back to the first time I saw those indignant eyes cut into mine. My smile fades.

Pixie was six. I was seven. And my Transformers were missing.

I remember running around the house, completely panicked that I had lost my favorite toys, until I came upon Pixie sitting cross-legged in the front room with my very manly robots set up alongside her very dumb dolls.

I immediately called in the authorities—"Mom! Pixie took my Transformers!"—and wasted no time rescuing my toys from the clutches of the pink vomit that was Barbie.

"Hey!" She tried to pry them from my hands. "Those are the protectors. They kill all the bad guys. My dolls need them!"

"Your dolls are stupid. Stop taking my things. Mom! *Mom!*"

Haunted eyes stare back at me in the mirror as I slowly finish shaving.

I wish I would have known back then how significant Pixie was going to be.

I wish I would have known a lot of things.

3

PIXIE

I enter the kitchen and grab my apron off the wall. It's bright yellow with dozens of red cherries all over it and trimmed with ruffles. It's the happiest apron in the world and my name is written in permanent marker on the front. Gah.

"Good morning!" Mable looks up from a bowl of egg yolks with a smile. Her thick, gray hair is pulled back in a bun, and her chubby cheeks are rosy like always. She reminds me of a sassy Mrs. Claus—minus the furry red dress and spectacles.

"Morning." I tie the yellow-and-cherry madness around my waist before moving to the industrial-sized sink in the corner to wash my hands.

I've known Mable, and pretty much every other inn employee, my entire life. Nearly everyone Ellen hires is from our hometown— a tiny dot on the map named Copper Springs. It's a typical small town, with struggling business owners, troublemaking teenagers, and churchgoing folks who pray for both. And it's a place I'd be fine never visiting again.

"How did you sleep, dear?" Mable asks, whipping the yolks with a fervor I do not share. The kitchen and I are not friends; we are simply allies in a time of war. The only position Ellen had available this summer was "prep cook," and as much as I hate cooking, I hate being broke more.

But I don't suck at cooking. Years of making food for myself and my mother, a woman who thought feeding me was a grueling chore, taught me how to put a meal together without disastrous results. At least now I'm getting paid to slave away in a kitchen.

"Aside from the blasting noise of Levi's TV?" I say. "Fine."

She eyes my half-wet ponytail. "Cold shower this morning?"

Everyone who works at the inn knows how Levi and I fight. Not just because sometimes we slam doors and yell but because everyone who works at the inn knows about *us*.

For the first few days after I moved in, this really bothered me. Because I knew the real reason the employees whispered, and the real reason made my chest hurt. But I don't give a damn anymore. If Levi and I provide some sort of tragic entertainment for them, so be it.

I look down at the list of menu items for the morning. "Yes. The spawn of Satan strikes again."

Mable laughs like she always does when I talk about Levi, her round cheeks glowing. Even though she's like sixty, I'm pretty sure she has a cougar crush on him. And if I didn't love Mable so much, it would totally gross me out.

"That Levi is something else," she coos.

"Something selfish, maybe."

She pours the yolks into a pan. "Something delicious."

Gross.

But true.

"What's delicious?" Haley, the curvy thirty-five-year-old who runs the front desk, enters the kitchen through the back door and peers into a bowl of chocolate chips before popping a few in her mouth. Haley gossips almost as much as Mable. She also has a minor addiction to chocolate.

I watch her shovel more of the chips into her mouth.

Okay, major.

"Levi," Mable answers, wagging her eyebrows.

"Mmm. He is scrumptious." Haley tucks her shoulder-length black hair behind her ear and gives me a dirty smile. "I'd lick him from head to toe and back to head again."

Good God. It's like I work at Hotel Horny Women.

"Levi is not scrumptious," I say, trying to think about omelet ingredients instead of how Levi's stomach muscles rippled when he leaned into the hallway this morning. "He's annoying."

"He doesn't annoy me. Does he annoy you, Mable?" Haley says.

"Not one bit." Mable smiles.

Haley reaches for more chocolate chips and I smack her hand away. "That's because you two didn't grow up with him and practically live at his house your entire childhood."

An uncomfortable silence falls over the room.

"No," Mable says after a few moments, her voice carefully quiet. "We didn't."

Haley clears her throat and forces a smile at Mable. "Got any of last night's cake left?"

Leave it to Haley to break up the tension with dessert.

I busy myself getting things ready for breakfast as Mable and Haley start gossiping about the guests.

Most guests who visit Willow Inn are retired folks who come to the country for fresh air and a quiet retreat. And some of them stay for weeks or months at a time, and make it an annual occasion.

So several of the guests staying here this summer have visited before and, since Willow Inn is a small establishment with semi-regular clientele, they sometimes get to know one another, and things around here can get rather friendly.

Mable's voice is dripping with drama. "…and then Marsha Greenberg told Betsy Peterson that she was no longer welcome at their bridge table because of the *incident* with Mr. Clemons." She looks up from the cutting board, scandal on her face, onions in her hands. "Can you believe that? Especially after what happened with Vivian Whethers last month…" She jabbers on, Haley bobbing her head emphatically as she forks chocolate cake into her mouth.

You'd think senior citizens relaxing at a quaint inn in the middle-of-nowhere Arizona would be low-key and rather boring, but they're just as bad as college kids. They flirt and drink and sleep with one another, and it's just nasty. Entertaining. But nasty.

Haley gasps at Mable's ongoing story, which I've failed to follow because I'm busy over here actually working.

"No, she did *not*." Her mouth drops open in disbelief.

"Oh, honey, you know she did," Mable says, and makes a disapproving *mm-huh* noise. "I told you that woman was trouble."

Haley shakes her head and takes another bite. "Trouble, indeed."

Wow. Remind me never to vacation at an inn when I'm older, for fear my daily activities might become the talk of the kitchen staff.

The old-fashioned phone by the door rings with a merry *ding-a-ling-a-ling*, and I can't help but glance at the thing. It's red and giant and hideous and it *ding-a-lings* loud enough to wake the dead. Ellen thinks the spinning dial and long coiled cord add charm to the inn. I think Ellen's full of shit and just hasn't gotten around to replacing the prehistoric device yet.

On the second ring, Mable wipes her hands on her apron—which is an appropriate shade of light blue and features no fruit or fringe—and answers the antique phone with a chipper "Good morning!"

She listens for a moment before promptly disappearing through the swinging door that leads to the dining room, speaking in hushed tones. Ever the gossip, Haley strains to hear what Mable's saying through the door but gives up and turns to me.

"So." She finishes the last bite of chocolate cake. "I hear you and Levi get to have weekends off this summer. Lucky ducks."

Hardly.

I'm pretty sure the synchronized time off is part of Ellen's diabolical plan to get Levi and me to spend some quality time together. Joke's on her though, since I plan on ditching this place every weekend. No need to hang around Levi and our pet elephant more than necessary.

"Lucky, indeed," I say dryly.

She rounds up all the chocolate crumbs on her plate and starts smashing them with her fork until they stick. "Got any big plans this weekend?"

"Not really. Just hanging out with Jenna and Matt."

She licks the fork. "Who's Matt?"

I pull some bell peppers from the fridge. "My, uh, boyfriend."

I have this weird habit of saying "uh" before the word "boyfriend." I can't help it. It's like saying "Jiminy" before "Cricket" or "more" before "cowbell." It just falls out of my mouth.

"Oh right, the *boyfriend*. I almost forgot about him," Haley says. "Are you sure he's real? You don't ever talk about him and I've never seen you guys together."

"He's real." I rinse off a knife and start cutting vegetables. "It's just hard with him living down by ASU and me all the way out here."

Arizona State University is a hundred miles south of my hometown, and somewhere right in between the two, on a desolate stretch of freeway, stands Willow Inn. So yeah. Middle. Of. Nowhere.

She licks the fork again even though it's squeaky clean. "Does Levi know about this real boyfriend of yours?"

I slant my eyes at her. "I can't imagine how he wouldn't, what with the gossip grapevine around here in full bloom. And I don't know why he'd care, anyway. He's like a brother to me." My heart cringes at the word and I try not to overthink why.

"A brother." She slowly nods. "Right...right—shoot!" She looks at the clock and drops her shiny fork. "I've got to get to the front desk. See ya." She hurries from the kitchen just as Mable swings back in from the dining room.

I watch Mable hang up the phone without making eye contact with me, and my gut tightens. She moves to the counter and begins putting together a breakfast quiche. I continue chopping vegetables. Minutes pass.

With a slow inhale, Mable calmly says, "That was your mama on the phone."

I slice a bell pepper in half. "My mama can go to hell."

My statement makes the room feel thick, so I look up and try to lighten the mood. "Hey, and maybe while she's there she can ask the devil if he wants Levi back." I smile brightly, but the thickness lingers.

There's a reason I chose not to go back home after school

ended, and that reason gave birth to me nineteen years ago and has regretted it every day since.

Mable finishes layering the quiche and slides the dish over to me to finish. "She says she's coming to see you in a few weeks. She wants to have dinner with you."

I grab some cheese from the fridge and mutter, "Well, that should be fun."

She gives me a tight smile because she knows how not-fun Sandra Marshall can be. One of the side effects of being from the same tiny town.

The door to the dining room swings open again and this time Levi walks through, a box of tools in his hand.

Cougar Mable immediately lights up. "Morning, Levi!"

"Morning, Mable." He smiles at her. He scowls at me.

I notice his face is now clean-shaven and a part of me misses his scruff—what? No. NO. I do not miss his scruff. Missing scruff is for weirdos.

I scowl back at him and start grating Swiss cheese.

"Where's the fire alarm in here?" he asks in his work voice. It's a very different voice than his get-out-of-my-way voice or his if-you-want-hot-water-wake-up-earlier voice.

Mable points to the wall, looking far too happy to be of service, and I keep my eyes down as he moves past me. As I sprinkle cheese over the quiche, I can't help but notice how grated Swiss kind of looks like white scruff.

I'm not a weirdo.

Quiche finished, I turn to start sautéing vegetables and my gaze automatically darts to Levi. He's so distracting. His arms are all raised, and his shoulders are all broad, and he's fixing crap, and it's just…it's just…annoying.

You know what else is annoying? The fact that the freaking fire alarm is right by the stove.

With a huff and a puff and some choice words in my head, I grab my sliced bell peppers and force my feet to the stove. I throw the vegetables into a frying pan, grab a wooden spoon, and ignore Levi's close proximity.

My body hums.

I ignore that too.

I steal a glance in his direction and watch as the corded muscles in his forearm flex as he unscrews something on the alarm box. Why does he have so many muscles in his forearm? That can't be healthy.

I drop my eyes to the frying pan and focus on bell peppers, because bell peppers are interesting and they don't have backs the size of Alaska or copious amounts of forearm muscles.

The forearm muscles that I'm not thinking about lightly brush my shoulder, and the humming inside my body knots together and zips around like a bumblebee on crack.

I casually turn down the heat on the stove, like that's the reason I'm suddenly a human vibrator, and go back to stirring. Levi goes back to screwing.

Bell peppers.

I'm thinking about bell peppers.

Levi brushes against me again, except this time his forearm grazes my breast and my body immediately goes wild, like I'm some love-starved teenager, and the humming dives low in my belly and the stove gets hotter and my breaths get shallow and suddenly bell peppers are the sexiest vegetable on earth.

Welcome to Hotel Horny Women, home of scruffy cheese and sensual produce.

From the corner of my eye, I catch his Adam's apple bobbing with a nervous swallow, which can mean only one thing. The boob brush was an accident.

Well, crap.

If he had been trying to cop a feel with his Hulk-ish forearm, I could have responded with some kind of snarky "you're a pervert" comment. But it wasn't on purpose and somehow that makes it sexier, and now the cracked-out bumblebee is buzzing in my nether regions and my hands are starting to tingle and why the HELL is this stove so hot?

I turn the burner down another notch and take a slow, deep breath. I have a boyfriend. A great boyfriend. So this sexual frustration I feel around Levi is nothing to get my bee-loving panties in a bunch about. I just need to calm down.

Levi lowers his arm for a moment, his eyes still on the alarm, and stretches his neck.

Ah, the neck stretch. The universal sign of stress. Well, at least I'm not alone in my frustration. My hot, distracting, pants-are-so-inconvenient frustration.

Wait, *what?*

Who said anything about pants? I am NOT thinking about pants—or lack thereof. Damn you, bell peppers!

I toss the wooden spoon to the side and move back to the counter, where the threat of being turned on by a handyman or, you know, a sautéed vegetable is much less severe.

I stare at the scruffy quiche and bite back a groan. What was I thinking, living under the same roof as Levi? There's no way I'll survive the summer.

Hell, I can barely survive breakfast.

4

LEVI

*S*exual tension is like a ruthless pigeon. Feed it once and it will follow you around forever. It never tires or goes on vacation. It just *lingers*. And it's lingering all over me every time I'm around Pixie.

Like right now, in the kitchen.

I carefully keep my eyes fixed anywhere but on Pixie's blonde hair or the yellow bow of her apron at the base of her back as I finish my task. But I can still hear her. The shuffling of her stained sneakers as she scoots around the counter, the soft inhale-exhale of her concentrated breathing as it flows between her lips…

Yeah. I have to get out of here.

I quickly finish with the fire alarm and spend the next hour checking the remaining ones around the inn before heading for Ellen's office.

Along with the lobby, kitchen, and dining room, the down-stairs has two small converted bedrooms. One is the library, where guests play chess beside tall windows and pretend to enjoy books by Ernest Hemingway, and the other is Ellen's bright yet incredibly cluttered office.

The wooden planks just outside her open office creak as I step into her doorway, and she looks up from a pile of papers, sticky notes, and pens.

"What's up?" She smiles.

"The fire alarms look to be in working order, but they're pretty ancient," I say, not stepping fully into the room for fear of being swept into one of her famous conversation traps. "You might want to think about installing a whole new system."

She nods and chews on the end of a red pen. "Yeah, I figured as much. I'll add it to my ever-growing list of *New Crap the Inn Desperately Needs.* Thanks for checking everything."

"No problem." I turn to leave.

"Your mail's still at the front desk," she says to my back, halting my exit. "It's been collecting dust for almost three weeks now."

I slowly turn back around. "Is that right?"

Her eyes narrow. "Don't make me open it up and read it out loud to the waitstaff. 'Cause I will, and then you'll have to face the music."

I scratch my cheek, which feels oddly bare since shaving. "I've never understood that phrase. There's nothing scary about music."

"Says the guy who's afraid of his mail."

I cock my head. "Must you bust my balls at every given opportunity?"

"Someone needs to." She smiles, but it's half-sad. "Just pick it up so I don't have to listen to Angelo complain about how untidy the desk is, okay?"

Angelo's incessant need for things to be clean and organized spills over to all areas of the inn, not just his bar. And it is *his* bar, as he likes to remind everyone.

"I'll be sure to pick it up today," I say, wiggling a hinge on the door I've just realized is loose. "Anything else?"

"Just the lobby chandelier." She grins.

I sigh. Chandeliers are a pain in the ass. They're heavy and cumbersome and contain more wires than any lighting fixture should. I honestly have no idea why people still use them. And by people, I mean Ellen.

Her grin widens.

"You don't have to look so amused," I say.

"Oh, but I do," she says. "I find the look on your face right now *very* amusing."

Ellen knows of my severe distaste for her choice in lighting fixtures. She doesn't care. *It's pretty and it adds charm*, she says. There's nothing charming about a five-hundred-pound hanging lantern.

"Whatever," I say, moving down the hall. "I'll fix your precious chandelier."

"I love you!" she calls after me.

I shake my head but can't help smiling.

After turning off the main electricity, I retrieve the inn's only ladder from the maintenance closet and set it up in the lobby beneath the chandelier. It wobbles as I climb to the top, and I make a mental note to add "ladder" to Ellen's *New Crap* list. This one is probably older than the alarm system.

I carefully begin unhooking a few chandelier wires under the close and obnoxious scrutiny of one of the inn regulars, Earl Whethers.

I'm not sure what it is that draws retired men to my side while I'm fixing things—maybe they find handiwork fascinating, or maybe they're horribly bored—but I sometimes feel like the Willow Inn sideshow.

Take Earl for instance. He's *pulled up a chair* in the lobby and is now watching my every movement with expectant eyes.

And for my next act, I shall fall from this prehistoric climbing contraption and break both legs—with no hands, because they'll be dangling from this hanging candelabrum after being torn from my body during my amazing fall!

I should set out a tip jar.

Earl scratches his white-whiskered chin. "You sure you know what you're doing, son?"

"Yes, sir."

The skin around his faded blue eyes crinkles as he squints up at me. "You look too young to be running the maintenance around here. How old are ya?" He crosses his arms over his short and stocky frame, once probably stacked with muscle, and leans back. His balding head shines a bit in the light streaming in from the lobby windows.

"Almost twenty-one," I say, shifting the chandelier to my left arm and clenching my jaw under its weight. I find the problem wire and slowly untangle it from the others.

"Did you disconnect the electricity before climbing up there?"

"Yes, sir."

"Did you check for frayed ends before you started pulling at those wires like a chimpanzee?"

A chimpanzee?

"Yes, sir."

"Did you—"

"Leave the poor boy alone, Earl." Vivian, Earl's wife and one of the inn's more outspoken guests, enters the lobby with her short blue-black hair wrapped in pink curlers and her thin, pursed lips coated in pink lipstick. She's tall and slender and manages to look poised even when she's gripping a martini and slurring her words— which is often. "He doesn't need you distracting him."

"I'm not distracting him, Viv. I'm helping him." Earl gestures to me, like I'm an idiot.

"Uh-huh." Vivian glances up at me through a pair of dark brown eyes. "You just go on and do your fixing, honey. Don't mind my meddlesome husband." She walks to the front desk and starts complaining to Haley about the bar's hours.

"Meddlesome, my ass," Earl mutters.

Vivian and Earl travel from Georgia every summer to stay at Willow Inn. Their visits are never shorter than four weeks and they make themselves right at home, hence the pink curlers.

They make an odd couple, with Vivian being a good five inches taller than her husband and at least a hundred pounds lighter. Side by side, they look like a pink giraffe and a white-whiskered monkey.

Earl watches me wobble. "Have you ever had professional electrical training, son?"

Good Lord.

I steady myself and keep my eyes on the wire. "Did you catch the game last night, Earl?"

He starts rambling about idiot referees, and I know I've bought myself a few minutes' reprieve from the tutorial on everything I'm doing wrong.

"All I'm saying," Vivian's Southern drawl carries through the lobby, "is the bar should be open before noon."

"Yes, well. I'm sure Ellen has her reasons for the bar's hours." Haley lowers her voice a smidge. "It's probably because of everything that happened with Mr. Clemons last year."

"…things are different now." Earl's voice pulls me back.

"What's that?" I ask.

"I was just missing the good ol' days."

For the next ten minutes, Earl picks apart my electrical skills and chats my ear off about how the world was so much better when he was young and how people these days don't know anything about hard work. He says these things to me as I'm balancing on the world's oldest ladder while holding a lighting device that weighs more than I do.

"What can I say," I grit out as I finish with the chandelier. "We're a lazy generation."

I climb down the ladder and turn the electricity back on before returning to the lobby. Earl is still in his front-row seat, eagerly waiting to chat my ear off about politics.

Like hell I'm touching that subject.

On my way to the light switch, my eyes catch on a flyer pinned to the activities board by the front desk. It's an advertisement for the annual Copper Springs Fourth of July Bash, one of the few festivities my hometown actually does well.

Every resident attends, and the town spares no expense on live music, games, food, and pyrotechnics. This will be the first year since I was nine and had a mad case of chicken pox that I won't be in attendance.

I flip the light switch, and the chandelier lights up in all its ridiculously complicated glory.

The Amazing Levi, ladies and gentlemen. I'll be here all week.

Just as I'm turning to walk back to my ladder of doom, Pixie rounds the corner and slams into me. Chest to chest, body to body.

The smell of lavender wraps around me as she looks up through startled eyelashes and, for a moment, it's thirteen months ago and everything is okay. Nothing is broken. Nothing is lost. Her green eyes slowly sink into mine, soft and safe, and I like it. I like it a lot.

Panic floods my veins.

Desperate to rectify any hope, or memory—or God, anything *good*—I see reflected in her gaze, I give her an annoyed look and make my voice as sharp as possible. "Can I help you?"

The softness vanishes and a sneer twists her face. "Nope."

She moves past me with a jerk and my heart starts to hammer. I head back to the ladder, my thoughts jumping in and out of memories.

The fourth grade when Pixie would drink all my chocolate milk when I wasn't looking. Junior year when she would sing along with the radio at the top of her lungs as I drove her home from school.

It feels like a lifetime ago. It feels like yesterday.

"Mm, mm." Earl stares after Pixie's retreating form. "I love watching that girl walk away." He makes another appreciative throat noise, and my fists tighten around the rickety ladder as I fold it up.

"Easy, Earl," I warn.

I swear to God, between Ellen and Pixie and all the assholes that gawk at them, someone's going to get their face smashed in.

A gravelly laugh tumbles from his mouth. "Nothing about that girl looks easy."

I sigh. Tell me about it.

After a few more repairs, I finish for the day and head back to the front desk to collect my mail. Angelo is leaning over the counter, speaking to Haley in his thick Jersey accent.

"Vivian Whethers was trying to get a martini from me before breakfast had even started. That woman can drink her share of liquor, I'll tell ya that much." He leans closer to Haley like he's spilling some huge secret. "And I swear to God she leaves her sticky fingerprints all over my bar top on purpose."

Haley giggles. "She probably wants to leave her sticky finger-prints all over more than just your bar top."

"Well, that's too bad for her." He winks at Haley. "'Cause Vivian ain't my type."

I try not to make a face as I step behind the desk. I'm pretty sure Angelo and Haley are sleeping together, which is unsettling because Haley is sweet and bubbly and Angelo is... well, terrifying.

He's nearing fifty, but carries himself like an angry forty-year-old. He's built like a bulldog and resembles one too, with his shaved head, golden canine tooth, oversized jowls, and sleeves of tattoos. I wouldn't be surprised if he was a mob boss with minions and a shovel resting beside a bulk supply of hand sanitizer in his trunk.

"How goes it, Levi?" he says, turning his head in my direction.

"It goes." I frown at the beige envelope topping the pile of mail Ellen set aside for me. Its placement is no accident.

"Good to see you're finally picking up your letters," he says. "They're an eyesore, ya know."

"Oh, I know," I say. They're hurting my eyes as we speak.

Gathering the stack, I go up to my room and toss the top letter on my desk, where it joins five other beige envelopes. All unopened. All making my chest tight.

I'd rather fix a thousand chandeliers than deal with one of those envelopes.

5

PIXIE

I will pee on your bed." This is my big, scary threat.

Levi used all the hot water again this morning, so I marched into his room in a rage. I never go into Levi's room. It's a personal rule of mine.

Our relationship—if you can even call it that—works because it's simple. We never talk about the past. We sometimes argue. And we always stay out of each other's business.

But here I am, in the business of Levi's room, gripping my towel as cold, wet hair drips down my back. I haven't had a hot shower for four days. *Four days*. This nonsense has got to stop.

"You seem stressed." Levi, whose jeans are so low on his bare hips that I can tell he's going commando, tilts his head. "You know what you need? A nice hot shower...oh wait." He gives me an impish smile.

I might just pee on his bed right now.

"Joke all you want, Levi. But the next time you're out fixing a broken window or a fire alarm, I will sneak into your room and pee on your bed."

I'm dead serious here. If I don't get a hot shower tomorrow, I really will pee on his bed. Or at least find a cat to come pee on his bed. But either way, there will be urine on his sheets and I won't feel bad about it.

The impish smile grows. "I can think of better things for you to do in my bed, Pix."

Silence.

If his plan was to make me uncomfortable by flirting with me, it totally backfired. Because the second those words left Levi's mouth, his body stiffened in awareness and the space between us became electric. So now we're staring at each other's lips and we're both breathing heavier than necessary, and neither of us is really dressed.

I shift in my towel and feel the material slip a bit as I pull my eyes from his mouth and try to coax my face into a look of something less *come-and-get-me* and more *ew-you're-pathetic*.

I'm gearing up for my comeback—which will be brilliant and kick-ass as soon as I nail it down—when his eyes drop to my chest, and all the air leaves the room.

He's not looking at my cleavage.

He's looking at the raised red scar peeking out from the top of my towel. The scar that cuts diagonally across my torso, running from my left hip bone to the top of my right breast. The scar I normally keep hidden under strategic shirts and dresses.

It's hideous and jagged, but I don't hide my scar because it's ugly. I hide it because it's a reminder of pain and loss. And Levi's eyes are fixated on it.

Pain. Loss.

My heart starts to pound and I no longer care that my shower was cold or that we have weird sexual tension. I don't care about Levi's forearm muscles or the way the bathroom smells like his soap.

I care about my scar and what it means. It hurts me. It hurts him.

It's the only thing we still have in common, the only thing we absolutely avoid, and now it's glaring at us—marked on my skin in permanent red, rising along with each of my breaths.

The horror in his eyes has me hollowed out and helpless, and I have no words. Unable to speak, I numbly turn and head down the hall to my room, shutting myself inside a millisecond before my body starts to shake. I lean against the door and try to take a deep breath.

I'm fine.

I'm fine.

I hear Levi's bedroom door slam closed with a heavy *thud*, and the vibration runs down the wall and shakes against my back.

He's not fine.

I'm not fine.

6

LEVI

*F*uck.

I clench my fists until my arms are shaking. I want to hit something, and I want to scream. God, do I want to scream.

Fuck.

I shove my hands in my hair. I grit my teeth. I stare at nothing.

I slam my fist into the wall and throw my weight behind it, welcoming the sharp sting that smacks against my knuckles and travels up my arm. I punch the wall again and this time the plaster cracks, giving me an odd sense of satisfaction. Another punch and the drywall gives way, leaving a hole, as crimson streaks of blood run between my fingers. I beat at the wall until the pain catches up with me and my fist begins to ache and throb.

Standing back, I rub my uninjured hand across my mouth and survey the destruction. A giant black hole stares back at me as a few leftover pieces of bloodstained drywall crumble to the floor.

Ellen is going to be pissed I broke the wall. But hell.

I'm the fucking handyman.

7

PIXIE

I avoid Levi for the rest of the week and he avoids me too. The only real benefit of all the avoidance is the abundance of hot water every morning. Either Levi has decided he no longer needs showers or he's taking them when I'm not around.

I should be happy about this.

I'm not.

Looking into the bathroom mirror, I frown as a blonde curl falls in my face. I didn't straighten my hair after my hot shower this morning, so now it's back to its natural state of wavy chaos. I haven't worn my hair curly in nearly a year, so the weightlessness of my untamed waves feels foreign as I run a flat iron down my locks until there are no more curls.

My phone beeps on the counter and I look at the screen. Crap. Another text from Matt. I keep forgetting to call him back.

Are we still on for tonight?

Yep! I text back, making sure to add a smiley face. I really suck at the whole keeping in touch thing.

It's Saturday night and I have plans to meet Jenna and Matt in Tempe to go barhopping. I spent all week looking forward to ditching the inn, but for some reason I'm no longer excited about leaving.

Rummaging around in my makeup bag, I find my eyeliner and lean over the sink as I carefully start applying it. I hate putting makeup on. I find it to be a waste of time and, frankly, a bit dangerous. Like right now, all it would take is a minor hand cramp for me to poke myself in the eye and render myself permanently blind. Who the hell cares if my eyes are lined in black or green or chicken poop? No one, that's who.

"Hey, you," comes a silky voice behind me.

Jenna, my heavily tattooed college dorm mate, enters the bathroom wearing skintight pants and a black shirt that shows off the caramel skin of her flat stomach. Her dark brown hair is straightened and pulled back into a long, sleek ponytail. Her eyes are shadowed in dark purple, she's got a spiked bracelet on her left wrist, and every piercing she has—including her nose and the seven holes running up each ear—is filled with either a diamond stud or a small black hoop.

Jenna always looks like an angry rock star.

She steps out of her shoes and climbs onto the bathroom counter with the grace of a jaguar before sitting cross-legged beside the sink. "Miss me?"

I lower the eyeliner and look around in confusion. "Where did you come from?"

"Yes," she says. "Your answer is supposed to be, 'Yes, Jenna. I missed you like crazy and I wish we were still living together.'"

When the semester ended, Jenna got to move into a fancy apartment with two of her cousins, while I got to shack up in the hallway of frigid water and awkward tension. So not fair.

"Yes, Jenna. I missed you like crazy," I repeat. "Now, where did you come from?"

"The girl at the front desk told me you'd be up here," she

says. "She also told me the woman in room three is a lush and that someone named Earl has a foot fetish. Chatty lass, that one."

"You have no idea." I return to lining my eyes with the sharp stick of potential blindness. "But why did you drive all the way out here? I thought I was meeting you in Tempe."

She shrugs. "I thought I would pick you up so you wouldn't have to drive. And besides, I wanted to check out your new place." Her eyes cruise around the bathroom. "So this is where you live?"

"Yep. I sleep in the bathtub."

"Nice." She nods. "And where does the handyman sleep?"

I shoot her a look. "Please tell me you didn't come all the way out here to meet Levi."

"I didn't come all the way out here to meet Levi."

"Jenna."

"Oh, come on," she pleads. "He's like this mythical creature from your past that you keep hidden away. He's like a puzzle to me. A jigsaw puzzle. One that's missing like four pieces and the picture guide that goes on the box. I must meet this puzzle."

When Jenna and I first met last year, I wasn't looking to become friends with anyone, let alone a crazy Creole girl with ink all over her body and a plethora of voodoo dolls in her suitcase. Yet somehow she managed to crowbar her way into my life—and the vault of my past—and pry out a few scraps of sensitive material, such as my history with Levi.

"He's not a puzzle or a fictitious creature, and I'm not hiding him," I say. "How's Jack?"

Shrewd golden eyes narrow at me. "And she changes the subject. Curiouser and curiouser."

I point the eyeliner at her. "Don't talk like Alice in Wonderland. You know that creeps me out."

She takes the eyeliner from my hand and starts to add another layer to her catlike eyes. "I don't want to talk about Jack. I want to talk about Levi."

"Not happening."

"Why not?"

"You know why."

"Come on—"

"Stop," I say more emphatically than I mean to.

She stares at me for a second. "Fine."

I turn around to examine my backside in the mirror. I spent all week in ratty jeans and stained T-shirts, so I'm trying to live it up tonight. And for me, living it up means wrapping my butt in a short piece of leather. I'm out of control.

"Is this skirt too short?" I tug the skirt down, but my booty is too bootylicious to be properly contained so the material bounces right back up.

"No. You look hot." She lowers the liner. "But what's with the granny sweater?"

She means the cardigan I threw on to hide my scar. I'm not ashamed of my scar—not at all—but I don't want to run into Levi with my chest exposed and risk a repeat of the other day. A knot forms in my stomach and I swallow to keep it from rising into my throat.

I glance at Jenna and shrug. "I was cold."

With a few more fruitless yanks of my skirt, I turn back around and start digging through my stuff for another deadly makeup utensil.

"So," Jenna says casually as she goes back to lining her eyes. "How's the sex thing going with Matt?"

Oh geez.

"It's not," I say.

She scrunches her nose. "Was your first time really so bad?"

My sexual experience is limited to a one-time disaster with a guy named Benji Barker—that was his name, I kid you not—and it was drunk and sloppy and just... bleh.

I always thought losing my virginity would be a memorable event with fireworks and theme music and maybe a parade afterward. But no. It was more like, *Hey, so thanks for the horribly awkward sex. Let's never speak again.*

"No," I say, searching the depths of the black hole that is my makeup bag for my mascara. "I mean, it was uncomfortable as hell, but it wasn't bad. I just haven't been able to get into it with Matt yet. Or the guy before him. Or the guy before that guy." I shrug again. "Maybe I'm a lesbian."

My fingers finally wrap around a tube of mascara and I pull it out in triumph.

"You're not a lesbian," Jenna says.

"I could be."

"No way." She looks at me with the eyeliner in midair. "If you were a lesbian, you would totally check me out. You never check me out."

"Well, maybe you're not my type," I say in between batting lashes and coats of black goo.

She rolls her eyes. "Oh please. I'm everyone's type—"

"Pixie!" calls someone from the hallway.

Levi.

I haven't heard his voice for three days, and all my senses immediately go on alert. My eyes snap to the mirror just as his reflection appears in the bathroom doorway, and my heart stammers at the sight.

He's wearing dark jeans and an untucked shirt that fits his frame perfectly. The top two buttons of his shirt are undone, showing off the tan skin of his thick throat, and I suddenly sympathize with vampires everywhere. Who *wouldn't* want to take a bite out of that?

WHAT?

Where did that thought come from?

"Hey, Pixie. Ellen wanted me to…" Levi's words trail off as his gaze runs down my body and lingers on my butt. Desire flashes in his eyes, and my insides start to heat and tighten in response.

Our eyes lock in the mirror.

Am I blushing? Crap, I'm blushing.

He clears his throat and starts again. "Ellen wanted me to give these to you. She says you lost your own set? These are her backups." He lays a set of inn keys on the counter by my hip, his hand so close to my belly I can feel his body heat seeping in through my leather skirt.

I nod. I swallow. I try not to pass out.

Or you know, bite him.

"Oh, right. Thanks," I say, my voice all ragged like I just finished running a marathon or something. I'm so cool.

"I'm Jenna," Jenna says loudly, holding out her hand.

Levi and I blink away from each other, and he raises his eyebrows like he hadn't noticed Jenna until right that second.

"Oh, hey," he says in his smooth-operator voice. He has many voices. "I'm Levi."

"Levi," she repeats with a Cheshire cat grin as they shake hands. "It's *very* nice to meet you."

I glare at her, but she refuses to acknowledge me.

"Right." He glances at me. "Good to meet you too." He

pauses. "So yeah. Later." Then he rigidly moves from the bathroom mirror.

I stare at the empty hallway that replaces him, suddenly feeling empty myself.

"Ohmygod." A low chuckle falls from Jenna's mouth and she drops her head back. "I totally get it. Everything makes so much *sense* now." More laughter. "You're so not a lesbian."

I pull my eyes away from the hallway and toss the mascara back into my bag. "Whatever." I look at my reflection with a grimace. My straightened hair looks all wrong.

"*Whatever*," she mocks, going back to her eyes. "You conveniently forgot to tell me that our mysterious Levi is HOT."

"Please shut up." I pull my hair up. Still wrong.

"Mega hot. Why did he call you Pixie?"

I let my hair fall back down. "It's a nickname he gave me when we were kids. Quit layering on eyeliner. You look like a walking cry for help."

"No, I don't," she says, putting the liner away and examining her reflection. "I look like a misunderstood bad girl who paints poetic pictures about death."

I blink at her. "Exactly."

Picking up all my belongings, I leave the bathroom as Jenna steps back into her shoes and follows after me. In my room, she throws herself belly-first onto my bed and leans over the side, eyeing the three paintings I have drying under the window.

"Whoa." She crawls off the bed and over to the nearest canvas, running a finger along the edge. "These are beautiful." She touches another one. "Depressing as hell, but beautiful."

"They're not depressing." I search through the mess of my room for my oversized purse until I find it wedged between an unopened box of stuff from my dorm and a stack of out of state college pamphlets.

"Everything you paint is depressing. It's all black and white and gray." She squints at a dark painting of a tree.

"Yeah, well. I like the contrast." I start cramming clothes into my purse. I'm not sure what my overnight plans are yet, but I'm pretty confident no one will be willing to drive me all the way back to the inn later.

Jenna flops back down on the bed and watches me shove a cotton T-shirt and a tiny black thong into the bag. "Are you thinking about staying at Matt's place tonight?"

I throw in a toothbrush, a hair tie, and a book. "Maybe."

There's no pressure with Matt. He's one of those rare good guys.

My palms start to sweat as I search for my favorite black bra, find it, and toss it into the purse along with a pair of socks and a tube of sunscreen.

She plays with her bracelet. "You guys have been together for like four months, right?"

"Uh, yeah."

"If you're not comfortable with Matt, then maybe you should move on."

I look up. "Who says I'm not comfortable with him?"

"Your vagina."

I let out a snort because, gah, it's true. My vagina is super picky and, apparently, still mad at me about the Benji thing.

I keep shoving random items into my bag like I'm packing for Gilligan's Island and not an overnighter in a metropolitan city. Do I need a scarf? No. Am I cramming one into my bag just in case there's a flash blizzard? Yep.

"Seriously, Sarah." Jenna sits up. "Why are you still dating him?"

Because having a boyfriend is a normal thing to do and I'm desperate for normal.

"Because he's loyal and patient and kind." I sound like I'm describing a pet dog. "Matt's a great guy," I add. "I just need to relax and get the sex thing over with."

She crosses her arms. "You realize how stupid that sounds, right?"

I point at her. "Don't you dare get preachy on me, little Miss Sex-a-lot."

"First of all"—she holds up a finger—"I may have had a lot of sex, but I haven't had a lot of partners. Second"—she adds another finger—"every guy I've slept with has been a choice I made without any hesitations. And third"—three fingers—"we're not talking about me. We're talking about you."

"Yeah, well. I'm sick of talking about me."

"Sarah doesn't want to talk about something real? Shocking." She pins me with her gaze. "Sex is not a requirement for a relationship. It's a perk. And if you don't want to get perky with Matt, then don't."

"I want to get perky with Matt."

"You sure?"

"Yes." Kind of.

"Okay. In that case..." Standing up, she reaches into the pocket of her rock-star jeans and pulls out a massive handful of condoms before sprinkling them into my purse, where they slip down among the many scarves, pop-up tents, and emergency snakebite kits I've deemed critical for tonight's bar crawl.

I packed for a deserted island. Jenna packed for a porno.

I blink at her. "Did you just rain condoms into my purse?"

"You betcha." She smiles. "But seriously, if you change your mind about tonight, you and your grandma sweater can always crash at my place, okay?" She sits back down. "So how are things going with Levi? Have you two talked yet?"

"Can we not do this right now?"

"You never want to do this. You're always so weird about him."

"I'm not weird about him."

"You're super weird about him."

"Can you just stop?" I snap.

"Stop what? I just want to know if you guys—"

"I don't want to talk about Levi!" I snap again. Like a bitch. I just bitch-snapped her.

The room goes silent.

With a slow nod, Jenna quietly says, "Okay. We won't talk about Levi."

Guilt washes over me and I hang my head. I shouldn't get snippy with Jenna like that, and yet I do it all the time.

"Sorry." I bite my lip.

She shrugs and gives me a small smile. "Don't worry about it." Without further argument, she drops the Levi thing and smoothly transitions into a conversation about her summer plans.

Jenna. She's good at being patient. She's good at being my friend.

And sometimes that scares the crap out of me.

8

LEVI

*Z*ack is living in a mansion. That's really the only word to describe the enormous house I'm walking through. I've already passed three staircases, two grand pianos, and an indoor pool—and I'm not even halfway through the first floor.

Loud music bounces off the marble floor and vaulted ceiling as I weave through the heavy crowd. There are people everywhere. Drinking, dancing…riding life-sized lion statues while topless… business as usual for a Zack Arden house party. And a perfect distraction from all the things I can't seem to escape at the inn.

Something furry wiggles past my leg and I look down to see a goat. A *goat*. Just hoofing along like it's perfectly normal for a farm animal to be kicking it at a house party.

I blink for a moment and then continue through the drunken mass of college students until I eventually find a kitchen the size of a restaurant and, thus, my ridiculous best friend. Zack is standing on a chair in the center of the large room with his arms raised above a group of gathered partygoers and a red plastic cup in one hand.

With short black hair, a Latino complexion, and a set of dimples girls can't seem to resist, Zack is a legitimate lady-killer—and he knows it. I watch as he winks at a nearby brunette before turning back to the crowd with a smile in his dark brown eyes.

"My good people!" he shouts, "There is plenty of beer to go around, but there is only *one*"—he holds up a finger dramatically—"cornhole champion!"

The crowd raises matching red cups with drunken cheers and hollers, everyone eager for the tournament to begin.

This is Zack's thing. Cornhole.

The game of cornhole is basically a glorified beanbag toss where players take turns tossing bags at a hole in a wooden board. Throw in a few rules and drinking consequences, and you've got yourself a party favorite. I'm pretty sure Zack would abandon his potential football career if it meant he could play professional cornhole for the rest of his life.

From across the room, he catches sight of me and tips his chin. I nod back before I realize his face has morphed into a shit-eating grin.

Ah, hell.

"And for your viewing pleasure," he yells above the noise, pointing to me, "I give you ASU's favorite quarterback, Levi Andrews!"

Eyes and red cups turn in my direction, and more cheering ensues. I shoot him an I-hate-you smile as dozens of people rush toward me.

I spend the next twenty minutes fielding an onslaught of pats on the back, sexual invitations, and inquiries about where the hell I've been for the past six months—a question I still don't know how to answer—before untangling myself from the well-meaning strangers and heading to the backyard.

Backyard is an understatement.

What I'm looking at resembles more of a golf course with a water park. Acres of green grass stretch behind the house broken up by a series of pools and small waterslides. I'm surprised I didn't have to pay admission at the door and sport a neon wristband to get back here.

The cornhole tournament is already under way, with a dozen boards set up in a large, flat square of grass just off the back porch. Ornate lanterns hang strategically about the yard, shining brightly on the game and spectators below as music plays into the night from a well-hidden surround sound system. And a guy wearing a Speedo, a top hat, and a plastic margarita cup around his neck is manning a large scoreboard on the patio.

Zack's voice sounds into the yard. "And...Kirkland misses the board completely like a wimpy little girl. Drink up, douche bag."

Looking to the side, I see Zack standing on a raised wooden deck holding a megaphone to his mouth as he officiates the tournament.

"Jensen!" he scolds. "Quit rubbing the beanbags on your balls for good luck. I've seen you with the ladies, dude. Your balls are anything but lucky."

I make my way over and step onto the deck just as he's lowering the megaphone.

"Thanks for the spotlight introduction," I say. "You're a dick."

Zack smiles and hands me a beer from a cooler at his feet. He gets himself one as well. "Good to see you too, fucker. What took you so long?"

"Your shitty directions." I open the beer and take a drink. "Did I see a goat earlier?"

"Yeah. That's Marvin."

"Sure."

"I'm goat-sitting him all summer for this hot brunette I met at mass on Sunday."

I squint at him. "You're not Catholic."

He grins. "I know."

This is Zack's other thing. People.

He's a chronic people-meeter. Church, school, sporting events, estate auctions, gas stations. He goes everywhere and meets everyone.

"Is that where you met the poor sucker who owns all this?" I gesture at the yard and mansion. "Church?"

"No. *That* guy I met at a poker tournament. He sucked at blackjack, so this place is mine until fall semester starts."

"So you have a goat and a mansion all summer?"

"Yes. My life is awesome." He pulls the megaphone back up. "I saw that, Angela. Your pretty ass has to drink." He scans the lawn and scowls. "Motherfu—someone take the beanbags away from Jensen!" Pause. "You're out, Mathers! Bested by the tiny chick with the weird yet strangely erotic blue pigtails." He turns back to me and lowers the megaphone again. "So where've you been lately? I've been inviting you to shit for weeks."

I shrug. "I've been busy."

He takes a drink. "Funny how you didn't seem to get busy until your new neighbor moved in. How is our little fairy, anyway?"

My thoughts go straight to Pixie's ass in that little black skirt. "I don't know."

"Is she still yelling and painting and breaking hearts?"

"I don't know."

"God, she was a riot." He chuckles. "Is she still going to ASU?"

"I don't know," I bite out, bringing the beer back to my mouth.

"Ooh. Sensitive." He eyes the cuts on my knuckles. "What happened there?"

I glance at my busted hand. "Some drywall pissed me off."

"So you beat the shit out of it with your throwing arm?"

"Something like that."

"Right," he says slowly. "Speaking of your throwing arm…" He moves his eyes back to the tournament. "Training starts soon."

I try to look uninterested. "So?"

"Coach says you're not enrolled." He keeps his eyes on the game while I silently curse Coach McHugh and his fat mouth. "Now, how the hell are we supposed to have a kick-ass team when our quarterback doesn't even go to the school?"

I rub the back of my head. "I was kicked out, remember?"

"No." He draws out the word. "You were put on academic probation. Dean Maxwell said all you have to do—"

"I know what he said."

"Good." He nods once. "Then do it and I'll see you at practice. In the meantime, let's get you relaxed." He smiles at an attractive blonde walking by. "Hey, Savannah. Have you met Levi?" He pulls her closer and gestures to me. "Levi is our starting quarterback."

The blonde's face brightens at the word "quarterback," and she turns eager eyes my way. "Nice to meet you, Levi."

Zack leans over and says, "You're welcome, buddy," before bringing the megaphone back to his lips and resuming his officiating duties. "Aw, come *on*, Jensen…"

He steps away, leaving me with the blonde, who has already started giggling and touching my arm for no reason. Let the distracting begin.

9

PIXIE

*T*wo college girls with fake IDs walk into a bar...
So cliché.

The bouncer didn't even check out the birth dates on our IDs. He simply checked out Jenna's butt, which beats mine in the booty-licious department by at least two jiggles, and waved us in.

Behold, the power of the booty.

I follow the cherry blossom tattoos on Jenna's exposed lower back as we weave through the almost-drunk, pretty-drunk, and has-anyone-seen-the-floor-oh-wait-I'm-lying-on-it-drunk crowd.

I ditched the cardigan at the door and shoved it in my Purse O'Plenty, so I'm looking perfectly slutty in my push-up bra and low-cut tank top. I don't usually take such liberties with my wardrobe, but I was feeling feisty when I got dressed tonight.

Jenna and I squeeze our way through a cluster of people and my feisty boobs accidentally brush against a nearby stranger. His eyes drop to my chest.

I had my boobs long before I had my scar, so I know the difference between a guy checking out my rack and a guy feeling sorry for me. And this guy's not checking out my rack.

Whatever.

I move forward and keep my eyes on the cherry blossoms.

They're pretty. Very girly and delicate and not at all like Jenna, yet somehow they suit her. I wonder if cherry blossoms would suit me.

"You made it." Matt's face lights up as we approach the bar. He's already there with his roommates, Ethan and Jack, saving us seats. He pulls me in for a quick kiss, then pulls back and whistles as he looks me over. "Nice outfit." His eyes rove over my very visible scar.

I quirk a teasing brow. "Am I showing too much tragedy?"

He meets my eyes and smiles. "Not at all. I think you look badass. Like a pirate or something."

"A pirate?"

"Yeah. Like a sexy Captain Hook."

"He's the least sexy pirate ever."

"Okay, Jack Sparrow, then," he says.

I frown.

"Captain Morgan?" He looks supremely uncomfortable, like he's not sure if it's okay to joke about my scar, and I almost feel sorry for him.

I wrinkle my nose. "How about we stop comparing me to sea criminals and alcohol mascots?"

"Brilliant idea. I'm a stupid boy." He smiles at me, but I can see small red splotches of nervousness creeping up his neck.

"What do you think you're doing?" Ethan looks at Jenna as she squeezes into the barstool between him and Jack. "You can't sit next to me. You'll ruin my game."

"What game?" she says. "You're a white guy wearing a gold chain. You have no game."

"Oh, I have game. And you're cock-blocking it. How am I supposed to pick up hot chicks when a hot chick is sitting right beside me?"

Jack leans over. "For starters, maybe don't call them *chicks*."

"I'm not cock-blocking you," Jenna says.

"Yes, you are," Ethan says. "You do it every time. Switch seats with Jack."

"Oh my God, you're such a girl." She stands back up and waits for Jack to move.

"Musical barstools. Yeah, that's not lame." Jack grudgingly scoots over so he's next to Ethan, and Jenna is next to him, and I'm next to Jenna, and Matt is next to me.

"Happy now that my hotness isn't screwing up your sex life?" Jenna glares at Ethan.

He gives a slight bow. "Me and my penis thank you."

"God." She rolls her eyes and leans over to me. "We need new friends, Sarah. Like immediately."

"Hey," Jack says in offense. "What did I do?"

"You're Jack," she says. "That's enough."

Jenna and Jack always bicker, but I see the way they look at each other and I'm pretty sure the only thing keeping them from tearing each other's clothes off at any given moment is the fact that they're usually in public. And really, I wouldn't be surprised if that didn't hold them back much longer.

"What can I get you guys to drink?" The bartender—who looks like she could be a supermodel—directs her question at Jenna and me, but her eyes travel to Matt. I can't really blame her.

Matt's pretty in that Abercrombie kind of way. All blue jeans and designer shirts, perfectly styled blond hair and a killer smile. He's stunning, really. And he's totally humble about it, which makes him even hotter.

I'm not really sure why he's with me. He could do better. Not that I'm hideous or anything, he just…he could do better.

When I first met Matt, he pursued me for weeks with his soft brown eyes and dashing manners. I was such a wreck at the time and had no interest in starting a relationship with anyone. I'd gone on a few disappointing dates and decided that boys were the last thing I needed in my life, but something about Matt made me feel...normal. And soon enough, all that charm and goodness of his wore me down until I was agreeing to a first date. Then a second. Then a third. Before I knew it, he was calling me his girlfriend and I wasn't correcting him.

He made me feel unbroken and I clung to the illusion.

We place our drink orders, and the supermodel bartender gives Matt a sexy smile before walking away. He pretends not to notice and squeezes my knee affectionately.

"So how's life on the prairie?"

Bell peppers flash in my mind.

"Boring," I say. "How's your internship at Edgemont going?"

Matt's an artist, but of the left-brained variety. The kind that likes math and perfection and drawing ninety-degree angles on everything. His internship at Edgemont Design is the perfect launching pad for his future career in architecture.

"It's great, actually." His hand moves from my knee to my thigh, sending a pleasant warmth up my leg. "I'm making some good contacts. Hopefully, they'll consider keeping me as a part-time employee through the year, just until I graduate."

The hope in his eyes makes me smile. "They'd be crazy not to. You're amazing."

I mean it. Matt really is talented, and I have no doubt he'll go on to build epic skyscrapers and buildings and whatever else he sets his mind to, because he's that kind of guy. A go-getter. An overachiever.

He's only two years older than me, but he's a good decade ahead of me in maturity and, well, life in general.

He's got a list of life goals and a ten-year plan and probably some kind of color-coded flowchart to keep them both straight.

Me? I've got a fake ID and a loose itinerary for tomorrow. No flowchart.

"Thanks, babe." He wraps an arm around my shoulder and pulls me closer. He always smells good. Clean.

The drinks arrive, and I suck on the straw in my ginger ale while Jenna takes a gulp—not a sip, a *gulp*—of her Manhattan. Jenna orders cocktails like an old man and drinks them down like a desperate housewife. I love her.

Matt turns to me and lowers his voice. "So you didn't call me back all week."

I make an apologetic face. "Sorry about that. I just got so busy. You have news?"

He nods. "Remember Tyson, my roommate last semester?"

"Yeah," I say, watching as Jack reaches for the plastic spear of olives garnishing Jenna's drink. She swats his hand away.

"Well, he works at New York University now, in the admissions department," Matt continues. "And he said he might be able to get your transfer application reviewed again."

I whip my eyes to him. "Really?"

I've been applying for transfers all year. California. Colorado. New York. Virginia. I just need something else. Something other than Arizona and all the familiar people and places I can't hide from.

New York was the first school to get back to me with a denial letter. The others followed suit shortly after. Fickle undergrads majoring in art don't seem to be at the top of every university's wish list for transfer students.

So the idea that Tyson could get my application reviewed again—that I might be able to transfer after all—is thrilling. For the most part. My palms start to sweat.

He nods. "Yeah, but he needed you to submit an appeal by last Thursday."

My heart dips, but comes right back up. "Well, that sucks. I guess I'm stuck at ASU for now."

"Giving up so easily?" He smiles at me mischievously.

"What?" I eye him.

His smile grows. "I submitted an appeal for you."

"What?" I squawk.

He nods excitedly. "Tyson said I could fill one out for you and, since you refused to answer your phone, I took the liberty of doing just that. So there's still a chance you could transfer there this fall. We could go to school together."

My mouth falls open. "Wow."

Matt starts his graduate program at NYU next semester, which explains the smile on his face. But me…I'm equal parts thrilled and panicked.

"Aren't you excited?" His smile slips.

"Yes." I force my mouth into a grin and nod. "Very excited."

Balls of stress tighten in my stomach.

Jack goes for the olives a second time and Jenna slaps his hand. Again. "Back off my olives or I will voodoo your ass."

Even though Voodoo is a peaceful religion that has nothing to do with cursing people, Jenna takes full advantage of others' ignorance and plays the Voodoo card every chance she gets.

"Oh please. You're not going to voodoo my ass." He tries again, only to be smacked harder.

"Keep playing," she says. "See if you wake up with all your

appendages." Her eyes drift over to me and she cocks her head. "You okay?"

I lift my brows. "What? Yes. Yeah, I'm okay." I push out a smile. I'm okay. I'm totally, completely okay.

Hours go by until everyone is drunk except for Matt and me. I've never seen Matt get wasted. He's too responsible for that.

Again, why is he with me?

We don't mention NYU or school again, so the stress balls in my stomach slowly unwind until I'm actually enjoying myself.

When Jenna, Jack, and Ethan decide to move the party to the bar next door, Matt and I opt to head to his place to watch movies. Matt cracks joke after joke on the way there, and by the time we reach his apartment, my stomach hurts from laughing so hard.

After choosing a movie, we go to his kitchen and make popcorn. Five minutes and four handfuls of salty popcorn later, we're kissing against the fridge, the wall, the counter…until we're kiss-walking our way back to his bedroom. It's dark in here, the only light being the soft orange glow filtering in through the window from the streetlamps outside.

We fall on his bed and the kissing turns into something more, which is right about the time my eyes—and my mind—start to wander.

Why is his room so clean all the time? I mean, seriously. Everything is tidy and organized. His desk is spotless. His shoes are in neat little pairs in the closet. It's not natural.

And why is it so quiet in here? He lives in a campus apartment, for God's sake. His neighbors should be throwing a kegger and blasting music through the walls.

Before I know it, our shirts are gone and his hand moves down my rib cage as he settles on top of me, trailing kisses along my neck.

I stare down his broad back and frown. I should probably do something here, like sink my nails into his shoulder blades or grab his butt or something.

Meh.

I slowly flatten my palms against his back in a symmetrical way and try to relax my arms. Why is he always so warm? And why the frack is he still sucking on my neck?

He just ate popcorn and now he's tonguing my throat and leaving a trail of buttery germs in his wake. And I swear to God his scruffy jaw is going to rub my skin raw.

The butter germs start to spread lower as my eyes wander back to his desk. There's not even a pen out of place. Left-brained artists are so weird. Should I have my eyes closed? Why is he breathing so hard?

Focus, Pixie. Focus.

His hands run over my body but avoid my scar completely. He never touches my scar. I'm not sure if it's because it freaks him out or if he's just being careful. Probably a little bit of both, which is unfortunate because, well, my boobs are right there and I don't want my boyfriend to be afraid of my *boobs*—which are flawless, by the way. I might have a nasty gash marring the valley between the girls, but the boobies themselves are pristine. Still. Matt avoids my chest for the most part. Such a shame.

Is that a piece of gum on his ceiling?

My eyes flutter a bit as his hand glides over my thigh and up between my legs. My skirt has ridden up, so I'm pretty much just lying here in my panties, holding on to his overly warm back as his jeans press against the inside of my legs.

He brings his popcorn tongue up to my mouth and kisses me deeply. I force my eyes shut and try to concentrate on kissing him back as the scruff on his jaw scratches against my face like a bristle brush. I just know my face is going to be all red after this. Maybe I'll buy him a new razor. But not an electric one. Those aren't always reliable.

Who invented electric razors? What guy was shaving his face one day and thought, *You know what this flat knife against my throat needs? A battery. Perhaps I should invent a razor with a cord—*

Matt yanks back from me and sits up on his knees with a frustrated exhale.

"What?" I sit up and cover my boobs. "What's wrong?"

I notice his hair looks perfectly styled, not a single blond strand out of place. Aren't people supposed to have messed-up hair after sex—or almost sex? That's probably my fault. Shoot. I need to remember to mess up his hair.

He runs a hand over his mouth. "Maybe I should ask you."

"Uh..." I glance at his spotless desk again.

"You're not into this, Sarah."

"Yes, I am," I say quickly. Too quickly. "Sex. Let's do this." I roll my hips in an embarrassingly unflattering way and clap my hands together like I'm breaking up a football huddle.

Go team, go!

He shakes his head. "This happens every time. It's like the moment we start getting hot, your head goes somewhere else. If you don't want to have sex, that's fine. Really. But I can't keep doing this *almost-but-not-really* thing when you're not into it. It makes me feel like an ass. Like I'm pushing you or something."

"No, no, no. You're not pushing and you're not an ass at all. It's me. I swear I can do better. I will do better."

I stare at his bare chest, shadows of orange lining his hard muscles, and try to feel something naughty.

Nothing.

Maybe I *am* a lesbian.

He sighs. "I don't want you to do better, Sarah. I want you to *want* it."

"I do want it."

Right?

Right?

He looks at the bed for a moment before slowly climbing off and pulling his shirt back on. "Why don't you get dressed and we can talk about this later, okay?" He attempts a smile, but all I can do is nod back.

I hide my face in my hands and let out a long, heavy breath. Why don't I want to have sex with my superhot and totally sweet boyfriend?

What is wrong with me?

10

LEVI

*W*hat is wrong with me?

I pull into the inn, sexually frustrated and generally pissed at the universe as I park in the back of the lot. Everything was going fine with Savannah—that was her name, right? Savannah? Susanna?—until she mentioned she was an art major, and any hotness I'd hoped to indulge in with her instantly evaporated.

I turn off the engine and run a hand through my hair.

Art? ART? What the *hell*, universe?

The girl had a streak of green paint on the inside of her elbow, for God's sake. And she was blonde. And smelled like flowers. She was two stained sneakers and a green-eyed scowl away from being Pixie, so I smoothly excused myself from her company and went in search of a different distraction. But by that time every girl in the mansion was either trashed or taken, and really, who was I kidding? No distraction in the world would numb the hot ache in my chest.

Damn Pixie. Moving in next door and fucking up my sex life.

As I exit my truck, a black car pulls up to the front of the inn. I look at the time. 3:35 a.m. This is either a senior citizen arriving very early for check-in, which has happened, or it's some kind of trouble.

I stand in the shadows of the tall willow trees beside the lot and watch as the passenger door opens and a figure climbs out.

Despite the darkness and the distance between us, I instantly know it's Pixie. Her straightened hair hangs down her back, shining in the moonlight against her sweater as she steps forward in the same man-eating skirt she had on earlier.

Trouble it is.

A guy I've never seen before climbs out of the driver's seat, and I straighten my shoulders.

Maybe he's a cabdriver in the nicest cab ever. Maybe he was the designated driver tonight and Pixie got a little tipsy. Maybe he's a gay friend who gives her pointers on what to wear, like that damn skirt.

The designated gay cabdriver leans down and starts kissing Pixie.

Or *maybe* he's the icing on this cake of despair I've been eating all night.

Watching them kiss makes the ache burn hotter, and I absently push a hand against my sternum.

They part ways and Icing Boy drives away as Pixie lets herself inside the inn. I wait a moment before leaving the shadows and following after her. The front door creaks a little when I step inside. The lights are dimmed and there's not a soul around as I quietly walk through the lobby toward the east wing staircase.

Pixie's at the foot of the stairs, silently cursing as she rummages around in the large purse slung over her shoulder. The floorboards beneath my feet groan as I move forward, and she whips her head up, relaxing a twinge when she sees me.

"Oh," she says. "Hey."

I slow my pace. "Hey."

Her purse buzzes and she drops down on the bottom stair, effectively blocking my path upstairs as she starts clawing through its contents.

I shove my hands in my pockets and wait. "Lose something?"

She sighs heavily as she digs. "I can't find my phone because I packed liked a hoarder but I know it's here because it keeps ringing and I'm pretty sure it's Jenna because she's the only person I know who would blow up my phone in the middle of the night and I don't know why she's calling but now I'm thinking there's some kind of emergency which would be just perfect because my night can't get any better and *why* do I have so many pens in my purse?" She holds up a fistful of pens. "WHY."

I bite the inside of my cheek to keep from smiling at the flustered expression on her face.

A happy lilt sings from the depths of her bag, and she immediately drops the pens—which fall onto the step beside her before rolling off in every direction—and starts yanking things out of her purse, tossing them aside.

A shirt.

A granola bar.

A sketchpad.

A scarf.

More pens.

With the path to my room blocked and nothing better to do with my hands, I start gathering the runaway pens.

By the fourth ring, Pixie finds her phone and answers with a rushed "What happened? Did someone die?"

"Finally," I hear a relieved voice say from the other line. "Where are you? I came back to Matt's apartment to drop off Tweedledee and Tweedledum—"

"Jenna."

"But you're not here. I thought you guys were going back to his place."

Pixie glances at me, then drops her eyes. "We did. But then I had Matt drive me back to the inn."

Matt.

I keep my gaze on the floor as I finish collecting pens.

"The inn?" Jenna says. "Matt's staying with you at the inn?"

"No. He dropped me off—can we talk about this later?"

"He dropped you off?"

"Jenna. Please."

"Fine. We'll talk in the morning—ah! Gross. Ethan, I swear to God if you vomit on—ugh!" Muffled commotion comes from the other line. "God! Sarah, do me a favor and tell that boyfriend of yours that the next time we all go out, he's in charge of his drunk roommates."

Boyfriend.

Pixie and I lock gazes.

Matt the Boyfriend.

Pixie's not mine, and she never has been, so I have no right to care about Matt the Boyfriend. But still my stomach twists in an ugly way.

"I am not drunk!" yells a male voice in the background.

"You're hammered, Jack!" Jenna yells back.

The male voice laughs. "Hammered Jack. Jack hammer. I'm a jackhammer."

"You're a jack*ass*," she shouts.

"So we'll talk in the morning?" Pixie says to distant Jenna.

"What? Oh, yeah. In the morning. Later. Ethan, don't you *dare*—"

Pixie hangs up and drops her phone back into her purse. "Sorry about that. My friends are, uh... interesting."

I nod. "They sound fun."

"Yeah."

She clears her throat and quickly starts shoving the rest of her discarded things back into the purse. I hand her the collected pens and she takes them without making eye contact, tossing them back into her bag before resuming her frenzied cleaning. I help gather the remaining items.

We reach for her scarf at the same time and our fingers accidentally brush. We both jerk our hands back as if touching each other is poisonous, and suddenly I'm keenly aware of all things Pixie. The curve of her neck, the scent of her shampoo, the shape of her lips, the single undone button at the top of her sweater...

She looks up at me with big green eyes, and the awkward tension between us instantly transforms into a charged current, pulsing up and down the staircase. She parts her lips and it's like her inhales are magnetic, drawing me closer to her, pulling me into the circle of her body heat—

A lock of her straightened blonde hair falls into her eyes and reminds me that things are different now.

I blink, breaking the charge, and step away from the scarf.

Shifting her eyes away, she snatches up the scarf and something small goes flying from the folds of the material and skids across the floor.

A condom.

For a moment, we just stare at it.

I have no right to care. I have no right to care.

With pink cheeks, Pixie casually picks up the condom square and drops it back in her bag.

I clear my throat and point upstairs. "So I'm just gonna..."

She looks up and sees how she's blocking my passage. "Oh, right. Sorry." She scoots over to clear a path, her eyes avoiding me completely.

I carefully step past her and head upstairs, feeling my pulse heat and hammer in my head.

Cake? Check.

Icing? Check.

Trojan cherry on top? Check.

I I

PIXIE

*M*ust the morning birds chirp so loud?

Are they mocking me? I bet they're mocking me.

I can't really blame them. After my horrendous run-in with Levi last night, I would mock me too. The condom? I mean, seriously.

And what the hell is up with my phone suddenly being a loudspeaker? Levi could totally hear everything Jenna was saying to me last night, and the look on his face when she said "boyfriend" was just...ugh. He obviously had no idea I was dating someone, and the revelation seemed to unsettle him.

I pull a pillow over my face and let out a muffled groan as more birds join in on the uber-cheery chirp fest.

It shouldn't matter. Levi dates people. I date people. This is how it's always been. But for some reason I feel icky inside, like I should write a letter of explanation and maybe print out a boyfriend permission slip for Levi to sign.

I, Levi Andrews, give my explicit permission for one Pixie Marshall to date whomever she wishes without any feelings that might resemble guilt or betrayal or awkward confusion. Signed, Levi Andrews, platonic third party in all Pixie Marshall–related endeavors and keeper of the east wing hot water.

My phone rings and I ignore it. It keeps ringing.

Ring. Ring. Ring. Ring—God!

I stay buried under the pillow as I grab my phone and bring it to my ear with a grumpy "What?"

"Drunk Jack asked me to have his baby," Jenna says.

I move the pillow aside and blink a few times into the bright morning sun streaming in through the window. "What?"

"Yeah." I can hear the bewilderment in her voice. "He was all like, I love you, Jenna. Let's have a baby and name it Taylor."

"Taylor?"

"Can you believe that?"

I pull myself into a sitting position and yawn. "Pure madness. Who names their baby Taylor?"

"I love that you think this is funny."

"It is funny."

"No, it's not. Jack. He's just…he's just so confusing, you know? Sometimes he makes me want to scream and kick and just…ugh." She sighs dramatically. "But enough about me. There are more important things at hand. Spill it."

"Spill what?" I say groggily.

"Uh…your *night*? What happened with you and Matt?"

"Oh. That." I quickly fill her in on all my non-sex with Matt. "So yeah. I'm broken. I have sexual ADD or something."

"You're not broken. You're just…"

"A prude? Cold? Destined to die a spinster?"

"Waiting," she says. "You're just waiting. And there's nothing wrong with that."

"Right." My stomach growls, and I look at the time. Maybe if I hurry I can still make it downstairs to catch the end of breakfast. "Can I call you back after I have my coffee? I don't feel alive yet."

"Yeah, and you sound like hell."

"Gee, thanks."

After hanging up with Jenna, I roll out of bed and put on a bra before padding downstairs in my socks and pajamas. In the kitchen, Ellen is seated at the small table in the corner, reading the newspaper. Because Ellen still gets the newspaper.

"Morning, Pixie." She chomps on a piece of bacon. No one else is around, so I assume breakfast is over. Bummer.

I pour myself a cup of coffee. "Morning."

"I thought you were staying at Jenna's all weekend."

"Yeah, well." I sit down and wrap my hands around the warm mug. "Plans changed, and Matt brought me back early."

She eyes me. "Is everything okay?"

"Yeah. Everything's fine," I say, stealing a piece of bacon from Ellen's plate. "Matt submitted an appeal to NYU for my transfer application."

I can feel her eyes examining me. "I didn't know that was even an option."

"Neither did I. But good ol' Matt had me covered there." Why do I sound bitter about this?

She takes another slow bite of bacon. "When will you find out if you got in?"

"The end of summer, maybe? Who knows."

Ellen rubs a thumb down the handle of her coffee mug. "Is New York still what you want?"

"Maybe." I pick at the tablecloth. "They have a great art program. I could move to New York, become a famous artist, live happily ever after…It sounds perfect."

She nods. "Oh, that reminds me. The canvases you ordered are in my office. I'll bring them up to your room later." She looks at something behind me. "You're here too?"

I turn to see Levi walking into the kitchen.

"And good morning to you too," he says to Ellen as he moves to the fridge and pulls out a water bottle.

He doesn't look at me, which is fine. Better than fine.

"I'm just a little disappointed, that's all," Ellen says, looking at both of us. "You two are the only employees with weekends off and yet you're both here. On a Sunday."

Levi shrugs.

I shrug.

"Weirdos," Ellen mutters, taking a sip of her coffee. "Hey. Do you guys want to drive into town together and grab some stuff for me today?"

"No," we say at the same time. Our panicked eyes meet across the kitchen.

"Wow," she says. "I guess that's a *no*."

Levi exits out the back door as I go back to picking at the tablecloth.

"Well, that wasn't obvious or anything," Ellen says, eyeing me over her mug. "You should talk to him."

"About what?" I feel sick inside, already knowing the answer.

"You know," she says casually, like she's not bringing up the mother of all taboo topics.

"And how, exactly, would I do that?" I tap the side of my mug.

Ellen turns a page in her newspaper. "One word at a time."

I shake my head, half-angry, half-broken. "If Levi wanted to talk about it, we would have talked about it a long time ago." With a final chug, I finish my coffee and stand up. "Thanks for letting me mooch your bacon."

"Anytime," she says, following after me with her eyes as I leave the kitchen.

I head back to my room and, once inside, my gaze falls to the easel in the corner and my inner ickiness eases up a bit. I prop a new canvas on the wooden stand and pull out a paintbrush.

My black and white paint tubes are still out from the last time I painted. I'm not sure where my colored paints are. Maybe in one of the unopened boxes I brought from my dorm? I don't know. It doesn't matter, though. I'm not really in a red or green or yellow mood, and haven't been for quite some time.

A few blonde curls fall into my eyes as I stretch my arms out, and I hastily blow them away. Once again, I didn't bother to straighten my hair after my warm shower last night—I needed to rinse Matt's buttery saliva trails from my skin—so of course my locks are a poofy mess, which is why I *hate* showering at night!

Holding the paintbrush between my teeth, I quickly pull my hair into a haphazard bun and imprison my curls.

Sunlight pours in through my bedroom window, warming the floorboards beneath my feet as I wiggle my toes and stare at the blank canvas.

Still staring.

A good twenty minutes goes by before I finally set my brush to it, and when I do, it's a giant black stroke. Then another. I brush at the canvas until it's nearly covered in darkness. I add white. I smudge it into gray. I change my mind and jab more black on there.

I don't know what I'm painting yet, but that's not unusual. I typically don't know where I'm going when I start a painting. The image just…happens, and sometimes it's not even a real image. Sometimes—most times, lately—it's just an array of colors and brushstrokes that *feel* like something more than *look* like something.

A few quick knocks pull my attention to my door.

"Come in," I call out.

It creaks open and Ellen steps inside with two canvases. "Here you go."

"Thanks," I say. "And thanks for lending me your spare keys yesterday too. My set is lost somewhere in this mess." I gesture at the mounds of laundry, books, and boxes about my room.

"No problem." She sets the canvases by the wall and watches me paint for a moment. "Why is everything you paint only black-and-white? What happened to those beautiful color paintings you used to do?"

Why does everyone care?

"Don't overthink it," I say. "I'm just in a phase."

"Right," she says with knowing eyes. "Well. Enjoy your day off." She turns and disappears into the hallway.

I go back to painting, thinking about all the times Ellen encouraged me to pursue my passion for art.

She bought me my first set of paints. My first real paintbrushes. She paid for my first art lessons and hung my first real painting—a bright orange sun shining over a purple lake surrounded by yellow flowers—in the center of her living room like it was a priceless piece of art. Like it was special.

I stand back and look at the muddled gray colors in front of me. I frown. It's not quite what I want to see. It looks...wrong, somehow.

My eyes skip to my bedroom window, drawn by a flash of movement outside. I see Levi running up and down the stone steps behind the lavender field. He does this almost every day.

Today it's cloudy outside and the sky is darker than usual, which means a storm is coming. My heart starts to race.

I watch Levi scale the steps again. His hair is all mussed up like he's been shoving his hands in it, and he's wearing a pair of gym shorts and his worn-out ASU T-shirt. I can't even count the number of times I've seen him in that shirt, running laps or bleachers. His dad, Mark, gave it to him for his sixteenth birthday, and I swear Levi wore it every day for two weeks after that. He was so determined to play football for ASU. He was always so dedicated and driven, so focused. He was a teenage boy with big dreams and few problems.

I wonder who he is now. Who's that guy running up and down those old stone steps?

I used to know him. I don't anymore.

Sharp sadness sinks into me, cold and dark, and I suddenly want to run outside and throw my arms around him. I want to bury my face in his chest and cry into his college T-shirt like a lost little girl.

I pull my eyes away from the window and look back at my gray painting.

I put my paintbrush away. It no longer looks wrong.

12

LEVI

*M*y feet beat against the stone steps in a constant rhythm as I ascend the steep incline yet again. The sky is heavy with clouds and the air is thick as I suck it into my lungs with each labored breath.

Pixie has a boyfriend and I have no problem with that.

Don't get me wrong, I hate the guy. But I have no problem with Pixie dating someone. It's good for her. Healthy. At least she's getting on with her life, which is more than I can say for myself.

At the top of the steps, I bend over to catch my breath and take a deep swig of water.

And the condom thing, well, that's just good planning. I'm not at all unsettled by the thought of Pixie having sex with Matt the Boyfriend—or any other guy, for that matter.

My knuckles go white around the bottle.

Not unsettled at all.

Loosening my grip, I take a few deep breaths and look out over the area. The lavender field leads down into an old amphitheater of sorts, complete with old stone benches curved into bowl-shaped stadium seating and crumbling staircases running up and down each side.

At one time, this place was probably used for small concerts or shows, but now it's mostly just rubble overgrown with dandelions and rogue sprouts of lavender. Guests sometimes come out here to take pictures or sit and read. It has that kind of feel to it. Quiet. Peaceful. I feel neither as I catch my breath.

With my muscles worked to their morning limit and sweat dripping down my face, I step away from the forgotten theater and climb up to the field.

The storm smell on the wind rolls over me, reminding me of a day last summer when I thought I had everything. A family. A future. Maybe even love. Funny how quickly you can lose the things you thought were certain.

Back inside, I take a shower and do my best to deplete the warm water. The first time I used all the hot water was an accident. It was two days after Pixie had moved in—two very uncomfortable days of tension and sadness—and I had exhausted the early morning repainting the inn's front porch. My hands and arms were covered in white paint, so I spent an excessive amount of time trying to scrub my skin clean as I showered.

I didn't realize I'd used all the hot water until twenty minutes after my shower when I heard Pixie squeal in the bathroom, then stomp into the hallway. She knocked on my door and proceeded to lecture me on the polite usage of a shared bathroom.

At first, I felt really bad about hogging the water, but then I realized her scolding was the longest conversation we'd had in months, and it took away some of the darkness inside me. Plus, I liked the way her cheeks crested with pink as she pointed at me and how her eyes narrowed when she thought I wasn't paying attention to what she was saying. From that day on, I went out of my way to ensure Pixie didn't get hot showers. Not very mature, but it was either that or drown in silence.

I finish with my post-jog shower and step out of the bathroom to an empty hallway. No Pixie tapping her foot outside the door with a scowl. No pink-crested cheeks. Disappointment starts to slide over my skin.

"Forty-two minutes!" Pixie yells from her cracked-open bedroom door.

Sometimes she times me. It's adorable.

"You're an asshole, Levi," she adds.

I grin as I walk to my room, all disappointment gone.

———

That night, I enter the bathroom a second before Pixie does, both of us with our toothbrushes at the ready. For a moment I just stare at her.

She looks the way I remember—blonde hair pulled back in a messy knot with curls escaping, paint smudged on her skin and bare feet—and I'm instantly transported back to a time when my house was filled with girly laughter.

It's hard to believe I ever found that laughter obnoxious.

She gives me a weird look, probably because I'm staring at her like an idiot, so I stretch my lips into a thin smile. Her weird look flashes into something else—hope, maybe? Sadness?—but quickly disappears as she gives me a strained smile in return. And now we're just standing here, fake-smiling at each other like morons.

I surrender my eyes first and step deeper into the bathroom so there's room for both of us at the counter. We start brushing our teeth, our eyes fixed anywhere but on each other.

Brush, brush, brush.

There's something intimate about brushing your teeth beside someone else. Perhaps it's because people who brush their teeth together are usually people who just woke up together, or people who are just about to go to bed together.

Our eyes meet in the mirror and quickly dart away.

She's wearing a dark T-shirt at least two sizes too large for her and a pair of ratty sweatpants. How is she still so pretty even when she's dressed like a homeless person?

Brush, brush, brush.

Her free hand is pressed flat on the counter between us. Speckles of black and white paint stick to her fingers and the side of her wrist. I wonder if the pads of her fingers are just as messy.

She was always great with a paintbrush. But when she'd get really into it, she'd ditch the brushes and just paint with her hands like a kindergartener.

In high school, she was all wild blonde curls and messy fingers, smearing paint on canvases like a crazy person. But then she'd step back from a masterpiece, and it always blew my mind how such a mess of colors and hands could create something so beautiful.

Brush, brush, br—

Pixie's toothbrush comes to a halt as she catches me staring at her hand.

"Whah?" she says over her toothbrush.

I stop brushing as well. "Yahr ah meh."

She looks confused. "Whah?"

I spit into the sink and rinse my mouth. "You're a mess."

The corners of her mouth slowly tip up, and I swear to God, even covered in toothpaste and drool, her smile is the most beautiful thing I've ever seen.

She says, "Ooh oot tah whyk meh mehey."

"I have no idea what you just said."

She spits into the sink and cleans her face as well. "I said"—she turns big green eyes to me and puts a hand on her hip—"you used to like me messy."

I scan her face, momentarily sucked into that warm happiness that is uniquely Pixie. "I didn't say I didn't like it."

The bathroom shrinks in on us until the walls and the shower curtain and the toothpaste in the sink are all gone, and it's just me and her and all the unspoken things between us.

Her smile falters as she looks up at me with little-girl hope and grown-up fear.

God.

All I want to do is hold her.

Her eyes begin to shimmer and that familiar panic creeps back in.

I whip my eyes away and rinse off my toothbrush before hastily leaving the bathroom. I need to keep my distance from Pixie. For her sake. For mine.

Once inside my bedroom, I fix my eyes on the gaping hole in the wall and stare at it until it's all I see. I broke the wall. That damage belongs to me.

The panic begins to recede.

13

PIXIE

I hate bowling.

The shoes are uncomfortable, the balls are gross, and I never win. But when Matt called yesterday and suggested we meet in Tempe tonight to go bowling, he seemed so excited that I didn't bother confessing my severe dislike for the activity. And honestly, after the way things ended last weekend, I'm just happy he wants to do anything with me at all. So bowling I shall go.

I hang up my apron and check the time with a frown. I quickly grab two leftover brownies from the lunch rush and head upstairs. I have only an hour to get ready. My hair still needs to be straightened, and I still need to pick out some clothes for bowling and anything that might happen afterward.

My stomach dips a little as I think about later.

Am I going to sleep with Matt tonight? Am I going to sleep with him *ever*?

Why is this so hard for me?

At the top of the stairs, I come face-to-face with Levi as he's exiting his room.

Ever since the toothbrush incident—yes, that's what I'm calling it—my heart's been doing this sad lurching thing every time I see him, and right now it's lurching like crazy.

"Hi, Levi," my overactive mouth says.

He stares at me, mid-door-closing.

Yeah. It's weird. We don't usually greet each other in the hall-way. Or anywhere for that matter.

"Uh...hi." He closes the door and eyes me curiously.

"Want one?" I hold out the plate of brownies like they're a peace offering. Maybe they are. Maybe they're my way of saying I'm sorry I have a boyfriend and condoms in my purse. And if that doesn't scream dysfunctional, I don't know what does.

"That depends." He eyes the brownie plate suspiciously. "Did you make them?"

In junior high, I went through this baking period and was determined to make the most delicious brownies ever. Every Saturday, I would slave in Levi's kitchen making brownies from scratch, and every Saturday they would end up tasting like bars of sour salt. I don't know how he did it, but I know—I just *know*—Levi was responsible for my disgusting brownies. I'm pretty sure he switched the salt and sugar, but I could never figure out how he made them sour.

I narrow my eyes. "No, I did not make them."

"Then...sure." He reaches for the smaller of the two brownies.

I shake my head. "Jackass."

He shrugs. "It's not my fault you make god-awful brownies."

"It's completely your fault."

"Oh yeah?" he says with a hint of a smile. "Prove it."

I'm on the brink of a smile myself when our hallway powwow is interrupted.

"Hey!"

I turn to see Matt at the top of the stairs and, for a moment, nothing in the entire universe makes sense.

I blink. "Wh—what are you doing here?"

"I came to pick you up." Matt smiles as he nears. "I wanted to surprise you so you wouldn't have to drive by yourself."

I keep blinking. "How did you know where to find me?"

And why the hell do people keep dropping in to *pick me up*? I know how to drive, dammit.

"The girl at the front desk told me you were up here." He leans in and kisses my cheek.

Levi's blue eyes shoot to mine, and I find myself irrationally angry with Haley.

Matt's staring at me. Why is he staring at me? Oh right.

I swallow and start gesturing back and forth. "Levi, this is Matt…my, uh, boyfriend. Matt, this is Levi…my, uh…" *Neighbor? Handyman? Toothbrush partner?* "My Levi."

Someone shoot me. Please.

Matt looks at me funny before holding out his hand to Levi. "Nice to meet you," he says.

Levi slowly moves his eyes from mine to Matt's and it's like watching two worlds collide as they shake hands.

What is happening right now?

I feel sick to my stomach. It's wrong. It's all wrong. Matt can't be here, in the same space with Levi, in the east wing of the inn.

Matt turns to me and wrinkles his brow. "You look different. Did you do something to your hair?" He gently pulls at a loose curl.

Levi's eyes are back on me, piercing me through like sapphire spears.

"No. This is just my hair," I say, functioning on autopilot because my brain is in shock. "My real hair."

What is happening right now?

"Oh." He smiles again. "I like it. You ready?"

"For what?"

"To...go bowling?"

Levi stifles a cough.

"Oh," I say, dragging my eyes back to Matt. "No. I'm not ready yet."

I'm not ready at all.

Levi nods at Matt. "It was good to meet you, man." He scoots past us and hastily exits down the stairs. He doesn't look back at me.

"Hey, you okay?" Matt tucks the loose curl behind my ear. I hate it when he does that. Maybe I *like* my hair all out of place and unorganized. My hair isn't his goddamn desk.

Oh my God, I'm losing it.

I force out a smile. "I'm fine. Let me just get dressed and I'll meet you downstairs."

I don't wait for him to agree. I just dart into my room and shut the door behind me, wondering why I'm on the verge of tears.

———

"But I don't *want* to bowl!" The pudgy little girl in the lane next to Matt and me stomps her bowling shoe on the glossy floor as she speaks to her mother. "Bowling is boring and the balls are really heavy."

Amen, sister.

The balls are ridiculously heavy. Fourteen pounds? What do I look like, He-Man?

"Quit making that face, Amanda," says the girl's mother as she sits with the small group of people they're with. "It makes you look ugly."

"I don't care."

"Well, you should," the mother says, raising her voice to be heard over the party music blaring from the overhead speakers. "You're already fat. The last thing you need is an ugly face to match that body of yours. Don't you want people to like you?"

I stare at the woman in horror as everyone within earshot shifts uncomfortably and looks away. The little girl bows her head in shame and silently collects her ball before rolling it down the lane. She keeps her eyes lowered as she makes her way back to her seat and the next person up gathers their ball. The little girl stares at her small hands.

I know that little girl. I *was* that little girl. Provided for, but unloved. Innocent, but resented. My mother was the queen of cruel words.

The first time I realized my mom hated me—and yes, I know that sounds dramatic, but the woman truly does despise me—was when I was five years old.

She was speaking on the phone to someone, I have no idea who, and I heard her say, "I hate being a mother. Sarah is so clumsy and messy and I swear she's retarded. She's scared of everything and cries all the time and she's annoying as hell. And she's not even pretty, so I can't even look forward to a beautiful teenage daughter. She'll probably be fat too."

I was five when I heard this. *Five.*

I was so startled and confused by the words coming out of my mother's mouth that I don't think the true maliciousness behind them registered. I walked into the room where she had the phone to her ear and stared at her questioningly.

She rolled her eyes at me and spoke to her listener. "And now she's eavesdropping on me like a little bitch. God, parenting is like a prison sentence."

It was so surreal to feel hated by the person I loved most in the world. And that was just the first of many hurtful words that would fall from that woman's lips. She didn't physically abuse me—at least not often—but sometimes words can be more damaging than wounds.

So when I met Levi's family, and his mother, Linda, loved me like her own and showered me with kind words and affection, I spent as many days and nights as I could in the comfort of the Andrews home. Linda and Mark Andrews were always trying to protect me from my miserable mother and give me what she wouldn't. They showed me love and family and compassion and all the other things I was starving for.

My heart twists as I think back on all that happiness, that warmth.

God, I miss them.

"Striiike!"

I blink over to Matt, who has his arms raised in victory as he stares down the lane. He spins around with a giant grin. "Did you see that?"

I smile and clap and pretend I saw the whole thing. "Whoo-hoo!"

"Your turn," he says.

Oh goodie.

I begrudgingly rise and lift my fifty-pound ball from the dispenser with an exaggerated grunt. I step up to the shiny lane—my feet sliding a bit on the polished floor so I have to catch myself like I'm baby Bambi—and halfheartedly throw the ball toward the white pins.

I knock over two. Thrilling.

I retrieve my ball for round two and knock over another three pins.

"Way to go, babe!" Matt says. "That's your best frame yet."

I pinch out a smile as we switch places and he prepares for his turn.

I hate this game.

As I take my seat, I glance at the neighboring lane and see the mother fussing with a barrette in the little girl's—Amanda's—hair. My mother always hated my hair. The curls drove her crazy. *A disgusting rat's nest*, she'd call it.

By the time I was in seventh grade, the rat's nest had grown to the middle of my back and I freaking loved it. It was wild and difficult to style, but it was my trademark, my identity. Pixie with the long blonde curls. Pixie with the happy hair. It made me feel girly and pretty.

My mom was always trying to get me to pin it back or twist it up into something that looked halfway respectable, but it was almost impossible to tame my unruly ringlets, so rarely ever did I cooperate.

One weekend I refused to pull my hair back and my mom threw a massive fit, but I didn't care. It was my hair and I was going to wear it down. Nothing could stop me.

Except a pair of scissors.

Sandra Marshall grabbed a thick fistful of my proud curls and swiftly cut them clean off. I watched in horror as the front left side of my identity fell to the floor in a sad heap of golden spirals. Then I cried.

There was nothing I could do to rectify the damage except cut the rest of my hair just as short to match.

"Maybe walking around like an ugly boy will give you some perspective on properly caring for your hair," she'd said.

I was thirteen and I thought I looked like a boy. I was thirteen and believed I was ugly.

I spent that weekend at Levi's house, crying to his mom about how kids at school were going to tease me and how no boys would ever like me. Linda did her best to style my hair in the most feminine way possible, but it was a lost cause.

Monday morning came around and I cried all the way to school. Junior high is hell on girls—especially in a small town—so with my head hung in shame, I braved the front doors and steeled myself for the endless teasing and whispering that was sure to ensue.

But it never came.

It seemed everyone in school was too preoccupied with a certain eighth grader's hair to care about mine. I traveled through the halls, listening to giggles and following wide eyes to the source of the school's entertainment.

Levi.

His hair was longer back then and he had dyed it purple—neon purple—and spiked it up all over his head. The school's star football player dying his hair a silly color wasn't jaw-dropping or mind-blowing, but it was outrageous enough to keep any attention off of me.

Levi and I didn't speak that day, but once, as we passed in the hall, he gave me a crooked smile and that's when I knew.

I was his completely.

Bowling pins crash against the floor and the loud noise ricochets in my ears as Matt jumps in triumph over his eight-pin knockout.

I glance over at Amanda, whose head is still down as she and her group finish their game and leave the bowling alley.

I hope she has an Andrews family in her life, or at least a Levi. Especially a Levi.

"Earth to Sarah." Matt waves his hand in front of my face.

I look up at him. "My turn again?"

"Yep. Go get 'em, tiger."

Rawr.

Matt and I bowl for a while longer and we're having a perfectly pleasant time—and by "we" I mean Matt—when he throws a giant-ass wrench into the evening.

"So," he says after throwing his fifth strike. "What are you doing Fourth of July weekend?"

I stand from my plastic seat and walk to the ball dispenser. "I haven't really thought about it. Why?"

He doesn't sit back down, but instead watches as I pick up my sixty-five-pound ball and insert my fingers into the dark holes of other people's dead skin cells.

Have I mentioned I hate this game?

"I was thinking about flying back home to San Diego for the weekend. And I want you to come along and meet my family."

I look up. "Wow. Random."

He laughs. "Not really. We've been together for a while and I think it's time to show you off. I've told my parents all about you, and they can't wait to meet you in person."

He told his parents all about me?

My mother doesn't even know Matt exists. Hell, *Ellen* barely knows. Should I have been prepping my family members for a Matt meet and greet? Shit. I really suck at the girlfriend thing.

I swallow. "I don't know..."

Am I ready to meet his family? Am I ready to go on a weekend trip with him? Wouldn't a weekend trip mean sex? My fingers start to sweat into the ball holes.

"Come on." He smiles. "I really want you to meet my family."

I scrunch my nose. "But...why?"

"Because you're important to me." His smile stays in place, but his voice lowers in sincerity. "And because I love you."

I almost drop my eighty-pound ball as I stare at him. We've never said the "L" word to each other.

Obnoxious party music and the loud echoes of falling pins fill the silence between us as he waits for me to respond.

Up until this moment, I wasn't sure if Matt and I would have a future or not. But standing here, in these ridiculously slippery shoes, with my fingers wedged in the sweaty holes of a ninety-five-pound sphere of nasty, I'm completely sure.

14

LEVI

*I*t's late and the kitchen lights are dimmed as I lock the back door. Just as I'm turning to head for the east wing, the dining room door swings open and a pissed-off Pixie flies past me, knocking into my shoulder as she huffs to the sink.

"Whoa." I turn around. "Who pissed you off?"

"Matt," she says through clenched teeth as she washes her hands. She yanks some vegetables from the fridge, grabs a sharp knife, and starts hacking away at mushrooms.

"Matt?" All my guard dog instincts immediately go on alert. "Why? What did he do?"

I'll kill him. If he hurt her, I will kill him.

"He told me he loved me!" She thrusts her arms out, the sharp knife in her hand glinting under the kitchen lights.

I lift a brow and wait because, surely, that's not the reason for the broken expression on her face. But she doesn't elaborate.

I pause. "So . . . ?"

"*So . . .*" She laughs without humor as she goes back to hacking. "Just when I think I'm making progress in my life and might be able to get back to normal, or finally have sex with someone other than drunk Benji, or just move on from this deep, sad place I'm in all the time, Matt goes and tells me he loves me and totally screws everything up!" She starts chopping more aggressively.

Pixie hasn't had sex with anyone other than Benji? I'm outrageously pleased by this information.

"I mean, who does that?" she continues. "Who declares their love for someone they don't even know? Does he know about my pet turtle when I was nine? No." *Chop, chop, chop.* "Does he know that my mother is evil incarnate? No." *Chop, chop, chop.* "Hell, five hours ago he didn't even know my hair was naturally curly! He knows nothing about me. And yet he wants me to fly away with him to meet his parents because he *loves* me? No. Just no!" *Chop, chop, chop.*

Pixie has been with only one guy, one time. Why am I so happy about this?

"And you know what else?" She points the knife at me violently. "I am *not* Captain Hook. If anything, I'm Tinker Bell." She returns to her wild dicing. "Tinker Bell!"

Tinker Bell?

Shit. I need to start paying attention.

"He's a crazy person," she says. *Chop, chop, chop.* "So clearly I had no choice but to break up with him."

I squint at her. "He told you he loved you...so you broke up with him?"

"Yep," she says, popping the *p.*

"Why?"

"Because Matt *doesn't* love me. So it's all just bullshit. Him. Me. Everything. *Bullshit.*"

"How do you know he doesn't love you?"

"Just because."

"Because why?"

She throws her arms out again and yells, "Because love isn't something that needs to be said out loud!" Her face flushes with passion. "It's something you just *know*. It's an unspoken thing. It's humble and quiet and constant..." She goes back to slaughtering the mushrooms, but lowers her tone a bit. "I mean, you can't just *say* you love someone and make it true. That's not how it works. Real love doesn't need to be declared or confessed. Real love just... is. You know?"

My throat constricts because I do know. God, I know. I know so much it's hurting me to look at her.

"So yeah." She swallows. "Matt doesn't love me and I don't love him and now I'm right back to where I started, which is exactly nowhere and I'm just so"—*chop*—"freaking"—*chop*—"sick"—*chop*—"of being nowhere. And nobody gets it. Nobody!"

I watch her for a moment, wishing I could take away the pain in those big green eyes of hers as they viciously hack up the remains of the mushrooms. She looks the way I feel inside most days. Hurt. Stuck. Desperate.

"I get it," I say quietly.

She stops chopping and looks up.

I press my lips together. "I know all about nowhere."

Our eyes meet beneath the dimmed lights, colliding in a tangle of shared emotions too raw to touch. How did we get so broken?

We might be legal adults now, but lately it feels like we're just as helpless as children. Just as lost and scared.

If my parents were here, they'd know what to do. How to heal Pixie. How to fix me. They always knew what to do. But since they didn't stick around for the fallout, we're navigating this thing on our own. And failing miserably.

Pixie stares at me for a long moment.

"I know you do." Her voice is barely a whisper, drifting through the air and gliding over my skin. She looks me over with longing and dammit if that's not everything I want in the world.

My eyes drop to her mouth, her throat, her hands. Every instinct I have is screaming to touch her. To cross the space between us and wrap my arms protectively around her small frame. To shield her from all the bad things, the sorrowful things. All the things I'm made of.

But that can't happen. We can't happen.

Neither of us moves as reality seeps in, slow and steady, and the moment evaporates into the dim kitchen. It's sad in the room, like there's something very much alive but fatally ill breathing in between Pixie's broken heart and mine. And we don't know how to fix it.

We need more distance between us. Distance is painless. Distance is safe.

She clears her throat and washes her hands. I double-check the door to make sure it's locked. And we go our separate ways.

15

PIXIE

*T*wo days later, I'm still not heartbroken.

I've never broken up with anyone before so maybe I don't really understand the concept, but I'm pretty sure I'm supposed to be feeling sad or lonely by now.

Nope.

All I've felt since my post-bowling meltdown in front of Levi—did I really blab to him how I hadn't slept with anyone since Benji? Ugh—is frustrated. And of course supremely embarrassed.

God, I can't believe I just lost my shit like that the other night. For a moment I forgot things had changed between us, and I just unloaded on Levi like I used to. He's done a good job of steering clear of me ever since and it's probably for the best. Who knows what I might blab out next time. My throat-biting desires? My unhealthy obsession with his forearm muscles? I need a muzzle.

This is what I'm thinking about as I reach the bottom of the east wing stairs. My face must be twisted into a look of utter shame and repulsion because Daren stops me on my way to the kitchen and says, "Hey, everything okay?"

I know Levi's not crazy about him, but Daren's not a bad guy. He's just a typical guy. He's one of those broken bad boys whom every girl wants to fix: guarded, cocky, desperate for approval but emotionally unavailable. Typical.

And he's way too attractive for his own good. The guy's not just hot. He's freaking beautiful. And he knows it.

But he hasn't had it easy, which is probably why Ellen gave him a job here and why I tend to give him a break. Even when he implores me with those pretty brown eyes of his—like he's doing right now.

Seriously. Too attractive for his own good.

"I'm fine," I say and move past him.

He follows after me, and it's all I can do not to roll my eyes. This is just how it is with Daren. He's always checking on me during work. I know he means well, but gah. Sometimes I wish my aunt wasn't such a softie when it came to hiring cute boys with damaged pasts.

I touch a hand to my chest.

Sometimes.

"Hi, Daren." Mable looks up from flipping pancakes as we enter the kitchen and smiles at him, but it's different from when she smiles at Levi.

"Hi, Mable." He turns to me. "So the Fourth of July Bash is coming up."

I put my apron on. "So?"

"So are you going?"

"No."

"Come on. It's tradition." He flashes his smile, and I'm reminded why every girl in high school put out for him. Every girl but me, of course. That smile is dangerous. "Everyone will be there and everyone misses you."

By everyone, he means all the random kids we grew up with.

And by people missing me, he means people are curious to see if I've stopped being a hermit yet. As far as my hometown is concerned, I've been keeping to myself like a shut-in lately. My friends in Copper Springs were cool about my social absence for a few months, but then their patience ran out and most of them stopped calling and inviting me to things. Not Daren, though.

"It'll be fun," he says. "You can bring your boyfriend. What's his name again?"

"Matt."

"Bring Matt."

"We broke up."

"Oh." He rubs a hand over his dark brown hair. "Okay, then bring a friend. Or, better yet, come with me." He's grinning again.

I shake my head. "I'm not feeling very festival-ish this year."

"Sarah," he says seriously, dropping his smile as he puts his hand on my cheek. "You can't be sad forever."

Screw you. Yes, I can.

I gently pull back from his hand. "It hasn't been forever. It's been less than a year."

"I know," he says in a quieter tone. "But this might be good for you, seeing people, seeing friends." His eyes scan mine. "Just think about it."

"I'll think about it," I say, mostly to get him off my back. I don't need to think about it—I don't want to think about it.

"Excellent." His eyes flick to something behind me. "We'll talk more later, okay?" He moves past me, but not before giving me a swift kiss on the *lips.*

What the . . . ?

I turn around to bitch him out—because I'm not a kissing booth—but my words catch in my throat when I see Levi at the back door, glaring at us with a dark look that's probably supposed to say *I don't give a damn* but comes across more like *I will shred Daren with my bare hands.*

Daren gives me a covert wink as he heads for the dining room door, and I make a mental note to scold him later.

I act casual until Daren is gone, smoothing down my apron and tucking a loose strand of hair behind my ear; then I look at Levi and wait for the storm.

He stares at me.

I stare at him.

Mable stares at pancakes.

Well, hell. Storms, I know how to handle. But this—this heavy silence bullshit—I don't know what to do with *this.*

He continues staring.

"What?" I snap.

"Don't be a whore," Levi says coolly.

Mable looks at him in horror, the spatula frozen in her hand as her mouth falls open.

"Ex*cuse* me?" I see red and suddenly know exactly where every knife in the kitchen is.

I know Levi doesn't like Daren, but why would he—how could he—I can't even—

"Look who's talking," I sneer. "I don't really think *you* have any right to pass judgment on whorishness. And besides, my life is *my* business."

He shrugs. "Fine, be a whore. But you can do better than Daren."

I slowly nod, anger and hurt filling up my lungs. "What, like you?"

His eyes sharpen as he looks me up and down. It's not a gross look, more like a refresher in who, exactly, I am to him. A refresher that breaks my heart more than any words ever could.

He finds my face again and lowers his voice. "Never me."

And then he leaves. The bastard just leaves.

I want to run after him and scream and yell and cuss, but there's a piece of me that knows I deserve his anger, his rejection. And that piece keeps me in my place and stings the back of my eyes for all the things I can't take back.

Things like Charity.

16

LEVI

*S*elf-loathing doesn't even begin to cover what I'm feeling as
I leave the kitchen.

I want to keep my distance from Pixie, yes. But calling her
names? Putting that hurt in her eyes? Is that what I want?

My gut twists, but there's no going back now.

And why was I so upset anyway? It's just Daren fucking Ackwood. Am I so far gone that I just go Darth Vader on Pixie's ass
whenever she talks to another guy? She's not mine. If she's okay
with Daren kissing her, then fine.

I crack my knuckles.

Who am I kidding? Daren's a prick and I don't want him to
touch her. Period.

But damn, I overdid it in the kitchen. Her eyes were so angry
and confused and...sad...

Fuck.

How could I have spoken to her like that? Like she was anything less than incredible? How could I have been so vicious with
my words when I know how much verbal assault Pixie endured
from her mother?

How could I have treated her just like the woman whose damage I once lived to undo?

I shove my hands in my hair as my heartbeat clogs up my throat. Then I blindly head to the maintenance closet in the west wing and start retrieving all the supplies I'll need to patch the hole in my bedroom. It's not on my To Do list, but I need to repair the wall. I need to fix what I did wrong—

Someone smacks me upside the head. "You called Pixie a whore? *Seriously?*"

I rub the back of my skull and turn to see a pissed-off Ellen. "How did you—"

"Mable," Ellen says. She's livid, and now I hate myself even more.

I sigh in shame. "I didn't call her a whore, exactly. I told her not to *be* a whore, which is different." And oh hell, that was the wrong thing to say.

"You stupid boy." Ellen smacks me again.

"Ouch." I'm not sure if I mean the smack or her words.

She leans in. "I know you have shit, Levi. I know the past kills you. But pushing Pixie away isn't going to ease the pain."

Her eyes have me trapped. They're locked and loaded and calling me out with nothing but concern. And for a moment, I see my mother staring back at me. Wanting more for me. Believing in me.

My heart thickens in my throat.

"I don't want to ease the pain," I say, completely serious.

Ellen watches me for a moment, hardness and sympathy warring in her eyes. "Yes, you do," she says. "And so does Pixie."

I watch her walk away, wishing I could undo the entire last year of my life.

With everything I need from the closet, I head up to my room. The hole in the wall gapes at me once I open the door, and I suddenly want to make it bigger. Smash it all to hell. Maybe break some bones, draw some blood.

I spend the next forty-five minutes patching up the damaged drywall and the rest of the day keeping myself busy with other repairs. Loose hinges, burned-out lightbulbs, busted pipes. Just anything to keep my hands busy and my head silent.

When there's nothing more to fix, I change my clothes, head outside, and start running the old stone stairs. Scaling steps. Climbing to nowhere. Home sweet home.

17

PIXIE

J'd offer you tequila to cure your crappy mood, but since you don't drink, I have the next best thing." Jenna holds a pint of strawberry ice cream and a spoon out to me. "Go to town, girl."

After my run-in with Levi this morning, I spent most of the day trying not to cry as I clanged innocent pots and pans and took out my frustration on the dinner asparagus. Mable didn't say a word, but she kept a watchful eye on me all day.

Ellen came into the kitchen at one point. She watched me slice vegetables with a vengeance and stir fettuccini like the noodles needed to be punished, and then she stroked a hand across my shoulder blades before leaving. It was simple, but it brought me the comfort I needed.

I managed to get through the rest of the day without manhandling any more food products, and then I hightailed it over to Jenna's. I needed to get the hell out of the east wing.

I take her offering. "I'm not in a crappy mood."

"Yes, you are, and it's completely understandable."

"It is?" I ask, filling my mouth with strawberry.

She nods. "Breakups suck."

Oh yeah. The breakup. I'd almost forgotten about that.

We plop down on the single couch in her tiny apartment, me with my pint of fat calories and Jenna with a rocks glass containing a concoction I'm sure Earl and his senior citizen golf buddies would appreciate.

"I'm confused, so let's recap," Jenna says, turning to face me as she leans against the arm of the couch. "So Matt told you he loved you."

"Yes," I say, nodding once.

"And then you dumped him."

"Yes."

She cocks her head. "Because somehow you know he *doesn't* love you?"

"Exactly."

Jenna sighs. "Girl. You might need something stronger than ice cream."

I try to muster up some grief over my ex-boyfriend. "I just wish Matt hadn't dropped the 'love' bomb, you know? We had a good thing going. Why did he have to mess it all up?" I shovel more strawberry goodness into my mouth.

"Yeah." She spins the ice around in her glass. "It's super annoying when dreamy guys say they love you."

I groan and drop my head against the back of the couch. "I know I sound like a baby, and I know breaking up with Matt seems over-the-top, but I just couldn't stay with him. I wasn't me."

Jenna takes the ice cream carton from my hands and eats a spoonful. "You didn't feel like you could be yourself around him?"

I think about it. "It's not that I couldn't be myself. I just... I just didn't *want* to be myself. He and I... we just didn't feel right. Do I sound crazy?"

"Yes." She nods. "But the good kind of crazy."

I rub my face. "This day has been super shitty."

She wrinkles her brow. "I thought you and Matt broke up a few days ago."

"What?" I sit up. "Oh. Yeah. We did." I take the ice cream back. "But then Levi and I got in this fight this morning and it was so stupid, but it just infected me, you know?" I cram an oversized bite into my mouth.

"What did you and Levi get in a fight about?" Jenna narrows her gaze. "Do I need to voodoo his ass? 'Cause I will."

"It was nothing really." I wave my spoon flippantly. "This Daren guy was trying to talk me into going to our hometown's Fourth of July lake party and Levi happened to be standing there when Daren kissed me—"

"Some guy kissed you?"

"Yeah, but it's not like that. It's—never mind. It's complicated." I sigh again. "But it pissed Levi off, which is understandable, but then Levi said some things he didn't mean, which is also understandable, but *God*. It hurt, you know?" I shake my head and look down at the ice cream. "And it made me miss Charity."

Jenna goes very still. "Levi's sister?"

I nod and stab at a few chunks of frozen strawberry.

Charity and I met in kindergarten and became instant best friends the day she invited me over to play at her house. That was the first time I was introduced to the Andrews family. To happiness. Love.

"This is my friend, Sarah," Charity introduced me to Levi. "Sarah, this is my brother, Leaves."

She always called him Leaves, like he was made of Thanksgiving decorations or something. I used to call him that too. Before.

Growing up, Charity taught me how to be beautiful and free

and brave, and she shared her family with me when I was desperate for one myself. She was my other half. We laughed and cried and talked about boys and had sleepovers and dreamed about the future. We were inseparable.

Jenna's golden eyes study me. "Do you want to talk about her?" she asks quietly.

"No." I stare at the ice cream.

"Do you want to talk about Levi?"

"No."

"Do you want to talk about—"

"No," I say sharply. I swallow and try to compose my violent tone as I look up. "I'm sorry. I don't mean to be bitchy. This is my fault. I know I brought it up. I know I should want to talk about it. But I just—I can't."

She nods with a half smile and shifts her weight on the couch. "That's okay." A beat passes. "Let's just talk about something else." She smiles again, but this time it's real and warm.

God, I love Jenna and her unflinching ability to roll with my closed-off past.

"Like what?" I take another bite and try to swallow down my emotions along with the dessert.

"Like…what are you doing next semester? Jack mentioned that New York might be back on the table…?"

My heart starts to race. "Yeah. Maybe. I don't know." The ice cream feels too cold in my hands. "What are *you* doing next semester?"

She shrugs. "Going back to ASU. Getting another tattoo. The usual."

"Another tattoo?" I lift a brow. "With what skin?"

She looks down at all the ink covering her belly, arms, and legs. "I'll find room somewhere. I want a sea horse."

"A sea horse?"

"Yes. Did you know the males carry the babies, not the females?"

I lift a brow. "And that's why you want to draw one on your body?"

"And sea horses don't have teeth. Or stomachs."

"I feel like these aren't good enough reasons to permanently draw one on your skin."

She tips her chin. "What *is* a good enough reason?"

I pause.

"Exactly," she says, pulling up a few sketches on her phone. "Okay. Which sea horse do you like best?"

For the next hour, Jenna and I sit on her couch and discuss sea horse tattoo possibilities until I've almost forgotten all about Charity and Levi and the way things used to be.

And they used to be wonderful.

When Charity and I were high school freshmen, Levi had a truck so he was our ride to school every day. He was also our ride home, which was only a problem during football season.

By that time, he was already a hotshot football player and the game was his life, and consequently, ours. He had practice after school, which meant we had to wait until the sun set for our ride home.

Most of the time, we just watched videos on our phones or whined about teachers and mean girls. Sometimes we did homework. But occasionally, we would hang out by the bleachers and watch the football team pummel one another and get yelled at by Coach McHugh.

I had a crush on the safety, so watching him run around in tight pants for three hours was not a problem for me. And Charity, well. Charity had a crush on every guy ever, so she didn't complain either. We'd sit there and happily sigh to the sound of play calls and colliding helmets.

On one of these occasions, Charity felt the need to make catcalls from our post in the upper bleachers. Don't ask me why. Probably just to piss Levi off. It worked.

After five minutes of god-awful meowing and almost-obscenities from Charity's mouth, Levi turned on the field and threw a football at us.

He threw a football. AT US.

Levi's grown a bit in the last four years, but he was no scrawny tyke back then, and a pigskin coming at you at a hundred miles an hour is effing scary, which is why we ducked as the football sailed just beyond where we were seated.

Fun fact: Levi always hits his target. So the football missing us was no accident. But still, it was terrifying—and quite effective since Charity never catcalled again.

The football of fury rolled down a few bleachers and landed at our feet, giving Charity and me the bright idea to play catch; this is a good example of just how desperate we were to kill time.

We chose a spot at the far end of the field and started throwing the ball back and forth, with less than desirable results. Whose idea was it to develop a ball with two pointy ends? Total nonsense.

Needless to say, Charity and I threw like girls and laughed our butts off at the cartwheel effect we somehow couldn't avoid as we chucked the stupidly shaped ball back and forth.

We didn't notice practice was over until Charity missed a catch and the football went dancing over to Levi's feet. He was standing there with his hands on his hips in that I-just-ran-fifty-miles-and-I'm-almost-out-of-breath kind of way.

He shook his head at Charity. "I'm ashamed to call you family."

She smiled. "Because I was whistling at your friends' cute butts?"

"That too." He nodded. "But ducking every time a football comes at you? That's unacceptable. It's not going to bite you. And *you*." He pointed at me. "Why are you using two hands? You're throwing like a moron."

I smiled because he was serious, and serious Levi cracked me up.

"Come here, both of you." He picked up the ball as we neared him. "This"—he pointedly looked at Charity, then me—"is how you throw a football."

He demonstrated flawlessly and proceeded to instruct us on doing the same. We failed miserably, but it was hilarious to try. We giggled and fumbled and flinched and annoyed the hell out of him. But he didn't give up.

Levi made sure to continue our football-throwing lessons until we were no longer an embarrassment to the good Andrews name.

By that point in my life, I considered Levi just as close of a friend as Charity. The three of us did everything together, and we had since we were little. We were the Three Musketeers. And even though time and adolescence changed the way we interacted in public, when it came down to it, the three of us were our own kind of family. Real. Unshakable. Constant. It was a special feeling.

I didn't know back then just how special it was, but I know now.

18

LEVI

I keep my distance from Pixie for the whole next week, not sure I'm ready to see how much she hates me. I've kept myself busy gutting the unoccupied east wing bedrooms. It's amazing how much work you can accomplish when you're plagued with guilt.

I still can't believe I called her a whore. Pixie, of all people. She's had sex only one time, for Christ's sake. A jealous tremor runs through my veins as I remember the night I found out she'd lost her virginity.

Two years ago, I picked up Charity and Pixie from a party where they had gotten irresponsibly wasted, and the moment we got back to our house, Pixie crawled onto the couch and moaned, "That party sucked."

Charity laughed. "Only because you lost it to Benji Barker and it was a total fail."

In that moment, I felt like someone punched me in the gut. I had no air, no sight.

"Total fail." Pixie hid her face in one of the couch pillows.

Charity clucked her tongue. "That's why you don't lose your virginity to another virgin, Pix. Neither one of you knew what you were doing. Bad call."

Still no air.

"Shut up, best friend." Pixie threw a pillow at Charity. "Maybe I wouldn't have made such a *bad call* if you'd stayed by my side instead of ditching me to go screw Daren Ackwood."

I whipped my eyes to Charity. "WHAT?"

My head was going to explode.

Charity turned to me with feigned innocence. "What? Daren and I have been dating for a while now and we have sex. A lot of sex. Get over it."

"Whore," Pixie mumbled, once again facedown in a pillow.

"Shut up," Charity said to the couch. "At least Daren makes me orgasm, which is more than I can say for you and novice Benji."

I tugged at my hair. "Oh my God. My ears are bleeding. My ears are bleeding."

Charity was sleeping with Daren Ackwood? And Pixie wasn't a virgin anymore?

My chest hurt. My stomach hurt. Where the fuck was all the air?

"God, I know," Pixie whined. "Benji Barker? Ugh."

Something tight and hot inside me snapped, and I spun to face Charity. "What the hell were you thinking, leaving Pixie alone tonight?"

"What?" Charity looked confused.

I yelled, "What kind of friend are you, ditching Pixie for some asshole?"

A hurt expression crossed Charity's face. "I didn't know—"

"Don't be mad, Leaves." Pixie pulled her green eyes up from the pillow and looked like she was going to cry. "Please don't be mad."

For the first time ever, I looked at Pixie like something that belonged to me. I wanted to throw her over my shoulder and have those green eyes all to myself. Always. I didn't want to share them with Benji, or any other prick.

"Mad?" I screamed. "I'm furious! You're hammered, Pix. That guy had no right to touch you when you weren't sober enough to make an intelligent decision! I'll kill him. I'm going to kill him. I'm going to rip him to pieces and—"

Pixie started crying. "I'm so sorry," she bumbled at no one. "I'm so sorry! It seemed like a good idea because neither one of us had ever been with anyone and he's not scary and I was that happy kind of buzzed and so was he and then it was all messy and awkward and it didn't feel good at *all* and then it was over and even more awkward and now my head hurts and Leaves is mad at me!" She started sobbing into the pillow and howled, "Leaves is so mad at me."

"Hey." Charity knelt beside her and rubbed her back, saying a slew of reassuring girl things while I paced the room. Pixie eventually calmed down, and when she passed out, Charity stood up from the couch and glared at me.

"What?" I stood there, stunned and angry and…sad. I was actually sad.

She put her hands on her hips. "I don't remember you freaking out like that when you found out I'd first had sex."

"That's because thinking about my sister having sex is gross. Thinking about Pixie having sex is…"

Charity waited with a cocked eyebrow.

"I didn't freak out," I said.

"You totally freaked out!" She threw her arms in the air. "God, Levi. Maybe you should just pee all over her so every guy she meets knows whose territory she is!"

That was the first time I realized how possessive I was of Pixie.

And then the other day, when I saw Daren kiss her, all my buried desires came roaring back to life.

God, I still can't believe I was such an asshole to her.

With a clenched jaw, I lift another roll of old carpet out from the east wing and haul it downstairs and out the back door. I toss it into a large pile beside the Dumpster, where it joins three other carpet rolls, an array of shredded baseboards, and peelings of old hideous wallpaper.

I hear the screen on the back door creak open and slam closed before the crunch of heavy feet on gravel meets my ears.

Turning around, I see Angelo smacking a box of cigarettes against his open palm.

"Levi." He nods, pulling a cigarette from the box and resting it between his lips. "Want one?" The unlit cigarette in his mouth bobs with his words as he holds the box out to me.

I wipe a hand across my sweaty brow and shake my head.

He shrugs and retrieves a lighter from his pocket before flaming the tip of his cigarette. He takes a deep drag and watches as I hack up carpet rolls and baseboards so they'll fit in the Dumpster.

"You've been working hard these past few days." He tucks the pack in his pocket.

"Yeah, well." I heave a roll into the trash. "Ellen needs the east wing ready by fall."

He nods. "And work keeps the demons out, am I right?"

I cut up a baseboard, not really sure what he's talking about. "I guess."

He looks out at the field. "Relentless little bastards, them demons. You can push 'em away for years, but they eventually find you." He takes another expert drag. "And then you gotta face 'em."

I say nothing as I chuck pieces of wood and wallpaper into the

Dumpster. He's probably referring to a murderous bookie he owes money to or a rival mob boss who wants him to sleep with the fishes or something.

A faint rumble of thunder vibrates the earth, and I look up to see dark clouds in the distance. Monsoon season has been threatening to start for weeks now. I wonder when it will finally pour down its first summer storm.

Angelo stares at the impending clouds and sucks a few more drags of smoke through his lungs before stomping out the cigarette.

He tips his chin at me and says, "The sooner the better," before heading back inside.

For a moment, I think he means the coming storm. But then I realize he was talking about facing demons, and I wonder if his sage mobster advice was directed at me.

After breaking up the remainder of the remodeling discards, I toss them in the trash and dust my hands off. Walking to the kitchen's back door, I open the screen just as Pixie opens the inner door, and we lock gazes under another faint rumble of thunder.

I drop my eyes and move to the side. She does the same, both of us moving to the same side so we're still in each other's way. We don't make eye contact as we jerk from side to side, trying to pass each other without touching. Awkward.

Finally, I stop and step back, letting her exit the kitchen with the bag of trash in her hand. As she walks toward the Dumpster, I quickly slip inside and head away from the kitchen as the smell of rain and wind laced with lavender chases after me through the open screen door.

19

PIXIE

When lightning strikes the earth, it scars the ground, branding it with heat and energy as it singes a path to where it can burn no more. I know this because I accidentally paid attention in science class once, but I think about it every time there's a storm on the horizon. Like today.

A bolt of lightning cuts through the sky and touches down in the distance, and I can almost feel its electric current running through my veins.

I throw the trash bag away and head back inside the kitchen.

It hurt to see Levi just now; to brush past him and smell him and not talk or touch. Will it ever be normal between us again? My chest aches as I ponder the possibility that we might not speak for the remainder of the summer. Maybe even the rest of our lives.

My heart lurches at the thought.

I start cleaning up for the day. The lunch rush was crazy and, thankfully, everyone has cleared out of the dining room, so I have a moment to catch my breath before dinner starts.

Angelo carries a carton of dirty glasses into the kitchen and, through the door, I see Daren's perfect form walking across the empty dining room. I hurriedly swing through the door.

"Daren," I call out.

He turns and smiles when he sees me. "Hey, Sarah."

"What was with the kiss the other day?"

His smile drops. "Oh. Yeah. Don't be pissed."

"I'm pissed."

He runs a bashful hand through his hair. "I know that was shady of me—"

"Damn straight."

"But someone needs to light a fire under Levi's ass," he says. "He wants you and he doesn't want anyone else to have you, but he's too much of a dumbass to act on it. And it's been that way for, hell, I don't know, years, at least. I just wanted to provoke him a little. Remind him that you're worth pursuing." He smiles again, but makes a face when he realizes I'm not amused. "It was lame. I know."

I roll my eyes in frustration, but I get it. Daren has always gone out of his way to push Levi's buttons when it comes to me. He and Charity might have had a rocky on-again, off-again relationship, but he was always a pretty decent friend to me.

I sigh. "Okay, well, next time you want to provoke Levi, could you do it without involving my mouth?"

"Yeah. I'm an asshole. Sorry." He gives me apologetic puppy dog eyes that only a heartless witch could resist.

"It's fine," I say. "Just be careful where you put your lips from now on."

He winks. "Oh, I'm *always* careful where I put my lips."

I bet.

"Ew. Just go." I make my way back to the kitchen and finish wiping down the counters before I wrap up another bag of trash and carry it out to the Dumpster.

As I toss in the heavy trash bag, a humid breeze lifts the ends of my hair and blows across my cheeks. I look up and see the dark clouds rolling in, and my thoughts fly to last summer.

It was one of those almost-stormy days, much like today, where the sun shone brightly between purple clouds as if the sky couldn't make up its mind about the weather. The air was thick and humid but the steady wind cooled my skin as I stood with a large group of friends at the ridge burn.

The ridge burn is a plot of forestland just outside of Copper Springs on Canary Road—a back road only locals used—that was struck by lightning years ago, leaving a cleared-out area of charred tree stumps and singed earth. It's not useful for much, but it was the perfect starting place for our annual game of capture the flag.

It was a long-standing tradition; our high school would play the rival school in a summer game of capture the flag—in which the team "flags" were actual town flags—to determine which school would have the honor of flying the other town's flag all year.

Copper Springs had lost the prior two years, so the stakes were high for me and my peers as we met with our opponents in the charred clearing. We partnered off, as we did every summer, but due to Charity being all chummy with Daren, and Levi arriving late, I ended up being partnered off with Levi. Which was fine by me because Levi was awesome at capture the flag.

The goal of the game was to snag the other team's flag before being tagged by an opponent. Tree houses, crate boxes, forts, tents, and tunnels were strategically set up throughout the four acres of the ridge burn as places to hide along the way. Each team had a home base set up at opposite ends of the playing field, and that's where we started.

Levi and I carefully maneuvered our way to the other team's

flag and snatched it before being tagged. That was the easy part. The tricky part was getting the flag back to our own team's home base.

We quietly crept through the forest as the clouds darkened above us and thunder rumbled through the air. Our fort was clear on the other side of the ridge burn, so we'd have to hurry if we wanted to reach it before the summer downpour fell on us and made running difficult. We could see our home base in the far distance. Levi looked at me. I looked at him. We nodded at each other, once. I clutched the other team's green-and-yellow flag in my fist and took a deep breath. Then we were off.

We rushed through the trees, smiles on our faces as we tried to outrun the storm. Droplets began to fall, catching on our cheeks and eyelashes as we charged through the darkening afternoon. We were fast, but the storm found us, and soon the clouds split open and rain poured down, deafening the day and mudding the ground.

"Come on!" Levi shouted with a smile, grabbing my hand as we splashed through mud and broken leaves.

I took his hand and laughed as he started spitting out the water coming down on him. We were already drenched, so there was no use in running, but we did anyway.

Lightning cut through the sky, a streak of silver in the dusky clouds, followed by another roar of thunder. It was an odd contrast to the sharp rays of sunshine slicing through the same darkness above us. Half day, half torrent. Beautiful and frightening. But I was nothing but brave with Levi holding my hand.

"We're not going to make it," I said, barely audible above the loud rain.

He looked around, then yanked me to the side with a smile. "Over here, Pix."

I chased after him, the storm chasing after us, as he led us into a thicket of trees where a few forts were hidden.

Shelter.

He pulled us into the closest one; it was half-destroyed, so we plastered ourselves against the far wall where what little was left of the roof still stood. Well, *Levi* plastered himself against the wall. I plastered myself against his chest. Both of us stifled smiles as our opponents ran past the fort, completely oblivious to our presence. We were so going to win this time.

We stood, chest to chest, perfectly still for a moment, waiting for the footsteps outside to fade away. I looked up at Levi, a grin on my face, and mouthed, *Suckers.*

He looked down with a huge smile and nodded.

His gleaming eyes dropped to my mouth and, in an instant, everything changed. We changed.

I was aware of him completely. The way he smelled, the feel of his breaths against my face, his hard body lined against my chest.

Neither of us moved even though the footsteps had all but vanished outside. My eyes fell to his lips, and his chest filled with a deeper breath.

Oh God.

I looked back up at him, and the only thing I could think about were his blue eyes, solid and steady, intense and drowning me slowly.

I should have moved away from him. I should have laughed off the awkwardness and removed my body from the warmth of his. But instead I just stood there, trapped in this new sensation between us.

His eyes fell to my mouth again, and I parted my lips.

He leaned his head down.

I tipped my head up.

Slowly, so slowly it hurt, our lips brushed against each other. Tentative. Careful. Unsure.

He kissed me softly. Once. Twice.

And then everything unsure about us flew right out the little fort window.

Our mouths came together in a desperate collision, hungry. It was a tangle of tongues and exhales, greedy and shameless. Hot breath glided across my face and down my throat as our wet mouths tried to conquer each other.

Lightning flashed outside, touching down close enough to make the air crackle with energy, and the resounding thunder made the fort walls shake.

He gripped my hips as my hands, still clutching the flag, slid over his shoulders and pulled me up toward the mouth I wanted so much more of. I whimpered desperately and I wasn't even ashamed. This was Levi. This was everything right.

His hands slid up my body and held my face, his warm palms cupping the sides of my neck as his thumbs stroked the edge of my jaw and the curve of my cheeks.

He kissed me like he owned me. Like I was his, and his alone, to kiss. And I wanted to be.

I felt precious and sexy at the same time. His hands fell back to my hips, where he pressed his fingers into the exposed skin below my shirt. He was touching my skin; he was lighting me on fire.

We kissed and touched in the little fort to the sound of angry thunder and heavy rain; falling on the wooden planks of the meager roof; falling on the dirt outside. Drenching everything I ever thought I knew about myself. Changing me—changing *us*—forever. And it was beautiful.

But that was before everything went to hell.

————

It's just cheesecake. It's harmless.

Yet I'm staring at it like at any moment it might grow teeth and gnaw off my arms.

"Just wrap it up, honey, and put it in the fridge for tomorrow," Mable says as she hangs up her apron for the night and finds her purse, completely oblivious to my current cheesecake phobia. "I'll make the toppings in the morning."

I nod.

Charity loved cheesecake.

"Good night, love."

"Night," I say halfheartedly as Mable exits through the dining room door. I hear a roll of distant thunder groan outside. Then nothing.

It's suddenly very quiet in here, and I can't help the memories that start whispering in the silence.

Last summer, Charity and I went to a party and got drunk. Wasted, actually. We always drank too much.

It was the day after my impromptu make-out session with Levi in the fort, and he and I hadn't spoken since. I wasn't sure how I felt about our kiss—or maybe I was and that was why I was getting trashed—but either way, I was anxious about Levi's feelings for me and the alcohol was making me feel better.

Charity was drinking and having a grand ol' time, until she walked in on Daren making out with another girl. They weren't technically dating at the time, but still she freaked out and they got into a giant fight. Charity came to find me in my drunken stupor, hysterical, crying her eyes out about Daren as I listened with fierce sympathy.

Even though Daren was our designated driver that night, I was emphatic about getting Charity the hell out of that party. I insisted we drive ourselves home.

"To hell with him," I'd said. "Let's get out of this shithole!"

"Yeah!" Charity said. "I'm the soberest of the two of us. I'll drive!"

We were stupid.

We climbed into Charity's little car and she peeled out onto Canary Road with me as her passenger. We were eighteen and thought we were invincible, listening to loud music as we both ranted and cursed Daren's name. Then, out of nowhere, Levi's truck appeared in front of us, blocking the road beside the ridge burn.

Charity slowed down with a curse. "How does my brother always know where we are?" She made a face. "It's like he has spies everywhere."

"Your brother's hot," I said with a drunk giggle.

"Ew. That's so gross."

I sighed and slurred, "I want Leaves to like me."

"God." She rolled her eyes. "He does. Leaves loves you. Leaves leaves you. Loves leaves you? What am I trying to say?"

We giggled as we neared the truck.

Levi was standing in the middle of the road, looking like a pissed-off superhero with his messy dark hair and steel-blue eyes as he motioned for Charity to pull over. The hazard lights of his truck blinked into the night as he watched her pull over and stop. Then he stormed over to her door.

Yanking it open, he said, "What the hell's the matter with you, Charity? Driving drunk? Get your ass out of the car!"

She started bawling. "You don't understand, Leaves. I caught Daren kissing Sierra Umbridge at the party and he's such an asshole and I just had to get out of that party, so Pixie said we should just drive ourselves—"

"I don't care!" He leaned in and turned off the ignition.

"Stop yelling at me!" Charity's tears dried up with her anger.

He grabbed her face and looked at her sternly. "You scared the shit out of me." His voice trembled as he looked into her eyes and released her chin. "Go get in my truck."

"I'm really not that drunk—"

"*Now*," he said, his voice getting all scary and low.

She shook her head. "No. I need my car in the morning for work and—"

"Fine." He growled. "Get in the backseat and I'll drive your car."

She huffed and clambered out of the car, stumbling in her high heels as she walked to the back door.

He climbed into the driver's seat and pierced me with his intense gaze, and I swear a piece of my heart broke with just that one look.

I tucked my lips in. "You seem mad."

"I *am* mad." He leaned over and made sure my seat belt was buckled before closing the door and putting on his own.

"I'm sorry," I said. "This is all my fault. I told Charity we should drive home. I didn't mean for you to have to drive out here and get us. I'm so sorry, Leaves. So, *so* sorry."

He met my eyes with a desperate gaze, and that's when I realized his anger was really just fear. Terrible and sad fear.

"Driving drunk is stupid." He looked away. "You know better, Pix."

A slow, hot tear rolled down my face. I did know better. I had disappointed him. I had scared him. I'd probably lost him forever too.

Charity climbed into the backseat and fumbled with her seat belt until it clicked into place. Levi pulled back onto the road, driving alongside the ridge burn as he yelled at us about how we should know better. And then...

I don't know.

Lights. Horns. Whooshing sounds.

And everything went black.

When I regained consciousness, I was in a hospital bed with IVs strung from my limbs, machines beeping at me, and breathing tubes shoved down my throat. I had a nasty gash in my chest from a thick shard of glass that had torn through my body, and my lungs were collapsing.

I was barely alive.

Levi was unconscious a floor below me.

And Charity was dead.

My best friend was dead.

I try to push the memories away as I stare down at the cheesecake. The memories hurt. They hurt so much. But it's no use.

They all come screaming back, cutting through me like that damn shard of glass until I'm lost and lonely and all flayed open under the dim kitchen lights.

And now I'm crying.

20

LEVI

It's my first game as starting quarterback at ASU. My parents are in the stands with Charity and Pixie, all of them cheering me on. The girls are both wearing jerseys with my name and number on the back, and Pixie has a sun devil painted on her face.

It's the happiest I've ever been. My dreams are within reach, and everyone I care about is rooting for me. I can do this. I will do this.

"Go, Leaves!" Charity calls from the bleachers. I don't know how I hear her, or how I know it's Charity's voice, but I just do. And I'm filled with pride—

I dart up in bed, gasping for air. A thin layer of sweat coats my chest as I try to calm myself. I stare across my dark room at the newly patched wall, my heart slamming against my rib cage, my lungs tight and hot.

I don't want to remember. I don't want to remember.

She was so proud...

The ache in my chest coils tighter and tighter until I can no longer stay in bed. I get up. I pace. I run my hands through my hair as I pad across the hardwood floor.

My window rattles with a bellow of thunder as a white fork of lightning strikes outside. The beige envelopes on my desk light up with the flash, daring me to ignore them a moment longer as my heart continues to pound.

Beige envelopes. Nightmares.

Relentless bastards, indeed.

I snatch an envelope up and tear it open, knowing full well what I'll find inside. The letterhead crinkles as I slowly unfold it.

Dear Mr. Andrews,

I realize your personal life took a tragic turn last year and a slip in your studies is understandable. But as the dean of students here at Arizona State University, I have no choice but to suspend your enrollment until you are ready to return to school with a refreshed perspective. That being said, the terms of your academic probation are temporary and can be rectified by submitting a single essay to my office on the concept of winning.

The concept of winning is not solely reserved for athletics. It applies to all fields of pursuit and, in your case specifically, academic standing. I hope to see your essay on my desk by the end of this summer so Arizona State University may welcome you back, both to school and to the football field, this coming fall.

Sincerely,
Dean Maxwell

Another streak of lightning cuts across the black night and the clouds finally break, releasing the heavy downpour they've been holding back all summer. The storm falls to the earth, loud, dark, and wild, as I reread the letter.

Then I crumple it up and toss it in the trash.

The demons can go to hell.

———

Rain has been falling steady all night, and the morning drizzle doesn't look as though it will be letting up anytime soon. My sleep was plagued with nightmares and truths, so I'm exhausted as I roll out of bed and quickly shower.

When I exit the bathroom, Pixie is standing there with her shower supplies and a blank expression on her face.

We haven't spoken in days.

We silently move past each other without speaking, without touching.

After getting dressed, I hurry from the east wing and grab my To Do list from Ellen. The first item is a broken drawer behind the front desk.

Just as I reach the lobby, Haley bursts through the front door, her giant purse falling off her arm as she rounds the desk.

"I'm here, I'm here!" she announces to no one, completely out of breath.

Haley has punctuality problems.

Her orange shirt is dotted with dark spots of rain, and her shoes squeak against the wood floor as she rounds the desk. She throws her purse down with a heavy *thud*, water droplets running down the material in thin rivers, and tucks her thick black hair behind her ears.

"Hey, Levi!" She waves at me even though I'm only a foot away.

I step over her giant bag.

"Hey." I start assessing the drawer damage as thunder cracks outside and vibrates the front windows.

"Ellen's not here yet, is she?" She looks around nervously as she clicks on the computer and starts rummaging through things, trying to act like she's been hard at work for an hour.

"She's in her office," I say.

Haley sighs in relief, picks her purse back up, and digs around inside until she comes up with a candy bar. "So...how have you been?"

"Fine." I remove the drawer and study the broken track.

She takes a bite. "And...how's the job going?"

"Fine."

"And...how's Pixie?"

I frown. "How would I know?"

She shrugs. "You live with her."

"I don't live with Pixie."

"You live *by* her."

"Which is not the same as living *with* her." I kneel on the ground and start working on the broken track.

"So you don't know how she is?"

"No."

A moment passes where Haley takes another bite of her candy and watches me closely. "You know what I think?"

I sigh.

"I think Pixie's sad," she continues. "And not because of the whore thing."

Damn gossip.

Haley says, "I think she's sad because she misses you."

I unscrew the broken track with more fervor than necessary. "Nah. I think it's the whore thing."

I can feel her eyes searing the back of my neck. "Would that make it easier for you?"

"Make what easier?"

"Missing her."

I stare at the drawer, cursing small-town nosiness and the uncomfortable conversations it brings, and open my mouth to spew a well-crafted denial—when the fire alarm goes off.

Chaos ensues, and guests start spilling out of their rooms and into the lobby, flustered and excited. Dropping my tools, I rush to the system control box at the back of the lobby and throw open the panel door to see which room triggered the alarm. My heart stops.

The kitchen.

It's all I can do not to knock guests over as I run that way. If anything happened to Pixie, if something exploded and hurt her, if she got burned—

Oh God. Oh God.

The screaming alarm drowns out all other noise as I skid around corners and through doorways. When I finally reach the kitchen, I see Pixie crouched on the floor with her back to me.

"Pixie!" I don't think. I just swoop down and pull her into my arms, icy fear shooting through my veins as I turn her to face me.

She looks at me in confusion, covering her ears from the blaring alarm, and it takes a few moments for me to register that she's not hurt. I look around. No fire. No smoke. She's fine.

She's breathing. She's alive. She has a smudge of something white on her cheek, but otherwise she's fine.

Her eyes fall to my chest and that's when I realize I'm clutching her to my body, one hand cradling her head and the other pressed against her back.

She's fine.

I slowly release her and we both stand. I rub a shaky hand over my mouth.

She must have seen the fear in my eyes because she starts explaining, raising her voice to be heard over the screeching of the fire alarm. "I heard the alarm go off and Mable and I started to leave out the back door, but I forgot to turn off the gas, so I came back in and then I knocked the powdered sugar all over the floor—"

"Pixie!" Mable gives a panicked wave from the back door. "Come outside."

Outside, I see guests and employees congregating under the gazebo at the back of the field, rain falling steadily on the lavender flowers surrounding them.

Pixie looks at me for a second before moving toward Mable. Once she's out of the kitchen, my heart starts beating again and I hurry back to the lobby. Ellen is guiding people out of their rooms and to the back doors as Angelo leads everyone to the gazebo.

"Where's the fire?" Ellen yells over the blaring lobby.

I shake my head. "There isn't one!"

"What?" She can't hear me over the alarm and the rushing guests.

I run back to the control panel and disengage the alarm, throwing the inn into silence. As the last of the guests hurry out the back door, I start running around the west wing just in case, looking in every room, sniffing the air. Nothing. I search the dining room, the bathrooms, but there's no fire anywhere.

As I make my way back to the lobby, I slowly start to relax. There's no danger. Pixie's fine.

"What happened?" Ellen asks, standing by the front desk, looking incredibly stressed.

"Something must have tripped the kitchen alarm," I say. "It was probably the rain seeping into the old wiring system."

"No fire?" Pixie, who clearly didn't follow Mable's orders and join everyone under the gazebo, comes up to Ellen with a concerned look.

"No fire," Ellen confirms.

My eyes catch on Pixie's, and we stare at each other. Powdered sugar is still on her cheek. Why is my heart pounding?

"Charity's on the phone."

We whip our heads to Haley, who is holding a phone out to Ellen.

"Charity from the alarm company," Haley quickly clarifies, looking at us apologetically.

"Oh." Ellen takes the phone and walks away as she answers.

"Good grief, woman! Answering the phones?" Angelo shouts at Haley from the back door. "What, are you trying to give me a heart attack? Get your cute butt out here, where I know you're safe."

"I'm coming. Geez." She hurries toward the door. "I had to get the phone, Ang. It was Charity from the alarm company..." Their voices disappear as the back door closes.

And then it's just Pixie and me, standing in the lobby, thinking about Charity and not making eye contact.

I should say something she needs to hear.

Something like, *I'm sorry I killed your best friend.*

Or, *I'm sorry I almost got* you *killed.*

Or better yet, *I'm sorry I intervened with fate and fucked everything up.*

But I say nothing. I realize my guilt isn't entirely rational, but that doesn't stop me from feeling it.

Pixie looks at me with unreadable eyes and swallows. "I'm glad you're okay. When I first heard the alarm go off—" She presses her lips together. "I'm just glad you're okay."

And for the second time today, my heart stops.

"Pix, I…if anything ever…" Am I brave enough to say something real here? Something honest? "I'm glad you're okay too," I say, because I'm chickenshit.

She nods, and we stand in silence.

I shift my weight. "About the other day—"

"It's fine." She waves me off.

"No, it's not." I shake my head. "It's not fine. I shouldn't have called you a whore. I'm an ass and I'm sorry. I really am."

She shrugs. "Let's just pretend it didn't happen."

I slowly nod. Sure. That's what we're good at: pretending things didn't happen.

21

PIXIE

When I was seven years old, I spent nearly every weekend at Charity's house. On one of these nights, while sleeping beside my bestie in our matching My Little Pony sleeping bags under the glow of her night-light, I woke up shaking from a nightmare, convinced there were monsters out to get me.

I tiptoed out of Charity's bedroom and headed for the bathroom—for some reason I thought bathrooms were monster-free zones—and on my way down the dark hallway, I heard a voice.

"What are you doing?" Levi whispered.

He scared the crap out of me, and I totally jumped and started crying and blabbing about my scary dream and how there were monsters everywhere and how I was going to die.

He looked at me like I was crazy as tears and boogers ran down my face.

"Don't cry, Pixie. Hey…" He stepped out of his room and hesitantly pulled me into an awkward boy hug. "If I see any monsters, I'll punch them until they turn into mush, okay?"

My tears and boogers started to subside as I shook in his skinny arms. If Levi would mush monsters for me, I knew I was safe.

"Want to see something cool?" he asked, no doubt trying to distract me.

I nodded.

He led me to an upstairs window overlooking their backyard, opened it, and climbed out onto the porch roof below, motioning for me to follow. I did, and we sat side by side on the roof and stared up at the night sky.

"This is what I do when I have a bad dream," he said. "There aren't any monsters out here." He sounded very matter-of-fact, in his Superman pajamas and messy hair.

As I took in the twinkling stars and quiet shadows of the night, I realized he was right. There weren't any monsters outside. Or at least none when I was sitting beside Levi.

That was the first time Levi Andrews was my hero.

And yesterday, when he thought I was hurt and he looked scared out of his mind, it was like he was that eight-year-old boy again. Protecting me. Looking at me like I was worth saving. And it made me want to cry for everything that we'd lost. Everything I'd ruined the night I let Charity drive drunk.

I swallow, trying to push the memory back into the cold corner of my mind where most of my childhood is locked up, and step out of my bedroom.

Levi's in the shower, hogging all the hot water again, and I'm both mad and relieved. Yesterday's scare broke the silence between us, and with it came an unspoken truce. And I'll take a cold shower over a cold shoulder any day.

When he finally emerges from the steamy bathroom, I put on my best "I'm pissed" look and stare him down in the hall-way. He's wearing only a towel, of course, and I'm momentarily distracted.

"Waiting outside the door, Pix?" He slants his eyes with a cocky smile. "Have you been missing me?"

I raise a bored eyebrow. "Only with my shotgun."

Okay, it's a cheesy line, but come on. It's early. And he's only wearing a towel. I can't be expected to whip out witty comments when I'm sleepy and aroused.

I try to step around him and enter the bathroom, but he blocks my path. With his bare chest just inches from my face, the textured skin of his nipple catches my eye and white-hot desire darts through me. It's all I can do not to lick him.

This is what I've been reduced to. Nipple-licking fantasies.

"If you want to see me naked that bad, all you have to do is ask." He winks.

"Move, asshole." I push against his chest with my hand, damp heat wrapping around my wrist, and move him out of the bathroom and into the hallway.

When he speaks, his chest vibrates and the current runs up my arm. "Ah, Pix. You know you love me."

I remove my hand from his chest. "I know I *loathe* you."

"Promises, promises," he says with a crooked smile as I start to shut the bathroom door.

But for a moment—for a super-tiny second, right before I close the door on his face—our eyes meet in a vulnerable gaze.

No facades. No snarky remarks. Just him and me, seeing each other. Knowing the hard things we wish we didn't and wanting to undo things we can't. It's raw and it's honest and it makes me want to cry.

But he blinks.

And I blink.

And then it's gone.

The bathroom door latches shut, and I'm left alone in the spearmint bathroom with my scar and an endless supply of cold water.

22

LEVI

*N*ote to self: Do not look in Pixie's eyes. From now on, stare at her mouth or her nose or...just anywhere else. But not her eyes. Her eyes see inside me and know the things I'm too afraid to say out loud.

On my way to Ellen's office I pass Haley, who quickly looks away.

She feels bad about saying the name Charity yesterday, and how stupid is that? People shouldn't be so afraid of Pixie and me that they can't even speak Charity's name around us. That's bullshit. Pixie and I are fine.

I rub the back of my neck because that's a lie straight from hell.

I turn a corner and pace down the back hallway.

Most people who lose someone close to them support each other through the tragedy.

Not Pix and I.

After Charity died, Pixie and I just stopped talking.

In fact, the first time I saw Pixie after Charity's funeral was just a few weeks ago, when she started working at the inn. And her presence took me by complete surprise.

I walked out of my bedroom and there she was, in her yellow dress, looking lost and found at the same time.

Little Pixie, whom I had spent my whole life loving and one night destroying, was standing outside my bedroom with pink toenails, a blue suitcase, and a look on her face that made me feel like I was home.

And God, I wanted to be home.

But guilt's a hungry bastard, so any thoughts I had about hugging her and begging her to forgive me for hurting Charity—for hurting *her*—were swallowed alive by the shame in my soul.

We stood in the hall, staring at each other in confusion for a minute before a very strained conversation took place.

"Uh…what are you…?" I had no words.

She licked her lips. "I just started working here. In the kitchen. For my aunt. School's out, and I couldn't stand the idea of staying with my mom."

"Oh." I nodded, staring at her mouth. "Ellen must have forgotten to mention that to me."

She shifted her weight. "What, uh…what are you doing here?"

"I work here."

"Oh."

I paused. "And I live here."

Her eyes widened briefly, then turned expressionless. "Really." She inhaled. "Ellen didn't tell me that."

Awkward silence.

I cleared my throat. "So if you're working in the kitchen, what brings you up here, to the east wing?"

She bit her lip. "Uh, my room's up here?"

"Your room?"

"Yeah, I uh…I live here now. Too." She pointed to the bedroom door next to mine, and I nodded, thrilled and terrified. Mostly terrified.

"So I guess we'll be sharing a bathroom."

Her eyes moved between me and the bathroom, then slid to our bedroom doors. "I guess so."

We locked gazes, and suddenly that stupid pigeon of sexual tension was in the air, swooping all around us.

Once again, I cleared my throat. "I'll be seeing you, then." Then I left down the stairs, trying to outrun the heat from her body and her pretty green eyes.

That was the first conversation we'd had since the night of the accident, and in all the conversations since then, we've never once mentioned Charity's name.

We exist as though Charity is still alive. I treat Pixie like she's my annoying little sister, and she treats me the same way. It works. It helps. And it's familiar.

Except we're not like siblings. At all.

I reach Ellen's office and rap my knuckles against her door.

"Come in," she says from within.

I let myself in and leave the door open. "Do you have my list for today?"

She looks up from her computer screen and hands me a piece of paper, looking exhausted and stressed out.

"What's up?" I take the list from her hand.

She sighs and rubs her temples. "Yesterday was a disaster. I can't have the fire alarm go off every time it rains. Guests will just freak out."

I shrug. "So install an updated system."

"Right. I know." She looks back at the computer. "I just don't know where to start. I've been looking up alarm systems all morning and there are so many and I have a ton of other work to do and a bunch of new guests are arriving this afternoon, and I'm just *so* overwhelmed."

"I'll do it." I smile, partly because I'm sincere in my offer and partly because Ellen reminds me of Pixie when she rambles like that. "I'll do research and figure out what type of alarm system would suit the inn best."

Her hazel eyes light up. "Really? Ah! Levi, that would be great."

Haley knocks on the open office door and finds my eyes. "You have, uh . . . visitors."

I frown. "Visitors?"

"Visitors."

"O-kay." I look back at Ellen. "I'll start doing research this week—sound good?"

She smiles brightly. "Sounds excellent."

Leaving her office, I follow Haley back to the lobby, where I find Zack staring at the Fourth of July flyer by the front door—and beside him is his goat, on a leash.

"Seriously?" I say as I near them. "You brought the goat inside?"

He turns. "He has a name, you know. Marvin."

"You brought the goat *inside*."

"Well, I can't leave him in the car. He cries and screams and it's very unsettling. It's like toting around a hairy toddler." Zack points to the flyer. "You didn't tell me about this."

"About the Fourth of July thing?"

"No. About the cornhole tournament *at* the Fourth of July thing. We are so doing this."

"No, we're not."

"Yes, we are."

Ellen walks past the lobby in her high heels, stops in her tracks, and turns back around to face Zack.

She points at Marvin. "Is that a goat?"

Zack nods once. "Yes, ma'am."

"In my lobby?"

"Yes, ma'am. But he's a friendly goat."

Ellen plasters on a polite smile. "I don't care if he's a tap-dancing goat. I want him out of here."

"Ooh. Harsh," he says. "But fair. Come on, boy." He pulls Marvin away from the activities board, where he was chewing on a flyer for bingo night.

Ellen turns to leave, her heels clicking on the wood floor as she sings out, "Thank you, Zack. Always a pleasure to see you."

"You too, Ms. Marshall," Zack calls out, lowering his voice as he watches her walk away with his lips parted. "Trust me, the pleasure is all mine..."

"Dude." I stare at him. "Stop it."

He yanks his eyes away from Ellen and mocks an innocent grin. "What?"

I shake my head. "Come on."

Zack and Marvin and I walk out the back doors and stand beside the lavender field as the morning sun slips behind a few left-over storm clouds. The smell of rain still clings to the humid air, but otherwise the storm has cleared out.

I cross my arms. "So why are you here?"

"Very blunt. I like it." Zack pulls Marvin away from the potted flowers Ellen has flanking the back door. "You're being a stubborn jackass."

I raise a brow. "Me? Or the goat?"

"Both of you, really." Zack tries to unwind himself from the leash as Marvin starts walking around him in circles. "But mostly you." I watch Marvin yank on the leash and nearly trip Zack.

"I doubt that," I say.

Zack unwinds from the twisted leash and exhales as he looks at me. "Coach said you haven't even responded to Dean Maxwell's request."

I run a hand over my head and mutter, "Not this again."

"It's one fucking essay, dude. You can do that. Hell, you can pay someone to do that."

"It's more than an essay," I say. "It's me. I lost focus. And I don't know if I even want to go back."

He steps over the leash as Marvin moves in circles again. "So what, then? You're just going to fix toilets for the rest of your life?"

I shrug, a thin burst of stress layering my skin. "Maybe."

That's my biggest fear. There's nothing shameful about being a handyman. In a way, it's actually pretty rewarding work. But it's not what I want for my life, and with every day that passes I feel any future in something other than handiwork slipping farther and farther away.

He curses and pulls Marvin away from the nearby lavender flowers. "You're unbelievable. And selfish."

"Me? Or the goat?"

Zack looks up. "YOU, dude."

"I'm selfish?"

"Yes," he says, completely serious. "Me and the guys chose to be on this team because Levi Fucking Andrews was going to be our quarterback. This isn't just about you anymore. Don't screw us over, man. Get your goddamn head figured out and come back and play."

Well...shit.

The kitchen's back door opens and Pixie comes out carrying a bag of trash. She throws it away, completely oblivious to us, until Zack opens his giant mouth.

"Sarah!" he shouts out merrily.

Her face breaks into a wide grin. "Hey, Zack." Her smile slips a bit as her eyes catch on mine, then quickly move back to Zack. "How've you be—is that a goat?"

Marvin bleats out a noise that sounds eerily similar to the cry of a small child.

"This is Marvin," he says. "He eats everything and yells like a distressed baby to get attention. I'm goat-sitting him this summer."

"Why?" She steps to the side as Marvin tries to lick her apron. "Did you lose a bet?"

He grins. "Better. I gained a phone number."

She shakes her head. "You will do anything for a hot girl."

"Present company included." He winks.

"In that case…" She gestures to me. "Think you can get this schmuck to stop using all the hot water so I don't have to take a cold shower every morning?"

I glare at her, but she simply cocks an eyebrow in return.

"Levi is depriving you of hot showers?" Zack turns to me and slowly says, "Interesting."

I look at Pixie. "Maybe you could set an alarm and hog the hot water yourself."

She says, "Maybe you could shower at night and save us both the trouble."

"Maybe you could quit nagging me."

"Maybe you could rock a half-beard for the rest of the summer."

"Wow." Zack appears thoroughly amused as he looks back and forth between us. He nods. "This feels good. This feels *right*."

Marvin goat-yells again.

"Whatever," Pixie says. "I have a job to get back to. It was good seeing you, Zack." She gives him a little wave before heading back inside.

"Later." Zack looks after her until she disappears, then turns back to me and smiles.

I stare at him. "What?"

He laughs. "I don't know what your endgame is here, but you really need to get your shit together."

I sigh and step out of the way as Marvin tries to bite my foot. "I know, I know. Everyone wants me to write the damn essay."

"No, I mean with Sarah," he says. "But yeah. The essay thing too." He lets out a whistle. "Damn, dude. You have a lot of shit to get together."

Marvin looks up and yells again.

"Tell me about it."

———

After I finish working for the day, I head back inside and to the stairs. As I round the banister, I come face-to-face with Ellen and a stack of mail.

"There you are." She smiles and presses the envelopes against my chest. "More mail."

"Gee. Thanks." I take the letters from her hands.

"Anytime." She moves past me.

I walk upstairs, enter my room, and throw the letters onto my desk. One of the envelopes skids across the surface and hits my laptop, bringing the screen to life. My e-mail window glares back at me with a new message. Stepping closer, I see that it's from my mom, and my chest immediately tightens.

I haven't spoken to either of my parents in months.

After Charity died, Mom and Dad went a little crazy. Instead of coping with their daughter's death, they took their sorrows out on each other. They fought constantly. They grieved endlessly. But not together. They didn't know how to console each other, so instead they slipped deeper and deeper into their own personal pits of grief.

They separated three months after the accident, and both of them left town.

My dad took a job in Nevada, where he promptly buried himself in his work and took up smoking. He didn't even bother to say good-bye before he left. I think the thought of making his move "official" with a send-off and a good-bye hug was just too much for him to bear.

But he called me once, after he moved. We spent the entire phone call rehashing a recent NFL game and kept away from any real-life topics. I haven't spoken with him since.

My mom moved to New Hampshire, where she was far away from Charity's memory and my facial features. After the funeral, she could barely look at me, the living son who so resembled her deceased daughter. And when she did chance a glance at me, her eyes would flash with pain before quickly darting elsewhere. Maybe she thought putting twenty-five hundred miles between my face and her eyes would make things hurt less.

"I'll call you and you can come visit," she said to me the day she left Copper Springs. I lifted her heavy suitcase into the white mini-van she used to drive Charity to piano lessons in and leaned down so she could hug me good-bye. She smelled like lemons. She always smelled like lemons.

She squeezed me tighter than necessary and mumbled a bunch of things about taking care of myself, but she didn't make eye contact. Not even when tears dripped down her soft cheeks.

She drove away, and I watched the white minivan disappear down the street like it was any other Tuesday. Headed to school, to piano lessons, to football practice.

Headed to New Hampshire.

That was last winter. I've talked to my mom twice since then, and both conversations were strained and short, like we no longer know how to interact with each other.

So her e-mailing me is a surprise. Not a pleasant surprise, exactly. Just an interesting one.

With a quiet inhale, I sit down at my desk and open her e-mail. It's addressed to me, but she copied my father as well.

Fantastic.

From: Linda Andrews
To: Levi Andrews; Mark Andrews
Subject: College

Levi,

I know things haven't been perfect for our family lately, and I know your father and I aren't helping any by keeping our distance from each other. But the two of us have been talking, and we're both concerned about you.

As you know, Dean Maxwell is good friends with your father, and he informed us that you haven't made any attempt to be reinstated at school. What is going on, Levi? Why are you not enrolled?

Your father and I realize that you're an adult now and can make your own decisions, but we want you to be happy. We want great things for you. We want you to play football and finish college, and go on to the live the life that you've worked so hard to earn. And we want to help you in any way we can. Let's come together as a family to get this resolved.

We hope you're doing well. And we love you so much. And miss you.

Love,

Mom and Dad

Several emotions pass through me as I reread the e-mail. Anger. Bitterness. Annoyance. The stubborn part of me wants to ignore it altogether and not respond. But the prideful part of me won't allow it. So I write them back.

From: Levi Andrews
To: Linda Andrews; Mark Andrews
Subject: RE: College

Mom and Dad,

It's nice to hear the two of you are on speaking terms, like grown adults who are still married should be, but I'm a little confused at why you're both so "concerned" for me.

I would think that the time for two parents to be worried about their child would be the first few months after that child lost his baby sister. But you guys didn't seem at all interested in my state of mind or well-being after Charity died. In fact, it was quite the opposite.

I realize you blame me for her death, and honestly I don't fault you for that. But I was a wreck after the accident. I really needed you guys, and you just took off and went about "finding" yourselves and "starting fresh." I didn't have that luxury. I had to stay.

I was racked with guilt and so messed up. I slowly failed all my classes at school and eventually got kicked off the football team at ASU. So yeah, my probationary status at school is a bummer, but it's far less severe than my psychological status during your flee-the-city phases.

So thanks for your concern, but you'll understand if I don't really feel like coming together as a "family" on this one. Clearly, I've handled far worse on my own. There's no need to start helping me now.

Love,
Levi

P.S. In case you were wondering, Pixie's doing just great too.

I click Send without a second thought and close my laptop.

23

PIXIE

*I*t's late, and most of the inn guests are already asleep.

I wait until I hear the TV click on in Levi's room before I start plugging everything I own into the wall.

We argued today. We avoided each other. And aside from the weird look we exchanged in the hallway this morning and our little spat in front of Zack, everything is back to normal.

Which means I owe Levi for the cold shower I had to take.

I turn everything on and the lights go out. I hear the TV die in the next room and crawl onto my bed with a smile.

"Pixie!" Levi's irritated voice rings through the walls and I'm feeling happier than a mature person should.

I hear stomping, and then he opens my bedroom door. Just opens it. Like he has the right to just waltz into my room. I could be naked in here; he doesn't know.

"You're going out to the fuse box this time." He steps inside, and now he's standing just a few feet away, pointing his finger at me.

I'm on the bed, trying to look casual, like lying in the dark playing games on my phone is perfectly normal. The only light in the room is coming from the glow of my phone and the half-moon outside, so we both look blue and soft. And in the blue softness, I see he's shirtless.

I see Levi without a shirt on almost every morning, but I've never seen him half-naked in the dark, and something about it makes my body feel electric.

"Not going to happen," I say.

He steps closer. "Well, I sure as hell am not marching outside to turn the power back on."

I shrug. "Fine with me. I don't need electricity tonight. I can watch TV on my fully charged phone." I wiggle said phone at him.

He sighs. "You don't understand. I was looking up the contact information for an alarm company I found so I can call and schedule the installation tomorrow. I need the Internet, Pix."

"Then use your phone."

"My phone is dead."

The boy never charges anything. He almost makes the whole fuse-blowing thing too easy.

"Well, that's too bad. I guess you're going to have to turn the electricity back on after all." I pretend to be very interested in my game.

"Let me use your phone. Just for a minute."

"No."

"Come on. It's for Ellen." He implores me with a pouty face I've seen him use on his mom a dozen times.

I scoff. "Please."

"Dammit, Pixie." The pout is gone.

"Maybe tomorrow you'll remember to charge your *own* phone. Or hey, better yet, maybe you'll let me have a hot shower." I make a big production of pressing random buttons on my phone.

He slumps his shoulders like he's accepting defeat, then whips out his arm and tries to swipe the phone from my hands. Sneaky bastard.

I pull my phone back and kick at him with my foot, but he grabs my ankle—because I'm not exactly a ninja with my kicking skills—and then we both freeze.

Because now I'm leaning back on the bed with my legs spread apart, and he's got one hand on my ankle and the other on the bed next to my hip where he was reaching for my phone, and his body is in between my legs, which are completely bare except for the tiny gym shorts I have on, and my right arm is raised over my head with my cell phone still out of his reach, but my back is arched and my shirt has come up so my stomach is completely exposed and I'm hot all over.

Hot. Heat. Everywhere.

I mean, really. We look like we're in the middle of having sex, but with clothes on. My body knows this. His body knows this. And our bodies are really, really happy about this.

He's looking at me with nothing in his eyes except *want*. And I like it. No, I *love* it.

This must show on my face because his hand—still wrapped around my ankle—moves up my leg an inch, and he watches my reaction.

I try not to react because, hell, he can't *win*. He can't just be asshole Levi all day long and then climb into my bed at night and touch me wherever he pleases.

Ugh. Yes he can.

I part my lips and he slowly, *slowly* slides his warm hand up my calf and, holy hell, I could orgasm right here. I might, actually.

My calf.

My *calf.*

He's touching my *calf* and I'm more turned on than I've ever been in my life.

His hand shifts again, and the only thought in my head is, *Go higher, go higher.*

Please, dear God, go higher.

24

LEVI

I could do it. She wants me to do it. She wants me to do whatever I want.

And I want...so...much.

I look at her bare stomach and stare at the skin below her belly button.

I could kiss her there. I could keep my palm around her calf and bend it to her body and lie down between her legs and lick a trail along the very low waistline of her ridiculous shorts. I look up at her, see the desire in her eyes, and almost do it.

But then I see the end of her scar peeking out from the bottom of her shirt and it's like a train hits me, crashing into me and shredding up my insides with hot metal and shards of split iron until I feel nothing but pain.

What the hell am I doing? This is Pixie.

Pixie.

I can't ruin her life and then *sleep* with her. That would be fucked up on so many levels. I'm not an angel, but I know the difference between right and wrong, and sex with the girl I maimed and nearly killed would be wrong.

Probably smoking-ass hot.

But wrong, wrong, wrong.

I force my eyes to stay on the scar, the only thing powerful enough to put distance between us, and with a deep inhale, I close my eyes and lift away from Pixie's bed. My body is in agony as I back away from her hot, open body.

She stays in the sinful position for a beat, then pulls herself up until she's sitting cross-legged. She takes a deep breath, and the light from her window shines blue on her chest as it rises with air.

I clear my throat and overenunciate my words. "Can I please use your phone?"

She slowly stands up and straightens her shirt before looking up at me. "No."

"Ugh." I pull at my hair. "Why are you such a pain in the ass?"

She makes a face. "Why don't you ever let me take a hot shower?"

I lean in. "If you want a hot shower, then shower at night."

"I can't shower at night. If I shower at night, then I'll have to dry my hair at night, and if I dry my hair at night, then I'll have to straighten my hair at night, and then I'll have to *sleep* on my straightened hair, and when I sleep on my straightened hair, it gets all poofy."

I blink at her.

"I don't like it when my hair gets poofy!" She thrusts her hands out like I'm supposed to know poofy hair is a nighttime-shower-related problem. "Why don't *you* shower at night?"

"Because I like pissing you off!" I raise my voice.

She raises her voice to match mine. "Why?"

"Because fighting doesn't hurt!"

It's the most honest thing either one of us has said to each other in nearly a year and it just hangs there, in the silence, like a gaping black hole.

Her lips part, and I see the fight drain from her expression.

No.

No, no.

Fight, dammit.

Lavender-scented body heat starts circling around me, tucking me into something lost and safe, making me feel wanted and worthy and all the other things I shouldn't feel.

She's all big eyes and fragile bones, with her pretty mouth tilted up as she scans my face and softly asks, "Does it hurt you to be around me?"

It hurts and it heals.

It aches and it comforts.

I swallow and quietly say, "Does it hurt *you* to be around *me*?"

Neither of us responds as we gaze at each other in the moonlight.

I step back from the sweet, warm haze Pixie just wrapped around me with her goddamn goodness and shake my head. Not saying anything, just shaking my head like an idiot, I leave her room.

25

PIXIE

*T*his morning the electricity has been magically turned back on, and I don't care about my cold shower as water runs over my shoulders. I stare at the simple white wall in front of me, thinking about last night.

The anger. The hurt. The cruel wanting we can't entertain against the backdrop of the thing we don't talk about.

Just thinking.

I rinse the conditioner from my hair and turn off the shower.

When Charity died, it was like the friendship Levi and I had died too. Our bond just sort of disappeared.

At her funeral, every instinct in my soul wanted to run after him and find comfort in the arms of the boy who was my hero, but I just couldn't do it. I couldn't face the shame I'd feel in his presence.

I had been reckless with Charity. I'd been reckless with *me*. And because of my poor judgment, Levi had lost his sister.

I didn't know how to face him, so I never did.

And now here I am, living next door to him and trying to ignore pretty much everything that comes up between us.

My scar. The ghost of Charity's memory.

The magnetic heat that just magically appears whenever we're near each other...

Yeah. Lots of ignoring going on.

I wrap a towel around my body and step into the hallway just as Levi steps out of his room. Our eyes meet, and at first it's really uncomfortable.

Like, *Oh crap. I was hoping to avoid you until the end of time.*

And then it's normal.

Like, *Hello, old friend whom I grew up with and trust with my life.*

And then it's dangerous.

Like, *Can I help you out of your towel and slip you into something more comfortable? Like my bed, perhaps?*

The tension in the hallway is hot and foreboding as his gaze strays from my face to every other part of my tiny-toweled body. And I'm checking him out in all his white-T-shirt-worn-jeans hotness, and my thoughts are going no place pure.

I feel the heat in my cheeks as I stare at the way his shirt pulls tight across his chest and molds to his muscles and, just when my body's getting too hot for a towel, his eyes snap to mine.

It's uncomfortable again. He goes back into his room and shuts the door behind him.

I stand confused for a second, barefoot and damp in the hallway, trying to figure out what the hell is wrong with us. It's like we can't get our chemistry right. It's either rude and mean, or sad and heavy, or hot and naughty.

Where's the happy medium?

26

LEVI

*G*od damn.

Pixie needs to start wearing a muumuu wherever she goes. I can't do this seeing-her-half-naked-all-the-time shit. With her long legs and flushed skin and her warm, wet body...

God damn.

I shake my head like that's going to clear up all the guilt and lust I have warring inside me and exit my bedroom for the second time this morning. I have work to do. I have stuff to fix.

Douche bag Daren is loitering at the bottom of the stairs, making my morning just fucking perfect as I head to the front desk.

"'Sup, Andrews?" he says.

'Sup?

He's a white boy in a polo shirt. *'Sup* is he's a poser.

I don't respond.

"Is Sarah upstairs?" He scratches his neck.

"She's busy." Apparently, I just spew shit sometimes.

"With what?"

Not with me, that's for sure. Though I could certainly keep her busy and—god damn, Pixie in her towel!

I sigh. "What do you want, Ackwood?"

He narrows his eyes. "Are you two...like...together?"

And now my head is swimming with all the possibilities of "together," and most of them—hell, *all* of them—involve no clothes and tangled body parts.

"Why?"

He shrugs, all confident and douchey. "You seem pretty possessive of her; that's all."

"Whatever, man," I say and move past him.

Pixie's not mine. I don't care.

I'm not sure where Daren goes after that because I force myself not to turn around. But damn if I don't want to track him down and put a leash on him.

"Morning." Ellen smiles at me from behind the front desk.

Haley's nowhere to be found, so I assume she's late.

"Morning. I called the alarm company this morning. Here's the estimate," I say, handing her a price sheet. "They can come out as early as next week to do the install. You just need to call them back to set up a time."

"Perfect." She smiles. "Your To Do list is on my desk. You're awesome, Levi."

I purse my lips and nod before heading to her office. I'm not awesome. I'm a loser who calls Pixie names.

But for some reason, Ellen doesn't hate me.

When my parents split, I didn't take their separation well. I knew they blamed me for Charity's death. Hell, *I* blamed me. But after they left town, things just went even more downhill.

I no longer cared about my grades or school in general. Football wasn't a problem for me because I got to step onto the field and do my job—and do it well—and step off the field without incident. It was the only thing I didn't hate about my existence.

But at one of our last games of the season this past winter, I absently looked up in the stands for Pixie and Charity, temporarily forgetting how drastically different my life had become. I searched the stands for my personal cheerleading section, and when reality hit and I realized that I would never see Charity—or Pixie—cheering me on ever again, I just choked.

I couldn't play. I didn't want to play.

Not then. Not ever.

I was failing my classes. I was failing as quarterback. I was spiraling down a winding staircase of guilt and grief. And then I got the academic probation notice from Dean Maxwell.

Needless to say, I had no desire to try at anything in life, let alone my studies, so I lost my football scholarship and, therefore, lost my room in the dorms. The day I packed up my things and drove away from ASU in my truck, I was a homeless college dropout without a job or a future.

I was halfway to Copper Springs when I realized I didn't have a home to go back to. Why I didn't call one of my buddies to see if I could crash at his place, I'm not sure. Shame maybe? I probably didn't want to explain how my parents bailed on me because, you know, I killed my sister.

When the Willow Inn showed up on the side of the road, I impulsively decided to stay there for the night and formulate a plan for my future in the morning.

Ellen was at the front desk when I walked inside. I forgot that Pixie's aunt owned the inn. She knew who I was and she knew I'd almost killed her niece, so she was surely going to kick me out.

"Hey, Levi," she said pleasantly as she looked at my duffle bag. "Need a room?"

I stared at her warily and nodded.

She smiled and started typing stuff into the computer before grabbing a key.

"How many nights?" She made it sound like I was just an average guest, but I knew twenty-year-old unemployed football players weren't her typical guests.

"Uh, just one," I said.

She glanced up, looked at my bag again, and said, "We're having a two-for-one special right now. Buy one night, get the second free. Want to stay two nights?"

"Uh, sure." I shifted uncomfortably.

"Follow me." She led me up to a room, left me in peace, and I dropped on the comfy bed, trying to figure out what the hell my next step was going to be.

The next afternoon, Ellen knocked on my door. "You used to work in construction, right?"

"Yeah." It had been one of the many summer jobs I'd taken to save up for my truck.

She sighed dramatically. "You don't by any chance think you could help me fix the downstairs banister, do you?"

I paused, because I didn't know shit about fixing banisters.

"I'll give you another night for free for your trouble?" she offered.

"Uh...I don't really know much about stair rails—"

"Oh, you can do it." She waved a hand. "You're smart and strong. I have total confidence in you."

"I guess I could try—"

"Perfect."

And that was the beginning.

Ellen kept finding things for me to fix around the inn and kept offering me another free night's stay for my work. Three weeks went by before I realized I'd been roped into a job that came with room and board.

I tried to bail, but the woman was convincing and, by that point, I was actually starting to like fixing things around the old place. It made me feel...well...not useless.

So we made it official, and I moved into the old wing of the inn, where I had several bedrooms and a single bathroom all to myself.

Until Pixie.

Everything was fine until Pixie.

27

PIXIE

I smell Levi before I see him, and this is why I have no business sharing a bathroom with the guy. If just the *smell* of him can drive me crazy, I certainly should not be anywhere near him when there's hot water and soap involved.

"The sink's broken?" he says.

I keep my back to him as I stir potato soup on the stove and point to the sink.

Things between us have been civil lately. Fake as hell, but civil. We haven't argued in several days, but we're not getting along either.

I'm not really over the erotic calf caressing Levi gave me last week, or the fact that it hurts him to be around me, but you know what? Screw him.

He's not the only person who lost Charity. I lost her too, and then some.

I lost the only real family I'd ever known and the house I considered my safe haven. I lost my childhood friend and the keeper of the "best" part of our "best friends" heart-shaped necklace. The only thing I had left after the wreckage cleared was Levi.

And then I lost him too.

He promptly headed back to his life at college and left me

behind in a town where nothing held any more significance for me and no one understood my pain.

Levi left me, and he didn't look back.

Sharp bitterness heats low in my stomach as I think back to the many days and nights after the accident where I was too hollow to cry, and the only thing that kept me from tearing my hair out was the hope that Levi would come back home so I wouldn't feel so lost, so alone anymore.

But he didn't.

And then, when I was healthy enough to be discharged from the hospital so I could start my first semester at ASU two weeks late, I thought for sure Levi would hunt me down and at least say hello. Maybe give me one of his awkward boy hugs and just let me be silent against his chest for a moment. Like maybe if we embraced and pressed our broken hearts together, for a moment—just a moment—things might somehow be better.

But he didn't.

The one and only time I ever saw him on campus was from across the library. I was seated in the back behind four textbooks when I saw him walk in through the squeaky double doors. He didn't see me as he headed for the reference section, but just the sight of him, the visual confirmation that he was alive and breathing and twenty yards away from me, made my broken heart leap.

I immediately stood from my table with every intention of following after him and…and…and what, exactly? What was I going to say to Levi, who so clearly had nothing to say to me?

Where have you been?

Why did you leave me?

I'm sorry?

Why did you leave me?

Please forgive me?

WHY DID YOU LEAVE ME?

I had nothing to say to him then, and I have nothing to say to him now, which doesn't seem to bother him one bit.

So yeah. Screw him.

My heart dips. I look at the soup.

Levi works for a few minutes, and the only sounds in the kitchen are the bubbling soup and the occasional *clang-clang* of his tools.

I shuffle about, finding mindless tasks to fill my hands. I'm stacking rolls and rearranging napkins and scrubbing the counter. Mindless.

I hear him growl in frustration and look over at his body, laid out on the kitchen floor, his head and shoulders tucked under the sink as he twists and turns things with his hands.

He's got one leg stretched out along the tile and the other bent at the knee, and the blue T-shirt he has on has ridden up his stomach a little, so there's this bronze patch of tight skin showing just above the waistline of his jeans.

I need a break.

Twitching my lips, I gingerly step over his lean, frustrating body with one quiet Converse sneaker and head to the dining room.

"Hey, Sarah."

Oh God. Daren.

He stops unloading a crate of club soda behind the bar and leans over the counter on his elbows. "Have you decided to go yet?"

"Go where?" I watch Angelo move Daren off the bar, then wipe the whole counter down with a white bar towel.

"To the Fourth of July Bash," Daren says.

"Oh yeah. That," I say, as Mable comes in and sets a lavender-

and-sunflower centerpiece on each table. It shouldn't work, lavender and sunflowers together, but somehow it does. "Uh, no."

He wrinkles his forehead. "No you haven't decided yet, or no you're not going?"

"I'm not going."

"What? Come on," he says. "Bring a friend. It'll be fun. You'll feel normal."

The idea of "normal" does something to me, and I hesitate, buying time as I watch Mable straighten a fork on table six before going to the kitchen.

"Please?" Daren implores me with those puppy eyes of his again.

God, he's such a whiny baby.

I sigh. "Fine. I'll go."

"Awesome." He smiles.

"But not with you."

His smiles drops. "Less awesome."

I shrug. "I'll bring a friend, and maybe we'll see you there. Maybe."

He smiles again. "I'll take it." He tilts his head. "So does this mean I'm forgiven?"

I lift my brows. "For kissing me without permission?"

"WHAT?" Angelo stops wiping down the bar and snaps murderous eyes to Daren. "You kissed Sarah without asking?"

Oh crap.

Daren looks like he might wet himself. "Uh, yeah. But I, uh, didn't mean—"

"It's fine, Angelo." I give him a small smile. "It wasn't a big deal. It was just a misunderstanding. We're cool. I'm cool." Angelo doesn't look like he believes me. "Really," I add. "I'm fine. I promise. And Daren already apologized, so see? Everything's fine."

Daren shrinks back as Angelo leans in to him and says, "I better not hear about you kissing any more ladies without permission. Ever. Understand?"

"Yes, sir."

"'Cause if I do, make no mistake. I will twist your head off, slowly, and shove it so far up your ass it comes out your throat; you hear me?"

Daren swallows. "Loud and clear."

"Good." Then Angelo goes back to wiping down the bar like he didn't just threaten Daren's life.

Biting back a smile, I turn and head for the kitchen.

I love this place.

28

LEVI

I'm staring at the piping above me, almost finished with the sink, when I hear Ellen enter the kitchen.

"There you are," she says to my legs. "The install guys just left, so it looks like our new fire alarms are up and running. But I'm going to schedule a drill tomorrow, just to make sure everything works properly. I'll let the rest of the staff know, but I'll need you to monitor the control box. Got it?"

"Fire drill. Got it."

"Thanks, Levi."

I hear her leave. As I finish tightening the last bolt, something thwacks my leg. Looking out from under the sink, I see Mable standing above me with a less-than-happy expression.

I sit up. "Did you just smack me with a spatula?"

"Yes. And I will do it again if I have to." She's dead serious.

I furrow my brow. "Is this about the whore thing? I know I was mean—"

She smacks me again.

"Jesus, Mable!"

"That boy was in the dining room talking to Pixie again," she says.

I blink. "Who, Daren?" It's all I can do not to say "douche bag."

"Yes, Daren. And I don't like him." She puts a hand on her hip.

I exhale. "Get in line."

She stares down at me expectantly.

I stare up at her, dumbfounded.

"Well?" she says. "Are you going to go get Pixie or what?"

"Why?" I stand up, immediately on alert with all these visions of Daren hurting Pixie and how I'm going to kill him when I find him. "Is Pixie in trouble?"

"Of course not."

"Then what the—ow! Mable, quit hitting me."

She points the spatula at me. "You are that girl's whole life, Levi." Her soft wrinkles bore into me. "Don't you dare let her get distracted by some guy who doesn't know how to love her."

And whoa.

When did we start talking about love?

I narrow my eyes. "What's that supposed to mean?"

She tosses the spatula into the sink I just fixed and makes her way to the exit. "You know exactly what it means."

29

PIXIE

I woke up this morning determined to be pleasant, but the moment I saw Levi enter the bathroom, my emotional barometer cracked. And suddenly I wanted to fight. Badly. I wanted to kick and scream and yell and get all kinds of angry.

Because he was right.

Fighting doesn't hurt.

"Oh, I don't think so." I wave my finger in the air as I barge into the small bathroom with him, setting my stuff on the counter and staking my claim to the shower. "My ass is taking a shower first."

He looks at said ass, then shakes his head. "Your *ass* is leaving."

He moves to pick me up and I skirt past his hands and duck under his arm, climbing into the dry shower with my clothes on.

"You want to get wet, Pixie?" He's got his wicked smile on, and I hate that I like it. "Because I can help you with that."

Of course my dirty head is going all sorts of naughty places with his words, and I fail to see his hand reach into the shower.

"What I *want* is a hot shower."

He turns on the water and the spray begins to douse the tank top and gym shorts I have on. I purse my lips as he grins at my slowly soaking pajamas. "Wet enough for you yet?"

Our eyes meet and the air around us begins to sizzle.

Because now we're both thinking about a whole different kind of wet, and the heat filling the small bathroom isn't coming from the steamy water running down my body.

I refuse to break our gaze, so I wait him out. His eyes flicker briefly, like maybe he's scared or nervous, but then they wander to my chest.

The wet tank top is hardly working as any kind of cover, so the exact shape and size and *tightness* of my nipples is very, very apparent.

I let him look. If he wants to be an ass, he can be an ass.

He lifts his gaze to mine, but then his cocky-as-sin expression falters for a moment. Like he forgot this was me, Pixie Marshall, standing pretty much naked before him. And the realization does something deep to his eyes and funny things to my stomach.

I suddenly want to cover my face.

Not my boobs.

Not my white shorts that easily show off how I'm not wearing panties.

I want to cover my *face*.

Because what he sees reminds him of everything he can't erase.

He stares into my eyes, and now I'm trapped in a deep blue sea of rage and regret and hurt and loss. And I don't want to be there. I want to be anywhere else. Because the deep blue sea is filled with a million things I can't bring myself to admit.

It hurts to think about his pain. It hurts to look at it. And it sure as hell hurts to swim in it.

But here I am. Swimming in Levi's deep blue broken sea, and I'm drowning right alongside him, just as hopeless and helpless as he is. Two castaways in an ocean of pain, and we're not even clinging to each other for dear life. We're just watching each other drift to the ocean floor, where silence and blackness might swallow us whole and take away the sorrow.

For long seconds we stand there, staring at each other as water beats down on me. And then his eyes fall to my mouth.

Oh crap.

My eyes fall to his mouth as well, and the atmosphere ignites. Now we're in this steamy, tense standoff—half in, half out of the shower—heads tilted toward each other and eyes locked on mouths. And I know I've already surrendered.

I know I'm mad at him, hurt by him, but when it comes down to it, I trust Levi with everything I am.

And he has me.

He has me when I'm seven years old and scared of monsters. He has me when I'm brokenhearted in the eighth grade because Tommy Marchim won't take me to the Valentine's dance. And he has me when I'm nineteen and in the shower with my pajamas on, searching his eyes for my hero.

He has me.

He's always had me.

And I've never wanted to be had by anyone else.

He leans closer, and the steam from the shower surrounds us like we're in our own private cloud. Right here, right now, yesterday, tomorrow—whenever he's near—I feel safe. Safe and loved. Because that's exactly what I am, even if he doesn't know it. Even if I don't deserve it.

I lean in closer too, not seeing anything other than Levi's body and a swirling cloud of hot fog.

Our faces are so close together I can feel each of his exhales sweeping over my cheeks. The silver flecks in his eyes glisten in the droplets falling all around us, reflecting off the white shower walls. The spray drowns out all other noise and makes it seem as though we're enclosed in our own little white rainstorm.

I trace my eyes along his scruffy face, taking in the small dark hairs that dust his jawline and match the color of his long eyelashes. Then my gaze roves over his full lips, and I absently lick my own.

And then he kisses me.

Like he was born to do it, like everything about him knows exactly how to kiss *me*. His lips fit to mine perfectly, and it's nothing like our first kiss.

It's desperate and starving, and blindly passionate, as we crush our mouths together in the white downpour.

I kiss him back like he's my very last breath, like I'd die without him—and maybe I would. I part my lips and our tongues meet, sliding over slick textured surfaces, as they dance and wiggle and taste and lick. And it's just…so…perfect.

I rise up on my tiptoes, trying to pull his mouth into mine because he's too far away. His tongue glides along the soft flesh inside my mouth. He's still too far away. I bring my hand to the back of his neck and tangle my fingers in his hair, tugging and making a noise of protest because I'm so damn short and can't reach him the way I want.

He grabs my hips and steps into the shower with me. Running his large hands down the back of my body, he lifts me up and presses me against the cool shower wall. I wrap my legs around his waist, my butt sitting in his hands as our hips push against one another.

And oh. God. Yes.

I'm eager and feisty and suddenly I'm like a kissing machine, just all hungry and frantic, and I'm making these moaning noises that would probably be embarrassing if I wasn't so freaking turned on.

He pulls back and tilts his head to the other side before bringing his mouth back to mine, sucking on my lower lip before giving his tongue back to me.

My hands are gripping his white T-shirt, which is now completely soaked, and I'm pulling at the collar for no reason other than I just need to *pull* something. But the collar of the shirt is wet and loose and my clenched fist has yanked it down so Levi's collarbone and top pec muscle are completely exposed, and there's this dirty little piece of me that wants to sink my teeth into the bare patch of skin.

My God. I must be part vampire.

And when the hell did I get so horny?

And then I realize. It's not that I'm suddenly horny; it's that I'm with Levi. And here in his arms I can be Pixie, damaged and flawed, wet and dirty, and it's okay. We're okay.

One of his hands leaves my butt and runs up my rib cage, his thumb pressing into the indentations between each rib, my skin soft and giving. His hand moves higher and cups my breast over the thin wet cotton of my shirt, gently squeezing. I move my hips against him, desperate for more of his touch, and he responds by brushing his thumb over the hard tip of my nipple. Back and forth. Back and forth.

I moan with each swipe of his thumb, and muscles low in my belly tighten in response. He palms my breast again and shifts against me. God, he's hard. And thick. And hot. And so many things I want to feel inside my now-aching body.

His palm moves down to my leg. His fingertips burn a trail of want into my skin as he runs his hand up the back of my thigh to where my butt cheek is completely exposed—because my white shorts have ridden up and are now acting more like a thong than running shorts—and grabs my naked ass, pressing harder against me.

And he's kissing me—God, he's kissing me—like he's starving, and I'm just kissing and rocking and rubbing and, hell, everything my body wants to do against his.

I move my hands to his back and under the hem of his shirt. His back muscles are hard and thick beneath my fingertips, rippling with his movement, as I start to pull his shirt up. He shifts against me, and I've never been more excited in my life. For real.

The wet shower has nothing on me.

His mouth moves to my jaw—yes—and then my neck—oh God—and then he has his teeth running along my collarbone while his hand rounds my leg and glides up the inside of my thigh and—holy hell! This boy knows his way around my body.

He slides his hand up under my shorts until he's cupping the naked V between my legs with his warm palm. I whimper in ecstasy as my body responds to his hot touch and grows more slippery as he begins to slide his fingers along parts of my body that really, *really* like being touched.

He kisses and sucks at my throat and chest as he slowly eases a finger inside my tight body while that clever thumb of his continues to slip and slide over my most sensitive spot. I squirm against him because I want more—need more—so much more. He slowly withdraws his finger and I whine and gasp in protest until he pushes it back in, all the while working his thumb against my hot, wet flesh.

I wiggle, I moan, I gasp, I beg as Levi kisses me and groans hot breaths of desire against my skin. He adds a second finger to the first and fills me thickly, pushing in and out of me as he increases the heavenly movement of his thumb.

My body begins to tighten and shake, my thighs quivering around his hips as he works me to the brink of sweet death, and I tip my head back, completely blind to everything but the white rainstorm. Then I cry out with pleasure as my body completely unravels and gives in to the magic of Levi's hand.

My insides pulse as Levi brings his lips to mine and kisses me deeply. I whimper against his mouth, and it's all I can do to keep my hands from falling off as I struggle to claw my way down his shirt and to the waistband of his shorts. I want to rip them off and fill my body with his until this blissful yet wanting hollow inside me purrs with satisfaction.

He kisses along my collarbone. I yank on his waistband. He pulls at my tank top—

And then the fire alarm goes off.

We both freeze. The drill.

The fire drill is today.

For a moment, we stay pressed together, breathing heavily against each other in the steam, our wet clothes warming between us.

But reality moves in fast, pushing through the haze. I've already made my decision. I am irrevocably and shamelessly interested in having Levi's body inside mine. Levi, on the other hand, has pulled his head back from my collarbone and is looking into my eyes.

Not my eyes. Don't look at my eyes.

If he sees me, he'll remember, and if he remembers—

"Shit." He pulls back, remorse and hatred in his eyes, and I want to scream.

But I don't. I stay where I am, pushed up against the wall with Levi's erection pressing against the still-quaking center of my body, and act like this is all just run-of-the-mill for me.

What's that now? Oh, no. I do this all the time. I'm always humping guys in the shower with my pj's on.

He gently lowers me to my feet; then he turns away.

He leaves the bathroom, the fire alarm still blaring, and I sink down to the shower floor, letting the water spray down on me as a shiver runs through my body.

It's the first hot shower I've had in days and I'm in my clothes, out of breath, and cold as hell.

30

LEVI

*I*t was a false alarm, the fire drill. The feeling of belonging when Pixie had her arms around me.

I don't bother explaining my wet clothes as I slosh downstairs to turn off the shrieking noise. Guests everywhere are fussing around, overreacting to the excitement.

Ellen's in the lobby, assuring everyone that there is no fire as she leads them out back, per alarm protocol. "This is just a drill," she explains. People hear this, but they still want to chat about the near-death experience they just had.

The only person in the whole place who just had a near-death experience was me. I almost died in the shower just now with Pixie on fire in my arms and my selfish body just burning alive with her.

What the hell was I thinking?

Never mind. I know what I was thinking.

Why the hell did I give in?

Never mind. I know that too.

But that doesn't make it right. And if I'm trying to atone for anything in my life, I'm certainly not going to find my salvation with the one person who should resent my very existence.

I walk to the back hall, passing by flustered guests who stare at me and my sopping clothes like I'm a crazy person, to the system control box and turn the alarm off.

There is an audible sigh of relief, a brief moment of silence, and then the chaos erupts again. More chatter about the "great fire" that didn't happen as people file out the back door.

I walk over to Ellen, who eyes me up and down. Her gaze lingers on my very stretched-out wet shirt collar and she raises a brow.

I don't explain.

She looks around. "Where's Pixie?"

Like we're supposed to travel in pairs or something.

"How should I know?" And shit, I said that with a ferocity that was only going to raise questions.

"You two share the same wing, Levi," she says. "What if there *was* a fire and she was trapped in it? The purpose of a drill is to practice being safe. Did you even look for her before you came downstairs?"

First of all, fuck that.

I would never leave Pixie to die. I might leave her wet and shaking in a hot shower with her clothes on, but I sure as hell wouldn't leave her at the mercy of a fire.

Second, whoa.

If Ellen doesn't know me well enough to know that I'd never let anyone—*especially* Pixie—die, then I should be shot dead on the spot.

I open my mouth to retort to Ellen in a very offensive and curse-filled way, when I catch the teasing glimmer in her eye.

Damn women.

"Pixie's fine," I say.

Ellen looks me up and down again. "You sure about that?"

Wow. I'm never living in a building filled with females ever again. They think they know everything.

"I'm sure," I say. "Do you need help with anything else?"

"Nope."

"Right, then. I'll make sure everyone has evacuated." I search the inn for any leftover guests, careful to avoid the east wing.

After the chaos dies down, I go back upstairs, taking my sweet time so I don't accidentally run into Pixie. When I reach the top, I grab some clothes from my room and head to the bathroom.

Pixie is gone and the bathroom doesn't smell like lavender, so I'm assuming she didn't stick around for very long after I left her in the water. The mirror is still fogged up, though.

My chest tightens as I turn on the shower.

I need a cold shower, which apparently won't be a problem because all the hot water is gone.

31

PIXIE

I sneak down to the laundry room while Levi's in the shower, carrying my wet pajamas in my hand. I don't know why, but I'm wearing the most hideous clothes I own—a pair of plaid sweatpants and a large gray T-shirt that has a ripped collar and a grease stain on the front.

I'm heavily clothed, but I'm still cold.

When I arrive, I'm sure I'm safe because Ellen never comes to the tiny laundry room in the west wing. Never.

"Hi, Pix," Ellen says behind me, and I want to cuss.

"Hi," I say in a far-too-cheery voice as I turn around. I try to tuck my wet clothes under my arm without drawing attention to the obvious wet mark they're branding onto my stupid gray T-shirt.

Ellen sees the clothes and smiles at me. "Doing laundry?"

I nod.

"With only"—she looks down—"two items?"

"Yep." I nod. "I'm just trying to stay on top of things. These are my favorite pajamas. And I washed them in the sink to conserve energy."

Okay, clearly, I suck at lying—Ellen knows this. And really, Pixie? Giving three excuses about *why* your clothes are wet when she didn't even ask is a dead giveaway.

I pinch my lips together.

Ellen stares me down. "Spill it."

"No."

"Spill it."

"No." I throw my two items in the washing machine and cross my arms. I'm an impenetrable wall. I'm a fortress of silence. I'm—

"Does this have something to do with Levi?"

"Yes."

Damn. I suck at being a fortress.

"Want to talk about it?" Ellen leans against the doorway and drapes her dark hair over her shoulder.

"No. I don't want to talk about it. I want Levi to talk about it. I want him to look at me and stop seeing Charity and all the sadness and I want him to let himself love me again." I'm totally talking about it, but now I can't stop. "I mean, what the hell? He and Charity were my best friends. They were my whole life, and then Charity died and Levi just…just *left* me! And now it's like we're totally different people." I say this loudly and realize I'm about to cry. "We're not the same anymore. We're not Levi and Pixie, Transformer and Barbie. We're not the Three Musketeers with dreams and futures. Charity is dead and my heart is lost and Levi is a mess and I don't…I don't…I don't…"

I start crying and Ellen pulls me into a hug, stroking my hair in a way my own mother would never have done. "I don't know how to love him anymore," I say into Ellen's soft shirt as tears spill from my eyes.

She squeezes me. "Sure you do. Love doesn't just stop, Pixie. It's always there."

I pull away and wipe at my face, frustrated for crying. "But he feels so far away from me. I just want him back. But I'm so…"

I search for the word. "I'm so *angry* with him. For abandoning me. For letting me hurt without him. For forgetting me."

She shakes her head. "He didn't forget you."

"He did."

"No. He was just hurting, Pix. Levi lost a lot after the accident. He lost Charity, and then he lost his parents—"

"But he didn't lose *me*." My voice cracks.

Ellen bites her lip and waits a beat. "Maybe he doesn't know that." She pauses. "Maybe you should tell him that."

"I can't." I shake my head, and a wild blonde curl falls into my eyes. "I can't. We're so messed up. I don't think it would even matter if I did. We're just too broken."

Ellen tilts her head and looks me over sympathetically. She tucks the loose curl behind my ear and lightly brushes my cheek with her finger. Then she smiles softly. "There's no such thing as too broken. Anything can heal." She kisses my forehead and wraps her arms around me. "Especially you."

32
LEVI

I need to move.

I can't sleep one door away from Pixie anymore— especially after feeling her up in the shower yesterday. I just can't do it.

Last night, I stared at my ceiling all night long, telling myself that if I ever tried to touch Pixie again, I was going to kill myself. And then I spent the next few hours staring at the ceiling, thinking of whether or not I actually *could* kill myself, and came to the conclusion that, no, I couldn't, because then Pixie would be at the mercy of douche bags like Daren and dirty old men like Earl and I was not cool leaving her in a world where Darens and Earls could look at her without the threat of me.

And *then* I stared at the ceiling and thought of all the ways I would hurt Daren and Earl if they ever tried to touch Pixie, which led to a very dark train of thought involving plastic bags and bleach.

So obviously, I need to move.

I shake myself as I walk downstairs and into the lobby. Enough thinking about Pixie.

Looking out the front windows of the inn, I see a familiar car pull into the parking lot, and my hands go numb.

Sandra Marshall.

Pixie's mother, Ellen's sister, and hater of me.

I watch Sandra exit the car and head for the front doors.

This is not good.

33

PIXIE

A quiet knock on my door has me leaping out of bed, thinking maybe it's Levi. We haven't spoken since our couples shower yesterday, and my nerves are pretty much shot from the silence.

But when I open my door, I see Ellen.

"Hey." I smile at her and try not to look disappointed.

"Hey..." Her facial expression goes crooked for a moment, and I know—I just *know*—my mother is here.

"Oh, no." I beg her with my eyes, *Save me.*

She makes a face of helplessness, and we both cringe when my mother's voice drifts up the stairs from the lobby.

"Why, Haley, how *are* you?" Oh God. My mother hates Haley. She hates Haley with a passion. *Run, poor woman. Run for your life.*

"Hello, Sandra." Haley's voice is polite and friendly.

"Fell off the diet again, I see?" my mom says. "Well, at least curvy suits you. You've never been one for the lean look."

"Mom!" I holler down the stairs, moving from my room, not caring that I'm still wearing my hideous pajamas from the day before. I need to spare Haley any further abuse.

When I see the woman who gave birth to me, I plaster on a smile so fake I think it might crack my face open.

"Hi there!" I say.

"Hello, darling." She gives me a fake smile as well. "I have a box of your old things at the house. You should come pick it up before I throw it away." She lifts one overplucked eyebrow. "What are you wearing?"

I look down. "Pajamas."

"Ellen!" my mother yells at my aunt, who has followed me down the stairs and is now standing behind me. "Is this how you let your employees dress?"

Always so casual with my mother, Ellen shrugs. "She's not on the clock yet, Sandy. She woke up five minutes ago."

Mom looks at me and frowns. "Go put real clothes on before some pervert sees you in your sleepwear and gets bad ideas."

I make a face. "I'm wearing oversized pants and a disgusting shirt, Mom. No *pervert* is going to—"

"Hush. Go change."

"She doesn't need to change," Ellen says sharply.

"It's fine," I say to Ellen as I turn around to head back to my room. I don't want to fight. It's not worth it. And I don't want Ellen to have to defend me. She's already done enough of that throughout my life.

A nervous twitch starts behind my left eye as I climb the stairs and hear Ellen snap at my mother about being kind to me.

I was thirteen the first time Ellen tried to get me to move in with her. She'd witnessed my mother's severe dislike for me throughout my childhood, and she'd tried to temper it for years—without success. Sandra Marshall was unhappy about her life and clung to her bitterness like it was a drug and she was an addict.

My mom was the head cheerleader in high school while my father—some guy named Greg—was the star basketball player, and they were this adolescent power couple or whatever. Until my mom got pregnant. She was seventeen.

I was young and beautiful and skinny, until you *came along and ruined everything,* she used to say to me. As if I were somehow responsible for my own conception.

Good ol' Greg couldn't handle the idea of his thin little girlfriend gaining weight and being sick and emotional all the time, so he spent more time bedding the rest of the cheerleading squad than he did hanging out with my mom during her pregnancy. Which broke my mom's heart.

But she refused to dump him because she didn't want to raise a baby on her own. Plus, she had plans to move to California with him, where they were both going to attend UCLA so she could become a news anchor. So she let her scumbag boyfriend cheat on her while she suffered through morning sickness and took on the body of a whale.

And then I was born.

Suddenly the baby thing got real, and life got hard. My mom and Greg were broke high school seniors who had no parental help, and Greg decided he didn't feel like being a daddy anymore. He skipped town when I was four months old.

My mother dropped out of high school, waved good-bye to her future as a news anchor, and got a job at a local diner, where she let her broken heart fester until it was black. With Greg out of the picture, the only person left to blame for her miserable life was the baby girl who had ruined her body and driven away the only man who would ever love her—that was her reasoning.

So I never had a chance.

Ellen, who was a few years older than my mother, jumped right in to help out with baby me. But Sandra Marshall was determined to be miserable. And with every year that passed without providing Sandra a way out of town or a handsome man to sweep her off her feet, she grew more intolerant of me.

Ellen's attempts at tempering Sandra's behavior failed. So as a last resort, she offered up her home—a place just a few miles from the inn—and asked me to consider living with her indefinitely. My mother wasn't horribly against the idea, but she was wicked cruel to Ellen for suggesting it. Because if Ellen took little Pixie away from Sandra, then whomever would Sandra have to blame for her unhappy existence?

I declined Ellen's offer under the guise of not wanting to move out to the middle of nowhere and live far away from my friends. But really, I just didn't want Ellen to have to take more heat than necessary from my mom and deal with whatever temper tantrums she decided to throw throughout my remaining years.

So I stayed in my mother's house and settled for visiting Ellen as often as possible. She used to drive into Copper Springs and pick Charity and me up from school on Fridays so we could stay the weekend at Willow Inn.

The summer we were fourteen, Charity and I got to stay at the inn for two weeks. It was two weeks of ice cream and movies and late-night fun with Ellen. That was the summer Ellen started calling me Pixie. I'm glad she never stopped.

Sandra Marshall's scolding voice rakes over my nerves as I hear her chatter away downstairs.

Goddammit, my mother is here. I thought I was free, but now the very person I've been trying to get away from my whole life is downstairs yelling at Haley about eating carbs.

34

LEVI

I occupy myself with outdoor jobs all day before heading back inside, hoping to avoid Sandra Marshall.

There are only three ways I can enter the inn. I can go through the front door—but Sandra might be in the lobby. I can go through the main back door—but Sandra might be in the library or by Ellen's office. Or I can go through the kitchen's back door.

Kitchen it is.

I wipe my shoes on the mat outside and let myself in.

"Hey, handsome." Mable smiles warmly at me. "I made honey croissants. Want some?"

"Always." I take a croissant from her and bring it to my mouth. Pixie's over by the sink, her hair pulled back from her face so her cheeks and nose look extra small. Her yellow apron is covered in flour and what looks like chocolate, and I notice she's wearing nicer clothes than usual.

Our eyes meet.

She looks away.

Sandra enters the kitchen and frowns at Mable. "Croissants are not good for a woman your age. Are you *trying* to die?"

Mable arches a brow. "Are *you*?"

"Oh, for God's sake, Mother." Pixie rolls her eyes as she starts kneading dough on the counter. "Quit insulting everyone."

Sandra isn't listening to her daughter, though. She's looking at me.

Here we go.

I'd been working at Willow Inn for only three weeks the first time Sandra Marshall came to visit her sister. I hadn't seen Sandra since Charity's funeral, and I didn't expect her to speak to me at all.

But she did.

"You work here now," she stated with disgust as I hung a painting on the lobby wall.

I turned around with a hammer in my hand, not sure if she wanted me to respond.

"My sister says you live here, as well," she added. "Do your parents approve of this arrangement? Oh wait. That's right. They've moved away." She clucked her tongue. "You just destroyed your whole family, didn't you? First your sister, then your parents."

I clenched my fist around the hammer.

"Can't say that I blame them." She looked me up and down with a pitiful sigh. "You look just like her." She shook her head. "Your poor mother. I bet she curses the day you were born." And then Sandra Marshall turned and left, walking out of the inn like she hadn't just ripped out my heart and verbalized every fear I had hidden inside.

I stood, hammer in hand, staring after her for long, hot minutes, waiting for my heart to stop pounding in fury. But I couldn't shake the pain in my chest. Because she was right. I was the reason Charity was dead.

And now we meet again, this time in the kitchen. Sandra's

evil eyes narrow in on me, and I'm the same guilty boy I was six months ago.

She purses her lips. "Judging by the muck and stench you're covered in, I guess you still work here."

I smile tightly. "Sorry to disappoint you."

"No, you're not," she sneers.

"Leave Levi alone." Pixie glares at her mother.

"I most certainly will *not* leave him alone. He almost killed you last year!" Sandra turns to me. "And you scarred her too. No man's ever going to appreciate her naked now. Does that make you happy?"

Mable gasps, all color draining from her face.

I feel like Sandra just punched me in the stomach.

"Mom!" Pixie looks humiliated.

"Well, it's the truth, Sarah!" she says. "You're only half-pretty to begin with, but with that giant scar through your skin—and across your chest, no less—it's just… well, repulsive."

All feeling drains from my fingertips as I stand frozen by the counter. I can't breathe. I'm torn between wanting to kill myself and wanting to kill Sandra Marshall.

I might do both.

"You hush your mouth, Sandy," Mable says. "That's no way to speak to your beautiful baby girl."

Pixie looks like she's going to cry, and my decision is made. I'm going to kill her mother first, then myself.

Sandra rolls her eyes. "Oh now, Sarah, don't get emotional."

"You need to leave, Sandra," I say. And I call her Sandra because formalities are way the fuck over.

She whips her eyes to me. "I'm not going to take orders from the *janitor.*"

"Then the *janitor* will be escorting you out," I say.

"Mom, can you just go?" Pixie's voice sounds small, and I hate the defeat I hear in it.

Sandra looks appalled. "And leave you here with this"—she looks me up and down like I'm a criminal—"filthy, despicable, sister-killing boy?"

And that's the end of any strength I had. Sandra played the Charity card, and all the oxygen has officially left my lungs.

"You are a horrid woman," Pixie says, straightening her shoulders. "You are truly awful, and I hate that we share DNA." She points to the dining room door. "Leave."

"But we haven't even had dinner."

"You didn't come for dinner. You came to be a bitch and remind me how very worthless I am. And you know what? Mission accomplished." Pixie throws the rolling pin down. "I'm ugly. I'm scarred. I'm worthless. Whatever." Her eyes harden. "I might be all of those things, but you know what I'll never be?" She pauses. "You."

She's more confident than I've ever seen her before, and I'm so proud.

"And *you*," Pixie continues, "are the ugliest thing in this room."

So fucking proud.

Sandra runs cool eyes over her daughter, staring her down in condescension, and mutters, "I knew I should have had an abortion." Then she turns and walks out of the kitchen.

I start to follow after her, but Pixie's voice stops me.

"Leaves, no."

Leaves. She called me Leaves.

My heart is pounding, my palms are sweating, and my soul is

screaming to run after Sandra and hurt her for all the hurt she's done to Pixie.

But Leaves...

Leaves stops me in my tracks.

I look at Pixie and she shakes her head. "I just want her gone, okay? Just let her go." She looks exhausted.

I nod once and watch as Pixie takes off her apron, hangs it on the hook, and exits the kitchen. I stand there for a long time, trying to figure out what to do with all the rage inside me. I'm so angry. Angry that Sandra put so many emotional scars on Pixie and angry that I went and put a physical one on her too.

When I finally move from the kitchen, I travel up the east wing stairs only to find Pixie seated at the top, like maybe she was trying to run away from everything but got discouraged and just sat down where she was.

I slowly climb the stairs and stop a few steps from her. "Your mom's a piece of work."

She nods. "My mom's a bitch."

"Yep." It's awkward for a moment, and I'm not sure if I should go to my room or stay where I am. But something about leaving Pixie feels... wrong, so I shove my hands in my pockets and stand still for a moment. "I've never seen you stand up to her like that before."

She sweeps a loose hair back from her face. "Yeah, well. I don't live with her anymore, so it's not like I'll have repercussions for days and days."

I nod. I look to the side.

She looks at her shoes.

"I'm proud of you." The words fall out of my mouth.

Pixie looks up and gives me a small smile, which just encourages my mouth to keep moving.

"You were pretty kick-ass back there," I say.

Her smile grows, and something inside me warms.

"Nineteen years too late, I guess," she says.

"No," I say quietly. "Never too late to be brave."

She rubs her hands over her face, and I have this overwhelming urge to sit down beside her and wrap an arm around her. I used to do things like that all the time. It used to be so natural for me. For us.

She glances at me and wrinkles her brow. "What my mom said, about my scar—"

I start shaking my head, panic and fear racing through my veins. "She was right."

Pixie looks like I just slapped her. "About it making my body repulsive?"

"What? *No*! God, no!" I want to kill Sandra all over again. "No. She was right when she said it was my fault. I'm the reason you almost died—"

"No, you're not." She looks confused.

"And I'm the reason Charity died."

"What?" She blinks. "Levi…*what*? Are you insane? A truck driver named Joe Willis who feel asleep at the wheel is the reason Charity died. The accident wasn't your fault." She looks baffled and raises her voice a notch. "And if anyone else is to blame for that night, it's *me*. I'm the one who decided we should drive home drunk."

"But *I* messed with fate, Pix. I basically forced the two of you to pull over, and then I drove you straight to death—"

"You were trying to protect us!"

"Yeah?" I'm yelling now. "And how'd that work out? Did I protect Charity? Did I protect YOU?!" My voice echoes up and down the east wing and my eyes start to burn.

It's so silent I can hear the beating of my heart and the very shallow breath Pixie just took. Her face is stunned.

My chest aches. My chest aches so much.

I head to my room and slam the door behind me.

35

PIXIE

I feel like a ton of bricks just hit me.

Levi doesn't just mourn the loss of Charity; he blames himself. The idiot actually blames himself. Just like me.

God, we're a mess.

I don't have any words for the emptiness inside me, and my feet feel like cement blocks, holding me in place as I stare at the floor. Turns out Levi has some monsters of his own, and I don't know how to be his hero.

36

LEVI

*T*he dam broke. The dam of tucked-away guilt Pixie and I had so carefully constructed over the past year split down the middle once Charity's name was mentioned, and now the inn is flooded with denial.

I can't look Pixie in the eyes. I don't want to know she's there or see my pain reflected in her gaze. I don't want to feel emotionally transparent in her presence or helplessly heavy in her sadness. So for the next few days, I act completely cordial in her company.

Any and all conversations we have are business related and robotic, and my eyes never go beyond the surface when they meet hers.

Stoic, that's what I am. Because anything else would force me to acknowledge the fact that Pixie feels guilty for Charity just like I do and that she might be broken inside just like I am.

So I hold the lobby door open when Pix and I reach it at the same time, and I say hello when I pass her in the hall, and I do these things with empty eyes and a hollow heart.

I don't feel a thing. It's safer that way.

The clicking of high-heeled shoes meets my ears as I spray glass cleaner onto a soft rag. Ellen is soon standing beside me, watching as I climb up the crappy inn ladder to reach a dirty window above me.

"So," she says in a matter-of-fact way as she holds a coffee mug between her hands. "Things between you and Pixie seem pretty tense. More tense than usual. Could that be because of all the shouting I heard the other night?"

Leave it to Ellen to wait until I'm on a wobbly ladder, with no escape, to strike up an uncomfortable conversation.

"We need to add 'ladder' to your *New Crap the Inn Desperately Needs* list," I say, keeping my eyes on the window I'm washing. Cleaning isn't really my job, but Eva is too short to reach these high windows, even on the top step of the ladder—not that I'd let her risk her life on this thing anyway.

Ignoring my attempt at changing the subject, Ellen sternly says, "What was all that yelling about protecting Pixie?"

I stop and look down at her, my body going completely still. "I fucked with fate."

"What?" She makes a face.

Setting the rag down, I run a hand through my hair and let out a long exhale. "I fucked with fate and I lost Charity."

She studies me for a long moment. "Have you ever thought that maybe you fucked with fate and saved Pixie?"

Silence.

She wrinkles her brow in a look of heartache. "Maybe Charity and Pixie were both going to die in that car when Charity was driving drunk," she says. "Have you ever thought that maybe you intervening that night saved Pixie's life?"

I stare at her, speechless, because no. I hadn't ever thought of that.

A beat passes, where neither of us speaks. Then Ellen casually takes a sip of coffee, glances at the window, and says, "You missed a spot."

37

PIXIE

I didn't just wear a bikini; I wore a neon-pink statement. And I wore it proudly.

If the good people of Copper Springs wanted to see me, they were going to see the whole damn disaster.

It's like parting the Red Sea as I walk down the lakeshore. People I've known my whole life are there, smiling and saying hi, and every single one of them is staring at my scar and moving out of my way like I'm some kind of leper.

In a way I guess I am. I'm diseased with the reality of Charity's death. So let them gawk. It's hideous, I know. But for the first time ever, I'm glad it's hideous. Because it's grabbing their attention and forcing them to remember.

"You know I think you're a badass, right?" Jenna pushes her sunglasses up her nose as we look for a clear spot on the beach.

"I know." My hot-pink bikini shows off more skin than I've ever shown in public before, and it kind of makes me feel powerful.

If I learned anything from Charity, it was to feel beautiful. To walk with confidence and gratefulness for who I am and what I embody. She always tried to undo the damage my mother inflicted by constantly building me up with positive words and compliments.

Charity was so deliberate about letting me know how valuable I was to her. How beautiful I was, inside and out. Did I do the same for her? Was I as good a friend to Charity as she was to me?

I straighten my back and move my hair off my shoulders so my chest is bare but for my bikini top. Charity would be proud.

God, I miss her.

She gave me a friendship most people live their entire life without finding.

And then she went and died.

Jenna and I find a clear spot on the shore and lay out our towels. As I'm smoothing mine over the sand, the sight of Daren's black sports car pulling into the beach parking lot catches my eye. He gets out and is immediately greeted by a slew of half-naked girls who are far too eager to touch him and offer him drinks. He lifts his sunglasses and scans the beach, smiling when his eyes find mine. He gives me a half-wave. I half-wave back.

His smile seems to crack a bit as we lock gazes, but he goes back to his harem before I can be sure.

"Who's that?" Jenna asks, watching Daren pull his T-shirt over his head before joining a nearby group of wasted beach boys.

"That's Daren," I say as I finish flattening my orange towel.

"The guy who kissed you?"

"The very same."

"Huh." She stares for a moment longer, no doubt falling into the sticky web of good looks and trouble that Daren can't help but weave everywhere he goes. "Not bad."

I snort. "Not good either."

"Good enough for me." She grins.

"You'd eat him alive."

"And I bet he'd be delicious."

I lift a brow. "Yummier than Jack?"

Her naughty facial expression twists into one of frustration. "Jack is not on the menu of conversation topics today."

I give her a knowing smile as we both sit down on our towels. "What's with you two, anyway?"

She sighs. "Confusion, that's what. Sometimes he's hilarious and wickedly fun, and I get the feeling he's into me, you know? But other times he annoys the shit out of me and I just want to slap him, and I get the feeling he wants to slap me back. And not in a hot, kinky way." She considers a moment. "Well, maybe in a hot, kinky way, but that just makes it more confusing."

"Oh, Jenna." I smile. "I like your life. It's entertaining."

"Happy to be of service."

We stretch out and lean back on our elbows, tilting our heads back to soak in the sun.

Jenna's jade-green bikini is almost as small as mine, showing off the inked canvas of her body. Rose vines stretch across her rib cage and tangle with shooting stars that fall over her shoulder and across her chest. Other designs mark her legs and arms, and her back is a winter landscape masterpiece.

She's fearless with her tattoos, stamping her body with whatever is truthful for her at the time. There's something honest about that—about devoting yourself to whatever is honest for you in the moment, even though you know life will change and you'll change with it.

People walk by and check us out. Some of them stare at my scar; some of them avoid looking at me altogether. I wonder if Matt was afraid to look at me too but forced himself to stomach it because he's a good guy.

"Handyman Hottie is here." Jenna looks over her sunglasses.

I follow her gaze and, sure enough, I see Levi walking our way with Zack by his side.

"Shit," I mutter, rolling over onto my stomach.

Levi and I have been in cold moods all week, ignoring each other at every possible opportunity. Bringing up Charity had been a mistake. Clearly, we couldn't handle it. And the fact that we both feel responsible for her death only makes things worse. Like maybe we're both more damaged than we feared.

A slight burning begins behind my eyes, and I blink to push it away.

I blame my mother for a lot of things—my crappy childhood, my inability to enjoy fattening food without feeling disgusting, my irrational fear of lizards—but mostly, I blame my mother for all the unspoken pain in the east wing.

If she hadn't opened every bloody wound she could find in the kitchen the other night, maybe Levi and I wouldn't be such a mess.

And don't even get me started on the orgasmic shower experience we had. Levi and I haven't uttered a word about that ordeal since it happened. Because that's what we do. We make out and then never speak of it again.

Dysfunctional to the max.

As Zack and Levi near, I press my chest against the towel and try to look like I'm sunbathing and not hiding. Levi has never seen my whole scar, and he will absolutely freak if he does now.

Jenna frowns at me. "Why do you look all stiff and awkward? And why is your face pressed into the towel? Isn't it hard to breathe?"

My voice is muffled from the towel, where it actually is hard to breathe. "Just tell me when he's gone."

"What?" She leans over to hear me better; then her face brightens. "Hi, Levi." She waves at him.

Don't call him over, dammit!

"Hey, Jenna." A pause. Then Levi's voice rumbles over my back and the hot-pink strings of my swimsuit. "Pixie."

I turn my face to greet him, keeping my front carefully tucked into the towel.

"Hey, Leaves." It's out of my mouth before I can take it back, and he stills at the name. I want to kick myself.

Zack looks at Jenna and slowly pulls off his sunglasses. "Why, hello, beautiful," he says. "I'm Zack." He shows off his dimples. "And you are... ?"

"Not going to sleep with you," Jenna quips, grinning right back at him.

His smile widens. "Well played." He puts his glasses back on, but not before checking out my ass. "And Sarah, as always, it's so, *so* good to see you."

"You're a pervert," I say, even though I'd rather walk around naked in front of the whole town than lie here with my scar out in front of Levi.

Zack shrugs. "You're the one wearing dental floss as a swimsuit—ow!" He rubs his gut where Levi just hit him and glares at his friend. "Relax, dude."

"Let's go," Levi says, moving on without a second glance at me. Zack follows.

I exhale slowly and catch Jenna's stare.

"What?"

"What is your problem?" She looks my body up and down. "You look like someone glued you to the towel. You're all rigid and awkward and your arms are at weird angles. What's the matter with you?"

Once Levi is far away, I turn over and lean back on my elbows like Jenna. Calm, cool, collected. "Nothing. I'm fine."

She rips off her sunglasses and narrows her gaze at me. Then at my chest. "You have *got* to be kidding me."

"What?" I feign innocence.

"You were hiding your scar? From *Levi*?"

I drop my head back. "You don't understand."

"You were marching around all proud and beautiful before he got here and then, what, you're afraid he won't like you if he sees your scar? Because let me tell you, any guy who's worth a shit won't give a damn about any scar."

"That's not—" I sigh, not sure how to explain it to her. "That's not why I was hiding. My scar makes Levi sad. And I...I don't want him to be sad." Oh God, there's the burning sensation behind my eyes again.

She frowns at me. "So you're afraid."

"What?" I turn to her. "I'm not afraid."

"Sure you are." She nods. "You're always afraid. That's why you're hiding your scar. That's why you keep trying to run away." She shrugs.

"Run awa—what are you even talking about?"

She waves her hands at me. "You want to transfer to New York. You want to move to a different state. You want to hide your scar from the boy you love. You want to hide your feelings from me. You want to *pretend*." She goes still. "Because you're afraid of dealing with things."

My mouth gapes open. "Jenna."

"Look." She sighs and takes her sunglasses off. "I know this thing between you and Levi is uncomfortable and difficult to navigate, but you have to deal with it. Shitty things happen, Sarah. If you keep pretending, all the shittiness is going to poison any chance you have at, hell...I don't know, moving on? *Healing?*" She waits until I meet her eyes. "Don't you want to heal?"

My heart starts to pound. "I don't know what you're talking about. I've already healed. I'm fine." I swallow, my throat suddenly dry.

"Oh yeah?" she says. "If you're so healed, why don't you go over to Levi with your perky boobs and loud-ass scar and chat about the weather?" I glare at her. "Do it, Sarah. You've moved on. You've healed, right?"

I shake my head and lie flat on my back, angry and ashamed, refusing to respond to her as I close my eyes against the hot July sun.

A moment passes where she doesn't say anything, but I hear her lie down on her back as well.

She speaks quietly. "I want to help you heal, Sarah. But you have to let me in first." She hesitates. "Please let me in."

My eyes burn again, and this time I let the tears come. There aren't many, and the few that do fall are mostly hidden by my sunglasses as they stream down the corners of my eyes and to my ears.

How can I let Jenna—or anyone—*in* when there's a chance they might not stay there forever? I can't risk attaching myself to someone who could suddenly leave my world indefinitely. I can't. I won't.

For a long time we just lie there, listening to the laughter and music filling the air around us as I silently cry. Jenna knows I'm crying. She doesn't say a word about it. She just lets me weep under the happy sun until my tears are dry and the silence between us feels clean.

When we do speak again, it's Jenna initiating the conversation and changing the subject to hot dogs and popcorn until our previous conversation feels a hundred miles away.

Jenna's good at being my friend.

Why can't I be good at being hers?

———

Before I know it, the sun is setting and the sticky summer day begins to cool. Jenna and I eventually put our towels away and throw on swimsuit covers as we join in some of the ongoing festivities. I introduce Jenna to some of my high school friends, which feels slightly weird and uncomfortable, but only for a little while. Eventually, I start to feel at home around the people I grew up with, and I relax.

No one has brought up Charity's name all night. I'm both offended and relieved by this.

"Your delicious friend looks like he's having a good time." Jenna tips her chin in Daren's direction, and I look over to see him slamming another beer before serving a deadly fast volleyball over the net erected by a few beach volleyball enthusiasts.

"Yeah…" I say, as his harem on the sidelines cheers. "He's a party favorite pretty much everywhere he goes." He serves again, lifting his arm high in the air as he smashes a second ball over the net.

The cheerleaders start hooting again. Daren tosses them his trademark grin, but his smile doesn't quite reach his eyes. Huh.

"Excuse me," says a voice behind us.

Jenna and I turn to see a pretty blonde—strike that, a beautiful blonde—standing in the lake's parking lot, looking like a lost super-model, with her tiny cutoff shorts, tight white tank top, and giant blue eyes.

Good God. What must it be like to be that gorgeous?

"Could you guys tell me how to get to the nearest motel?" she asks, her eyes darting to the volleyball game for a moment.

"Sure," I say. "Just jump back on the freeway and head north for another five miles or so. You'll see a motel just outside of town on the left." I smile and hold out my hand. "I'm Sarah, by the way."

"Kayla," she says, shaking it.

"And I'm Jenna." Jenna shakes her hand as well.

"Nice to meet you two." Kayla smiles.

"Are you heading to Copper Springs to visit family?" I ask.

Her smile tightens. "Something like that." She clears her throat. "Well, thanks for the directions. Oh, and happy Fourth of July," she adds, before turning away. Her long blonde hair swishes across her back as she walks through the parking lot, and every single male in the vicinity cranks his head to stare at her as she climbs into a small rental car and drives away.

Jenna looks at me. "I want to be that pretty."

I nod. "Seriously."

———

When the first stars of evening begin to twinkle in the heavens, I step away from Jenna—who's been on the phone with Jack for the past twenty minutes—and find a quiet spot away from the raging bonfire on the lakeshore.

Sitting on a large, flat rock, I take in my surroundings. The sky is a brilliant purple filled with beautiful storm clouds, and people are smiling and singing and dancing. But everything is all wrong.

I inhale deeply, feeling my lungs burn with emotion as I think about the Fourth of July Bash last summer.

Charity was tossing her head back, laughing up at the night. She was standing in the bed of Levi's truck, dancing to the radio and promising to see fireworks in Paris someday. She was alive.

The burning expands.

Levi was shaking his head with a smile, his eyes meeting mine every few seconds. He was going somewhere. Successful. Brave. Happy.

I was happy…

Thunder rumbles from afar, and my gaze drifts to the side, locking on to a pair of blue eyes that look just as haunted as I feel.

Levi is standing with a group of his old buddies, playing cornhole just a few yards away. And he's staring at me.

God, it hurts to look at him. To share the pain. But it hurts to bear it alone too. After Charity…it was like we toppled over a cliff, with nothing to catch us. Nothing to cling to.

And we're still falling.

"Remember how I said we need new friends?" Jenna plops down beside me on the rock, and my gaze is broken. "Well, we should have acted faster because that was Jack on the phone, and the boy is losing his mind because he lost Ethan."

"Does that mean you need to go?"

She makes an apologetic face. "Sort of."

I shrug. "Then go."

"Come with me."

"No way." I smile. "I don't do Jack drama. Or Ethan drama. I don't do boy drama, period."

"You're so wise." She sighs, then scrunches her nose. "But if I leave, how will you get home?"

Jenna drove me out here tonight because, apparently, the whole wide world is afraid that if I drive myself anywhere I might instantly combust or something.

"No worries," I say, and quickly send Ellen a text asking if she'll pick me up later. She responds with an immediate yes. "See?" I smile at Jenna. "Problem solved. Now go attend to your damsel in distress."

"Ugh." She rolls her eyes. "That's so what Jack is. An overgrown damsel with a penis. I swear to God, if he wasn't so ridiculously hot I would—I would—"

"Still want to screw his brains out?"

She makes a face. "Probably." She gathers her stuff, then hesitates. "Are you sure you're okay if I leave?"

"I'll take care of her," Daren says, interrupting our conversation as he walks over and throws a lazy arm around my shoulder.

Jenna looks at him with sharp eyes. "And why would I trust you?"

"Uh...why wouldn't you?" he says.

"Because you're a random kisser."

"I'm a—I'm a what?" He laughs.

"A random kisser," she says, overenunciating each word. "You randomly kiss girls without permission."

"Aw..." He cocks his head. "You sound jealous. Would you like me to randomly kiss you? I mean, we haven't really met, but I feel like we could have some serious chemistry here. And I'm not above kissing complete strangers."

She juts her jaw at him, then looks at me. "Is this guy for real?"

"He's harmless," I say as I casually remove Daren's arm. "And it's not like I need a babysitter." God. It's like I'm twelve years old again. "I'll be fine. Just go."

She looks unsure.

"*Go*," I urge her, flicking my hand. "Before Ethan winds up in jail or another country."

She kisses my cheek. "Okay. Love ya."

As she walks away, I call out, "Tell Jack Hammer I say hi and that I'm totally on board with naming your baby Taylor."

"Not funny," she sings at me as she walks away.

I sing back, "Very funny."

"Come on," Daren says, gently cupping my elbow and turning me around. "You're missing all the fun."

I look at him as we walk back down the beach. "Are you okay? You seem...down."

"Who, me?" He scoffs. "The only thing I'm down about is the fact that I don't have a cold beer in my hand right now. A dilemma I will quickly rectify." He grins at me, but even in the darkness I can tell his expression is strained.

"Okay." I don't want to push it. And even if I did, Daren isn't the type to just spill his guts to someone. Especially not to a girl.

We walk in silence toward a large bonfire. Music playing from some unidentified source grows louder as we near, as does the laughter of all the partygoers. I wonder where Levi is—if he's still here, if he wishes he were somewhere else.

When we reach the group, Daren says, "All right. I'm off to get my drink on. Try to stay out of trouble, would you?" He winks.

I shake my head. "*You* need a babysitter."

"Ah, what a fantastically sexy idea. I'll go look for one." He smiles, then disappears into the sea of people dancing in the firelight.

I stay beside the giant bonfire, where I can no longer see the stars in the purple sky. Or Levi.

38

LEVI

A flash of lightning in the distance is all I need to see to know we're headed for a monsoon, but the clouds have yet to burst, so the jovial atmosphere is still in full swing.

I watch Zack win another round of cornhole and move on to his next opponent with a hoot of victory. He whispers something into the ear of Sierra Umbridge, and I almost roll my eyes.

Zack wasted no time finding a girl to entertain him tonight. He also wasted no time meeting my high school English teacher, the town mayor, and the guy who drives the fireworks in from Phoenix every year—who goes by "Buck," apparently. Buck owns twenty-eight guns, a tabby cat named Priscilla, and has tentative plans to visit Miami next summer.

Sometimes I think Zack's goal in life is to meet every person on the planet.

"You want a beer, man?" Sam asks.

I shake my head and nod at the can of soda in my hand. "I'm driving."

"You sure? If you don't like this kind, I think Richards has a different case in his car."

"Nah, I'm good. Really," I add when Sam looks unsure.

He finally shrugs and walks off to finish his own beer.

I can't figure out why the hell everyone is being so chatty with me tonight. You'd think they hadn't seen me in years, rather than months. Davis is retelling football stories from high school, all my great highlights; Richards has been asking me dumb questions about my job; and Sam has been offering me food and beer all night.

What the hell is going on?

Richards, who is plastered as always, keeps glancing over at me in between dirty jokes and glory stories, and I figure if anyone will break down, it'll be him. I walk up beside him and stand there for a minute, waiting until the silence between us gets too awkward for him to ignore.

"Hey," he says, taking a gulp of beer.

"Hey."

"So…I know I never said this before," he begins. "I'm a real jackass, I know, but…I'm sorry, man. About Charity."

I nod, dumbfounded. "Uh, thanks. That's…random."

He shrugs. "Well, I saw Sarah's scar today—"

"Holy shit! You saw it too?" Sam butts in, drunk. "It was wicked. Shame too. She's got this kick-ass little body, and then *bam*, there's a gnarly gash cutting right between her tits."

My heart drops to the dirt.

"You guys talking about Sarah?" Davis leans in and shakes his head. "I couldn't believe it."

"Me neither," some guy I've never seen before says.

I clutch my soda so tight the can starts to crinkle. "When did you guys see all this?"

"Today, man," Sam says. "She was prancing around in that pink bikini, all proud. Just putting her marred skin on display and looking people in the eye and shit." He shudders. "Unsettling as hell."

I struggle to keep a straight face as I look around at my uncomfortable friends. Is that why everyone has been bat-shit crazy around me tonight? Because Pixie marched Charity's memory around the lake today?

I almost laugh out loud. I could kiss her for that—for being brave and obstinate and proud. She's amazing. I wish I could have seen that—

My stomach falls, joining my heart in the sand, as I realize why I *didn't* see that. Pixie was acting weird earlier today because she was hiding her scar from me.

She was hiding her scar. From *me*.

I throw my soda away.

I'm halfway across the beach before I realize I'm headed to Pixie. My fists are clenched, and the sour feeling in my gut is sloshing with every step I take.

I find her standing with a group of her high school friends. Not smiling, but participating as the pink straps of her swimsuit peek out from the dress thingy she's thrown on.

Her eyes catch sight of me as I near, and she watches me like she knows I'm coming for her.

"We need to talk," I say when I'm within earshot, a low tremor in my voice.

She pulls out of the group and steps to the side as I trudge away from the fires and music and drunk people. I see her shadow following after me as I move into the darkness by the cliffs, just as the first of the opening fireworks spark to life in the sky. Cheers and clapping echo behind us as we travel deeper into the shadows.

When we reach a secluded place, I turn to her, and for a moment we just stare at each other. More fireworks shoot into the sky, lighting up her face as she waits.

I'm suddenly scared stupid to talk about this.

"Let me see it," I say, my voice coming out a bit unsteady.

She crosses her arms over her chest and doesn't pretend not to know what I'm talking about. "No."

I blink, not quite sure how to respond to that. "So what, then? You're just going to hide it from me for the rest of your life?"

"Well, I'm certainly not going to strip down for you right here so you can see just how torn up my skin is."

"But you'll let the whole town see?"

"Would you rather I hole up like an ashamed hermit?"

"No! Of course not. That's not—" I purse my lips. "You know that's not what I meant. I just...I just don't want you to hide your scar because you're trying to shield me from reality. I don't need you to protect me."

Her eyes narrow. "You can't even handle seeing me in a towel."

"That's *my* problem, Pixie. Not yours."

"Like hell!" She uncrosses her arms. "How is that not my problem? You looked like you were going to throw up the other day—and that was after seeing only the *tip* of the scar."

"That's because I'd never seen it before."

"Well, maybe if you'd bothered to come visit me in the hospital while I was *fighting for my life*, you could have checked out all the gore firsthand and wouldn't feel so left out right now." Her eyes widen a bit, like maybe she didn't mean to say that out loud, but it's too late.

Her words sink into me like iron stakes, driving deep and wedging anger and regret between my lungs. I take a step forward. "I didn't come visit you in the hospital because I'd almost killed you. I didn't think you'd want to see me."

"Well, that wasn't your call to make."

"I was trying to be respectful."

She juts her jaw. "Is that why you abandoned me too? Out of *respect*?"

"Abandoned you? What are you talking about?"

"You *left* me, Levi. Charity died and you just disappeared, like I was nothing more than an accessory to your past. I lost Charity, and then I lost YOU. Did you ever stop to think about how alone I was back here in reality while you were off at frat parties and throwing footballs?"

Fireworks pop in the sky, orange and blue flashes filtering down on her cheeks as I stand, wordless.

She shrugs angrily. "Did you ever think for one minute that I might have needed someone to be here for me to mourn with? Or were you too busy thinking about your own pain? Because I lost her too, you know. I lost Charity and your parents and your home—just like you—but I didn't get to run away. I had to stay in this god-forsaken town and listen to people pretend Charity never existed while I healed enough to get out of this place and start college. You didn't think about me or look back, and that hurt, Levi. It hurt so much and…" Her features twist in pain, and she shakes her head. "You know what? Forget it. It doesn't matter anymore." With a wave of her hand, she spins on her heel and walks away from me as more colors fall from the sky.

My mouth and my feet are stuck to the earth.

She's totally right. I left her.

God.

I left her.

Just like my parents left me. But what I did was worse because Pixie was blameless. I was so caught up in my own personal hell that I put distance between us without even a thought as to how she might feel about me disappearing from her life. She was in that hospital, hurt and sad, and I just fucking LEFT.

"Pix!" I shout. "Wait—*wait*." I follow after her, but she has a head start and maneuvers quickly through the shadows of the rocks. Every few seconds or so, she's lit up by the overhead fireworks, but then her form is plunged back into darkness once the holiday sparkles fade away until she's completely gone. Blending into the crowds of people on the beach. Hidden in the shadows of laughter and music and noise. Gone.

Then the sky breaks.

39

PIXIE

*P*ouring rain doesn't make for a great fireworks show, but it sure as hell makes for a happy group of drunk people. Some of them are even swimming in the lake. Morons.

I can't believe I just snapped at Levi like that, but a part of me feels a little lighter because of it. I didn't realize how truly angry I was with him until just now. And I'm pissed. And hurt. But mostly pissed.

Desperate to get away, far away, from Levi and all the rage and brokenness inside me, but not in the mood to get drenched or, you know, struck by lightning, I look around for shelter.

"Sarah!" Daren's voice calls from where our friends are still gathered by the bonfire. "Where did you go? You missed the fireworks!"

I don't know how he thinks I could have possibly "missed" the giant pyrotechnics show in the sky thirty seconds ago. Clearly, he's not sober. But his voice reminds me that his car is parked nearby, so that's where I head, careful to ignore his distant pleas for me to return to all the fireworks/lightning/rainstorm fun.

I let myself into the passenger side of his car and shut the door so rain isn't pouring on me. Then I get out my phone to text Ellen to come pick me up.

Before I can press Send, Daren jumps into the driver's seat with a giant smile on his face.

"Sarah!" He cheers. "I caught up with you!"

Yay.

"Whatcha doing in my car?"

"Temporary shelter," I say. "I think I'm going to head home. I'm tired."

"No!" His protest is very dramatic, and I know he's wasted. "Stay with me a little while longer."

I shake my head. "I'm tired. I want to go home."

"Nope. You're staying with me." He smiles and closes his door, shutting himself inside with me.

The smell of liquor invades my nostrils, and now I'm annoyed. "I'm just not feeling it tonight, Daren. Sorry."

He ignores me and starts to ramble. "It's weird being here, right? I mean, last year I was here. And you were here. And so was Charity. We were all here. And now you and I are here again. But not Charity." He stares out the windshield. "It's weird being here."

I exhale, feeling his pain. "Yeah. Charity being gone is tough, but it'll...it'll get easier. It has to."

Right?

He nods.

I bite my lip, wanting to leave so I can be pissed at Levi in private. "So...I'm pretty spent. I think I'm just going to take off—"

"Old Man Turner died yesterday," he says quietly, his glazed brown eyes still staring out the window.

I suck in a short breath.

Well, that explains all the excessive drinking and sadness rolling off Daren in waves. For a moment, I have no words as I watch

Daren's profile. I know Mr. Turner was like a father to him. Or at least like an uncle.

"Daren, I . . . I'm so sorry." I press my lips together.

He blinks a few times and then turns to me with another forced smile. "No worries. I barely knew the guy." His bloodshot eyes brighten. "You know what we need to do? Party. Yes." He nods to himself. "We need to go party." He pulls his car keys from the pocket of his board shorts, puts them in the ignition, and starts the engine.

My palms start to sweat. "What are you doing?"

The panic in my voice is evident and, yeah, maybe I'm a bit of a drama queen when it comes to the whole drunk-driving thing, but seriously?

"Calm down." He gives me a lopsided grin. "We're not going far. Just to Shannon's house."

Shannon . . . Shannon . . . Who's Shannon?

"I don't want to go to Shannon's house," I say and try to open the passenger door. Stupid childproof locks. "Let me out."

"Why? We're not there yet, silly." He's still smiling, and I realize he's drunker than I thought. Drunk Daren—even super-drunk Daren—would never lock me in a car with him when he was drinking. He knows my story. Hell, he was in it.

But this isn't run-of-the-mill-drunk Daren. This is megadrunk Daren, and now I'm freaking out.

I play with the door handle again. "Open the damn door, Daren."

He rolls down the driver's side window and calls out to a group of people who are leaving the lake. "Sarah and I will meet you guys at Shannon's, okay?"

"No, we won't!" I yell out his window as droplets of rain splash into the car. Then I look at Daren. "There's no way in hell I'm going to let you drive drunk. If we're going anywhere, I'm driving."

I shift out of my seat and try to take the keys from the ignition.

He covers them with his hand like this is some giant joke. "Um, I don't think so? Do you know what kind of car this is? A Porsche. Which means it needs to be driven by a professional. And besides, we both know you can't drive a stick." He laughs. "At least not this kind of stick. Calm *down*," he says as I swat at his freakishly strong grip on the keys. "I got this."

"No. You got drunk." My heart starts to pound. "Let me drive."

"No."

"Then let me out right now."

He starts fumbling with the gears until we're in reverse.

Oh God.

"Ellen is going to pick me up. Let me out!" With Daren's window rolled down, people can hear me yelling and some of them are staring now.

He backs the car up. "Tell Ellen you'll be at Shannon's." He puts the car in drive and slowly pulls forward.

"No! Stop the car." The pounding in my chest grows violent. "Stop the car!"

The car stops, but not because of my protests.

Levi is in front of us and has just thrown his hands on the hood, making an outrageously loud sound echo through the car.

"What the hell?" Daren puts the car in park and leans his head out the window. "Levi?" He smiles drunkenly. "I didn't know you were here. Are you going to Shannon's too?"

Levi looks pissed as he comes around to Daren's window. He glances at me, then at Daren. "Why was Pixie just asking you to stop the car?"

He waves it off. "Ah, you know. She wants to drive the Porsche." He rolls his eyes. "Girls *always* want to drive the Porsche."

Levi leans back from his breath. "You're drunk."

"I am?" He laughs and slurs out, "Are you sure? Because sometimes my laid-back nature comes across as a lack of sobriety, but I *assure* you—assure you?" He laughs again. "That sounds funny in my mouth. Assure you. Assure—"

"Let Pixie out of the car."

He points a wobbly finger at Levi and squints. "No, man. She's not yours."

"Well, she sure as hell isn't yours."

"I'm not anybody's! God!" I say, angry and scared and just over the whole stupid thing. "Just let me out of the car, Daren."

He turns to me. "Quit bitching, Sarah."

And then Daren's not in the car anymore.

Levi has him by the neck and has just dragged him *out of the window* and around the car.

Holy hell. Things are about to get real.

Daren's body makes a hollow sound as Levi throws him against the hood and pins his throat.

Frozen in the passenger seat, I'm just staring through the rain-dotted windshield, while everyone in the parking lot waits for the whole Batman scene to unfold.

Daren tries to pry Levi's hand from his throat, but Levi holds tight, his body rigid and giant. It's been so long since I've seen Levi next to any guy who wasn't a football player that I forgot just how big he is. Daren doesn't stand a chance.

"Three things, asshole," Levi says casually, like yanking a guy out of a car window is an everyday occurrence for him. "One." He looks at Daren calmly. "Don't drink and drive. That's fucking dumb."

Daren's gasping.

"Two." Levi stretches his neck. "When a girl says no—to anything—that means no."

Daren smacks at Levi's strong arm.

"And three." Levi leans down and puts his face frighteningly close to Daren's and lowers his voice. "Pixie's. Not. Yours. And if I ever hear you speak to her like that again, I will yank the tongue out of your throat."

With one last shove, Levi releases Daren and straightens his shoulders.

Daren starts coughing and hacking.

I'm speechless.

Without looking at me, Levi opens the driver's door and waits. I scramble across the console and climb out, fully aware that everyone in the parking area is staring at us.

I'm still angry with him, but I follow him through the drizzle anyway. Because this is Levi. This is my hero. And you always follow your heroes, even when you're mad, even when you'd rather punch them in the mouth. That's how trust works. It's blind and unconditional and it takes you places you can't reach by yourself.

Just like love.

My heart squeezes and I drop my eyes to the wet pavement as we walk along. We don't stay a word to each other as we cross the remainder of the parking lot and get in his truck.

I buckle my seat belt and stare at the dashboard.

"Where's your friend Jenna?" he asks, putting on his own seat belt.

"She left already." I clear my throat. "Where's Zack?"

"He went home with Sierra Umbridge."

I nod, and that's the end of our conversation. He starts the engine and we pull away from the lake.

———

Rain beats down on the windshield, pattering in a peaceful way interrupted only by the rhythmic swiping of the wiper blades as we drive along.

Why does rain always look so sad but sound so peaceful?

I prop a foot up on his dashboard like I used to do when life was still good, and my paint-stained shoe reminds me of the first time I ever rode in this truck.

Levi picked me and Charity up from school, and we felt like rock stars, climbing into her big bro's big truck. He was so proud of getting his license. So sure of himself and happy. It's a beautiful thing, Levi happy.

My last class of the day was art, and I had paint on my shoes. When I climbed in, I accidentally left a blue shoe print on the floorboard of his new truck, and Levi was pissed.

I felt super bad, but I totally laughed at his attempt at anger. He was awful at staying mad at me. I took my shoes off and held them in my lap the whole ride home, my bare feet feeling oddly intimate against the soft floorboard beneath me.

It seems like a lifetime ago.

The wipers cut across the windshield again and I look down at my feet. The blue shoe print is still there. It's a little faded by time and dirt, but I can still see it. A reminder of me.

I reach down and trace a finger across the brightest splotch of blue. It's a gross floorboard and completely grimy, but I can't help myself.

We stop at a red light, and I can feel Levi's eyes on me as I stroke the blue stain. He probably thinks I'm crazy. Maybe I am.

Why didn't he just get new floor mats?

I sit back up and chance a glance at him. The red stoplight glows into the cab as we stare at each other, listening to the sound of rain falling on the windshield. Constant. Steady.

Red turns to green and our eyes pull apart.

40

LEVI

I haven't been in a car with Pixie since the night of the accident, and it all seems too familiar. My shoulders are tense and my knuckles white as they grip the steering wheel.

I clear my throat. "I'm sorry. For taking off after Charity died. I shouldn't have left." I clear my throat again because it's starting to close in. "I should never have left you."

She watches me for a long moment. "It's okay. It's not like I stayed by your side either."

"I'm still sorry."

Silence.

I inhale deeply and attempt to make light conversation. "So Ellen says you might transfer to NYU this fall."

"Yeah. Maybe. If I get in. What about you?" she asks. "Ellen said you dropped out of college after the season ended and haven't reapplied yet. What happened?"

Dropped out. That's a nice way of saying it.

"Studying wasn't exactly my top priority last fall, and I don't know if I really want to return."

A long lull follows as we stare at the dark road outside and the rain that blurs it. I manage to get her back to the inn without maiming her and slowly pull into a parking space. I don't move to get out and neither does she, so we're sitting in the dim light shining in through the windshield from the inn's front porch. I can smell her lavender shampoo.

"Thanks for the ride," she says, still not moving from the car.

I nod. "I'm sorry about everything tonight. Sorry I implied that you were mine. That was lame. I know you're not anyone's. I wasn't trying to be a Neanderthal, I swear. I was just... God, I was pissed at Daren for trapping you in that car and scaring you like that and—"

"I'm glad you were there." She smiles and shifts uncomfortably. "I'm sorry I hid my scar from you. That was... immature."

I shake my head. "I don't know why I pounced on you about it. It's really none of my business."

More silence. More rain.

She shifts again. "Do you still want to see it?"

I blink and then nod, even though the idea scares the hell out of me.

She slowly unties the dress cover thingy she has on and slips it down her shoulders until she's wearing only her bikini top. And cutting a thick diagonal through her chest is everything I did wrong. Red and jagged, it looks out of place against the flawless skin of her breasts and stomach.

I can't pull my eyes away from it. I can't.

"Levi."

I broke her. I broke everything.

My heart starts to pound in my ears.

"Levi," she says again, and I meet her eyes. "I'm okay."

"I'm so sorry." My voice cracks as my eyes fall back to the scar. I can't help myself as I touch a hand to her skin. I lay my palm flat against the center of her chest, my fingers in line with the diagonal, and feel her heartbeat pulsing beneath me.

She covers my hand with hers. "I'm okay."

I stare at her small hand, covering mine, for a moment. Suddenly overwhelmed with emotion, I gently slip my hand out from under hers.

She looks down and puts her hand on the door handle, biting her lip before looking back at me.

"And I am yours," she says quietly. "Even when you don't want me. I'm still yours."

She exits the truck and walks inside the inn as rain continues to beat on the windshield.

41

PIXIE

I don't regret it.

I've been so afraid of Levi seeing my scar, so scared that the red reminder of Charity would destroy him, that I failed to realize how healing showing him might be for me. The sight of my scar might have cut into Levi, but it patched up a bleeding piece of my soul that I didn't think I'd ever get stitched; the part of me that refused to see Charity's death in Levi's eyes; the part of me that denied his pain.

So I don't regret it.

Even now, ten days later, when Levi still won't look at me or speak to me, I don't regret it. Charity is dead. I am scarred. Levi is haunted.

These are the real things, the true things.

And the truth is easier to breathe in than the lie. Uglier perhaps. But far less suffocating without the cloud of denial I've kept around me all this time. Denial is thick and sweet, and for the past year it filled up my lungs until they threatened to burst. But truth…truth is clean and pure. And yes, it hurts when I inhale it, it hurts to cleanse out the sweet smoke, but breathing out is like new life.

With black paint staining my fingers, I step back from the

small canvas I've been working on all morning. It's not perfect. It's not even close. It's a mess of gray, with shards of black and slits of white, but it's what I want to see.

With careful hands, I hang the canvas up to dry beside the three other similar paintings I've been working on for the past few days.

Four paintings. One subject. A million unspoken things.

42

LEVI

*W*hen she was nine, Pixie found a dog on the side of the road and brought him to my house out of pity. She was always finding stray, ugly animals and taking them in like she was some kind of angel of all living creatures.

Of course we fell in love with the mangy puppy immediately, and Maverick—Charity named the mutt Maverick—became a member of our family. But two years later, Maverick died, and everyone, including myself, was devastated.

The night we lost Maverick, Charity and Pixie crept into my room and crawled into my bed with tears streaming down their faces, convinced the heartbreak would hurt less if the three of us stuck together and slept beside one another. They were right.

And in junior high, when Charity and Pixie snuck into that horror movie and were terrified that an ax murderer would come for them in the night, they crawled into my bed again, sleeping soundly under the illusion of my protection. They came to me for bravery and strength.

I don't feel brave or strong anymore.

It's the crack of dawn and I'm in the garden fixing a planter wall that's been lopsided for two months. Ellen didn't put it on my list of things to do, but it's been driving me crazy, so...yeah. The planter will be fixed today.

An elderly guest named Paul is sitting on the nearest garden bench, watching me re-lay the bricks for the planter.

"I used to garden," Paul says, eyeing me carefully. "Still do, actually. But only during certain seasons. Do you like to plant things?"

I lay a new brick down. "Not really. I'm more of a 'fixing things' kind of guy."

He laughs and the sound is hoarse and gritty, like he's been smoking for fifty years. "That's pretty much all planting is, fixing. You grow a flower or a vegetable—you spend months watering it and protecting it from the sun and critters—and then one day it starts to die and you have to fix it."

My thoughts go to Charity. I banish them.

Then my thoughts go to Pixie, and I don't banish them.

Paul leans forward on the cane in his hands. "It's the damnedest thing, a dying plant, and it makes a man want to give up. But that's the beauty of gardening, son. You can revive the things that wither."

I lay another brick and shovel back some dirt from the flower bed. "It sounds like rewarding work."

"Oh, it is. It is." He's silent for so long I think maybe he's fallen asleep, but when I look over at him, he's wide-awake and watching me lay the last brick down.

Finished, I stand and dust my hands off on my jeans and pick up my supplies.

"They're stronger, you know." Paul looks up at me.

I shield my eyes in the morning sun. "What's stronger?"

"The plants that you revive," he says. "When you bring something back from the brink of death, it fights harder to thrive." Paul leans on his cane again and smiles. "So is the story of life, I guess."

———

"Ellen says you still have the spare keys?" I say outside of Pixie's open bedroom door. This is the first we've spoken since the Fourth of July Bash.

"Oh. Yeah," she says. "I found my own set yesterday. Now, where…did I put…the spare keys…?" She glances around. "You can come in. This might take a minute."

I step into Pixie's room, not sure if I want to be here. It feels personal. And it smells like her, which makes my chest feel funny.

There's a tension in the air I've been trying to ignore all day, but with every passing minute it growers thicker and tighter. Tomorrow is almost here.

I can't think about it, so I concentrate on mundane objects as she searches for the keys.

Dirty clothes on the floor.

Paintbrushes in glass jars. Stained. Frayed. Chewed at the ends. She's always been such a mess. I like her messy.

My eyes wander and land on four paintings strung up against the wall, and my feet absently take me there. I blink as I take in the dark-haired girl with light in her eyes and mischief in her smile. She's fearless and pensive. Laughing and free. She's everything I remember and more.

Charity.

My stomach fills with longing, but not the sad kind. The meaningful kind. The kind of longing you feel when you think about your first roller coaster or your first perfect game. The longing that makes you wish you could experience it again, but so grateful you had it in the first place.

I touch a finger to the closest painting. "These are beautiful."

Pixie hesitates. "Thanks. Sometimes I see her and I just want to remember."

I nod because I get it. "I like that you remember."

She finds my eyes, and all I see is a sad little girl who lost her friend. Everything inside me wants to cross the space between us and pull her into my arms. The last time I felt this way was at Charity's funeral. There were people in dark clothes everywhere, saying things to me I couldn't hear. There were tears and prayers filling up the cemetery. And then there was Pixie.

Seated in a wheelchair five people away with bruises on her face and a thick bandage peeking out from her purple dress. The girl wore purple. Charity's favorite color. Tears fell down her cheeks, but her face was expressionless.

I wanted to hug her then. I wanted to pull her close and tuck us into each other, where there was no one else to mourn Charity. Just us. Because no one else understood. Just us.

"I found the keys." Pixie looks up at me, and I'm suddenly looking at Charity.

I'm watching her play with dolls and dress up like a princess and ask for a kitty every Christmas. I'm hearing her tell on me for lighting firecrackers in the backyard and whine when I get to stay up later than she does. I'm watching her cry on her first day of junior high when some girls made fun of her outfit, and lock herself in her bedroom when Jason Hampton broke up with her. I'm seeing her grow up, I'm sharing my banana splits with her, I'm watching scary movies with her in the upstairs bedroom so Mom and Dad can't hear us, I'm giving her a ride to the mall and yelling at her for taking my credit card. I see Charity and she's beautiful and happy. And worth reliving every memory.

I blink, and it's Pixie staring back at me.

"I miss her," I blurt out.

It's the first time I've felt safe enough to admit that to someone aloud. It's the first time I've been able to say that without feeling guilty.

Pixie nods like she totally gets it. "I miss her too."

She gets it.

43

PIXIE

There is nothing extraordinary about today.

It is just a day. A Saturday, to be exact. The morning birds are chirping outside. The wind is blowing through the fields out back. And I am alive.

Lying in bed, I roll onto my side and stare at the four gray paintings hanging on the far wall. Sadness does not flood into me like I anticipate. Nor does anger or peace. The only thing I feel, as the waking sunbeams slide over my sheet-wrapped body, is longing. Deep, wailing longing.

Not for the girl in gray—that girl is at peace and unbroken—but for the boy next door, who is anything but. And yet the boy next door feels farther away than the girl in gray.

I let out a long, slow breath as I stare at Charity's face. Today marks the one-year anniversary of her death. A year has gone by, but somehow no time has passed. I'm still here, at the precipice of my future, waiting for life to happen. I'm still the broken girl who woke up in a hospital bed without her best friend, without her hero.

I thought time stopped for me, but time is not something I ever had or ever will have. It simply is. It never begins. It never ends. So the sun rises and sets, and my scar heals and fades, and the morning birds chirp on.

There is nothing extraordinary about today, except that it has come and I have lived to see it.

But perhaps that is precisely what makes today more extraordinary than any day before.

With a deep breath, I get out of bed.

44

LEVI

I'm sitting against a log right at the edge of the lavender field with my back to the trees beyond. The air smells like Pixie.

The inn lights are mostly off, giving darkness over to the night and showcasing the many stars in the clear sky. It's quiet out here, no guests milling about the grounds or taking late-night walks, no storm.

I light the cigarette in my hand, take a drag, and tilt my head up to the stars as I exhale.

Everyone kept a wide berth around me today, no one brave enough to start any conversations with me or make direct eye contact. I'm not sure what they were afraid of. Me breaking into tears?

Angelo was the only person who even acknowledged the shittiness of today, and even he didn't use words. He simply walked past me as he was leaving for the night and handed me a single cigarette and a lighter.

He's a scary bastard, but he has a soul.

I'm not a smoker. Sure, I've smoked before. But I've always been an athlete, and a smoking athlete is a weak athlete. So I'm not big on cigarettes.

But today hurts.

So I'm smoking.

I hear crickets in the distance and the sound of wind sweeping through the purple fields.

I'm alone. I'm thinking. I wish I wasn't thinking.

I hear the back door to the kitchen close and see a form step outside with a trash bag. I know that form. I've felt that form against my body.

Pixie starts to turn away, but freezes when she catches sight of me in the shadows. How she sees me I'm not sure, but she's on her way over.

I stay seated and rub a hand down my face.

Her walk is slow and deliberate until she stops beside me, dressed in her work clothes. Even though we both had the day off, we still decided to work. Work keeps the demons out.

She watches me smoke for a moment. "Got one for me?"

I exhale a cloud of smoke. "No."

She plucks the lit cigarette from my hand. At first I think she's going to stomp it out and lecture me on the health ramifications of smoking. But she doesn't. She takes her own slow drag and breathes the smoke in before handing it back to me.

I take it from her, both annoyed and turned on. "You shouldn't smoke."

She sits on a rock in front of me, just a foot or so away, and I can feel my body respond to how close she is.

"I shouldn't do a lot of things." She looks at the stars. "Charity hated cigarettes."

I shift against the log.

"She would always try to smoke, but end up coughing and gagging." She tucks a strand of loose hair behind her ear. "It was fun to watch her try, though." A small smile plays at her lips.

I take another drag, watching her carefully. "I don't remember that."

"Yeah, well. I don't think she ever wanted you to see her try. You were her hero, you know?" She plays with a lace on her shoe.

"I don't remember that either." My lungs are shrinking and I can't quite get the air I need to keep my eyes from stinging.

"You were my hero too," she says softly. "You still are."

She drives her eyes into me, and all the memories I just ran away from, all the thinking I wasn't doing, it all comes swooping back in, picking me up with razor-sharp claws.

It feels like Charity is right here, sitting between us. It's tense and it's heavy, but, somehow, it doesn't feel wrong. Pix must feel it too because I see her shift on the rock.

I wish I could protect her from everything bad, always. I want to protect her from drunk driving and asshole guys, of course. But I also want to protect her from the sadness of losing Charity. The guilt.

"It's not your fault," I say.

Her eyes glide to mine in the darkness.

"What happened to Charity," I continue, "wasn't your fault. Not at all."

The moment Charity's name leaves my lips, a charge goes into the air, and at first I'm afraid of it. Like maybe I just unleashed an emotional hell that will take me another year to shove back inside my soul.

But then I take a breath and my chest rises freely, because saying Charity's name feels good. No. It feels safe.

Safe with Pixie.

She leans forward on the rock so our faces are directly in front of each other, and she looks right at me, silent. It's not sexual. It's not playful. It's Pixie asking for my full attention, and now she has it.

"It's not your fault either," she says.

I look down at her scar.

She follows my eyes and takes my face into her hands, tipping my chin up so I'm gazing at her soft face. "And what happened to me wasn't your fault."

I pull my head away and look at the dirt.

"It wasn't your fault—"

"Stop, Pix," I say quietly.

She's quiet for a few minutes; then she slides down the rock until she's right in front of me, knees in the dirt, apron on the ground.

"I forgive you." Her steeled eyes wait for mine to meet them and hold me there under the stars. "You have nothing to be forgiven for," she says, "but I still forgive you. Will you forgive me?"

I stare at her in horror. "For what?"

"For getting wasted with Charity at that party. For encouraging her to leave. For letting her drive drunk."

She's insane. None of that was her fault. None of that was—

"I forgive you," she repeats. "Will you please forgive me?"

The look in her eyes tells me we're not talking about blame. We're talking about heartbreak and loss and all the things we don't know how to deal with.

"I forgive you," I say, meaning it even though there is nothing that needs to be forgiven, and I'm looking at little Pixie, six years old and stealing my Transformers. Six years old and wiggling her way into my heart. She's still there, wrapped inside me like she's mine. And maybe she is.

Suddenly it's gone. The guilt, the heaviness. The fear of letting myself be happy, love fully. It's all gone. Because Pixie just forgave me. And maybe I just forgave myself.

The air around us is free. It's like a million tiny weights are floating up off my chest and into the sky, and I didn't know I could feel so much relief.

She moves to sit beside me, and my body tenses as hers slides down my side until she's leaning against the log. Reaching over, she takes the cigarette from my hand and brings it to her mouth. Tiny red embers glow in the darkness as she sucks smoke into her lungs and tips her head back, resting it against the log as she stares at the sky.

I shift down a bit, the side of my body rubbing against hers until our shoulders are level, and rest my head back as well, looking at the sky as Pixie slowly exhales beside me. A cloud of gray smoke feathers into the air above us, blocking the night sky until dissolving into the black and unveiling the heavens.

We gaze at the sky for a long, quiet minute, and the only sounds I hear are the crickets and Pixie's steady breaths.

I feel like a kid again. Stars above me, Pixie beside me. There's solace in the silence that floats between us, and I wonder if she feels it too. I could stay here all night, where the sky is bigger than anything in my life and lavender scents the air. I could stay here forever.

I hear the smile in Pixie's voice. "Remember when Charity and I tried to jump off the porch roof and you got all mad?"

I scoff. "What were you, like six?"

"Yeah. We were being fairies, remember? We had our costumes on from Halloween and we were going to fly." She says this in exaggerated wonderment and I laugh. I actually laugh.

Charity was a pain in the ass to keep alive. It wasn't just the porch thing. The girl climbed ridiculously tall trees and went cliff jumping and stuff. But the fairy thing, that was the beginning of it all. Charity and Pix were dressed up with my mom's makeup on and they were carrying these stupid wands. Ugh. They were so adorably annoying.

"I didn't let you fly," I say.

"No. You told on us."

I smile. "I sure as hell did."

And then we're silent for a moment, but the air isn't so smoky and I'm not so heavy.

"That was the first time you ever called me Pixie," she says quietly.

I inhale, thinking about little Sarah dressed up like a fairy in my backyard, all pink and sassy. "Yes, it was."

She pauses. "I like being Pixie."

I don't say anything, but I smile.

45

PIXIE

*I*nhale.

I pull the sharp heat and bitter taste of the cigarette through my lips, feeling my insides burn and my eyes blur as the smoke expands in my lungs. I don't want to talk. I don't want to cry. I just want to sit here, beside my hero, and remember.

Exhale.

The smoke floats into the quiet summer sky, swirling above us and fogging up the stars.

I bring the cigarette back to my mouth, but Levi gently pulls it from my fingers before it reaches my lips. Keeping his eyes on the sky, he deftly smothers the burning tip into the dirt as the smoke above us thins out until it clears completely.

Inhale.

The stars are more beautiful without the smoke obscuring their brilliance.

Exhale.

Much more beautiful, actually. Real.

We stay like that, shoulder to shoulder, eyes fixed above, for countless minutes.

Inhale.

Lavender. Summer air. Spearmint.

Exhale.

There aren't any monsters out here.

46

LEVI

*T*his morning, I feel like I'm whole again, like my lungs have expanded and made my chest a paradise for oxygen, as I finish showering and cross the hall to my room.

"Thirty-seven minutes!" Pixie shouts from next door. There's a lightness in her tone I haven't heard in a long time, and it makes me wish she would keep speaking, even if only to scold me.

"You need a new hobby!" I yell back.

"Jerk."

I smile at the wall. "Nag."

And the day begins.

I get dressed and retrieve my To Do list from Ellen. Scanning the items she's scrawled out, I glare at her. "Another chandelier?"

She smiles. "The one in the west wing hallway."

"You haven't used that chandelier in ten years."

"Right. Because it's broken."

"That hallway is already well lit. You don't need it."

"Yeah, but it's pretty. So fix it."

I shake my head and smile. "Fine."

She grins. "Have fun."

Fun is the exact opposite of what I have for the next two hours as I fix Ellen's precious hanging piece of hell, but my mood doesn't sour. I conquer all the items on my list earlier than usual and head back to the front desk to let Ellen know I'm calling it a day.

She cocks her head at me. "You seem chipper."

"Chipper?"

"Yeah. Happy. Upbeat." She looks at me suspiciously and then smiles.

"What?"

She just keeps smiling. "Nothing."

I stare at her, but she says nothing more and now it's awkward.

"So…" I say. "Anything else you need me to do before I wrap up for the day?"

"No. Oh wait—yes. Can you give this to Pixie?" She hands me a white envelope. "It came in the mail today, but I forgot to give it to her. And while you're there, can you check the garbage disposal? Mable said it was gurgling."

"Gurgling. Sure." I take the letter and head to the kitchen.

When I enter, Pixie looks up from a mess of baking ingredients and smiles. I smile back. A piece of myself that I didn't know was starving suddenly warms in satisfaction.

"Hey, handsome." Mable smiles at me. "Haven't seen you all day."

"That's because Ellen has an unhealthy obsession with chandeliers."

Pixie scoffs. "She has an unhealthy obsession with everything old and impractical."

"Tell me about it. Ellen wanted me to give this to you," I say, handing over the letter.

"Thanks." Pixie takes the envelope and nods at two plates—one red, one blue—of chocolate squares on the counter. "Want a brownie?"

"Sure."

She pushes the red plate toward me and I grab a brownie and head to the sink. As I reach for the garbage disposal switch, I take a giant bite and—

"Holy mother of hell!" I gag and spit the disgusting treat into the sink. "What the—" I start coughing and stare at the vile brown piece of crap in my hand.

Mable keeps her eyes down with a smile.

Pixie crosses her arms and raises an amused eyebrow at me. "That's what you get," she says, looking much too satisfied by my continuing gags and coughs.

"For what?" God, this is the worst thing I've ever tasted. I gag again.

"For switching the sugar and salt on me all those years ago and adding *vinegar* to the vanilla so my brownies came out tasting like sour bars of salt. I finally figured it out this morning and decided to whip up a batch and give you a taste of your own medicine."

I spit again and smile. "It took you this long to figure it out? Yikes, Pix. You might have to kiss that future in detective work good-bye." I throw the remainder of the nasty brownie away and gag again. The real kind of gag where I think I might throw up.

"And you might have to kiss what you ate for lunch good-bye," she says. "Please don't vomit in my kitchen."

This only makes me gag harder.

"God." She rolls her eyes and grabs a brownie from the blue plate. "These are the good ones. I swear."

"Get away from me, you wicked treat devil."

She laughs. "Wicked treat devil? Wow. You can do better than that."

"Evil dessert demon?"

"Still lame."

"Chocolate temptress of salty death."

"Now you're just reaching. Here"—she grabs something—"spare your mouth any future embarrassment." She shoves another salty-sour brownie against my mouth and I start hacking all over again.

She smiles as she tears open the envelope. She scans the thick piece of paper inside and her face goes slack.

I quit gagging and wipe my mouth. "What's wrong?"

A bewildered expression crosses her face. "I was accepted into NYU. I can transfer there this fall. I'd have to leave next week."

"Wow," I say.

Wow.

"That's wonderful, dear," Mable says, then frowns at the dumbfounded expression on Pixie's face. "Are you okay?"

"Yeah. Yeah, I'm just...I don't know." Pixie smiles and wrinkles her brow and bites her lip. In that order. "I'm surprised, that's all." She smiles again.

I smile at her, but for some reason my gut feels hollow.

47

PIXIE

I'm stunned. Shocked. Dazed. Terrified, even. But not because I was accepted to NYU. I'm surprised because I'm no longer excited to go.

I've been trying to transfer schools for the past year, and now here's my chance and I just…don't care. I should be jumping up and down and squealing. Or at least smiling in a way that doesn't have Mable looking at me in concern, but instead I'm just standing here, staring at the red plate of brownies.

"Congratulations," Levi says.

I meet his eyes, and our strained smiles collide.

"Thanks," I say.

"New York." Mable smiles. Hers isn't strained. "What a wonderful city. I've only ever been there once, myself, but it was breathtaking. A great place for an artist."

"Yeah. NYU has a great art program." I sweep up some sugar with my hands and clean it off the counter. "One of the best in the country."

"How exciting." Mable sounds genuine, but keeps glancing at Levi every few seconds.

"You deserve it," he says, pressing his lips together.

I nod. Nothing else. I just nod and sweep up more sugar.

He clears his throat and wipes a few brownie crumbs from his face and shirt before moving to the disposal, where he promptly gets lost in work after retrieving a few tools.

I concentrate on cleaning up flour and salt, baking powder and sugar, tossing the remainder of my baking mess into the garbage.

Soon, the counter is spic-and-span and there are no more ingredients to sweep or put away. I wrap up the good brownies and put them in the fridge for tomorrow, wondering why my stomach keeps twisting.

Mable hangs her apron on a hook by the door. "All right, dear. I'm headed home. Are you sure you don't need any more help?"

"Nope. I'm good. Have a great night, Mable."

"You too, love." She leaves through the dining room door as I survey the kitchen. Levi is frowning at the disposal with a wrench in his hand and some leftover brownie still on his shirt, and Mable's blue apron is gently swinging back and forth from the hook.

Finding a fork, I scrape the remaining prank brownies off the red plate and into the trash. They pile up, a tower of deceitful chocolate in a white sea of discarded baking ingredients.

Like a tidal wave rushing for land, it hits me, and I instantly know why my stomach is twisting like a pretzel.

And the reason has ocean-blue eyes and chocolate brownie crumbs on his sleeve.

48

LEVI

No," I say.

"Aw, come on, dude," Zack whines through the phone the next morning. "I would do it for you."

"You would drive an hour to come babysit my pet goat?" I tuck my phone against my ear and shoulder as I grab my mail from the front desk and start flipping through it as I head upstairs.

"Yes."

"You're a fucking liar."

"You owe me," he says.

"Since when?" I pass Pixie in the hall and give her a tight smile. She smiles back and shifts past me as we go our separate ways. She's probably thrilled about moving to New York. She should be. She deserves it. She deserves something more than... well, anything here.

Zack says, "Since I hooked you up with Savannah the boobtastic blonde."

I enter my room. "I didn't even hook up with her."

"Irrelevant. Now, come get Marvin so I don't get kicked off the team for bringing a goddamn billy goat to the first day of practice."

"I'm not babysitting your goat."

"Get your ass down here, Andrews. Or I'll call up Sarah and tell her about the night you got wasted freshman year and blubbered all about how you wanted to kiss her pretty teeth and smell her golden hair."

I stop walking.

"Golden hair," he says. "You called it *golden*."

I drop my mail on my desk. "I hate you."

I can hear the smile in his voice. "The best friendships are rooted in hatred and blackmail. See you in fifty-five minutes."

By the time I reach the practice field, I'm royally pissed off and have decided that I'm going to sell Marvin on Craigslist before practice is over so I'll never again have to do a goat errand. But I guess this is better than staying at the inn all day, thinking about today.

Charity's birthday.

It's definitely not as heavy as the anniversary of her death, but it's still something. A piece of her. A reminder that she's not here. It's a cruel twist, her death being just a few days before her nineteenth birthday. One of many.

I park and walk through the familiar stadium gates and tunnels to reach the field where my former teammates are doing warm-ups. I wonder if Pixie will ever go to a football game in New York.

Coach McHugh sees me and blows the whistle to signal a five-minute break. Everyone disperses from their sprints and congregates around the bench as Coach marches up to me.

"What the hell, Andrews? Why isn't your name on my fucking roster? And why aren't you dressed for practice?"

I scratch the back of my neck. "Because I haven't responded to Dean Maxwell and I'm not here to play. Where's Arden?"

Coach's face turns red like he wants to scream at me, but instead he screams across the field at Zack. "Arden! Get your ass over here."

Zack jogs up to us with a pleasant expression. "What's happening, Levi?"

I glare at him. "Where the hell is your goat?"

Coach shoots his eyes to Zack. "What goat?"

He shrugs. "I left him at the mansion."

"What mansion?" Coach asks.

I flex my jaw as I stare at Zack. "Then why the hell did you have me drive all the way out here?"

"Because it's time for you to get your shit together." He looks at McHugh. "Coach, I believe Levi is here to scrimmage with us."

I shake my head. "No. No, sir. I'm not here to scrimmage."

"It's shit-getting-together time and Levi has clocked in," Zack says.

"No, I haven't."

"Shut up, both of you." Coach looks me up and down. "Suit up."

"What? No. I'm not here to play, Coach. I'm not even enrolled in school—"

"Too bad. You're here and I need players. Suit up."

"But I—"

"Suit your ass up!" he screams loud enough to draw the attention of every member of the team, who of course are looking at me like they're glad to have me back.

Zack grins. I hate him.

But as I look around the field and smell the newly cut grass and upturned dirt, a piece of me aches to stay, to feel air rushing at me and to thrust a ball from my hands. And the idea of running and throwing and smashing into things sounds good.

I slowly turn to Coach and relent. "Fine. One scrimmage game."

Coach gives me a warning look. "What's that, now?"

"One scrimmage game, *sir.*"

"Good. Now quit gabbing and suit the fuck up!"

"Yes, sir," I say, biting back a smile as I jog off to dress for practice.

49
PIXIE

The kitchen screen door squeaks as I take out the last trash bag of the day. Mable left early, so I've been on my own for the past few hours, which is just as well. I haven't been much of a conversationalist today.

Partly because it's Charity's birthday and I wanted to indulge in a private stroll down memory lane in my head. But mostly because I made my decision about NYU this morning and I'm not sure how I feel about it yet.

I spent the past year struggling with my college plans because planning seemed pointless. Why bother plotting out the future when everything about life can change in an instant?

But life is going to happen to me no matter what. *Not* planning won't keep the future from coming. So I may as well try—or better yet, hope—for something my heart wants.

So I have a plan now. And it scares the crap out of me. But it also makes me feel alive.

I hear tires on gravel at the front of the inn and then a door slam. Levi's truck. I'd know the sound of his truck anywhere.

I throw the trash bag into the Dumpster just as he rounds the corner, looking worn-out and sweaty, but in that good kind of way.

The way that feels liberating and strong and helps you sleep soundly at night.

"Hey," he says.

"Hey," I say back, noticing he's got a football tucked under his arm. "Where've you been?"

"Uh, practice."

I lift my brows. "Football practice?"

"Yeah."

"Oh. Wow. Good. Okay. Good." I sound dumbfounded. I am.

He laughs. "I was surprised too. Zack kind of roped me into it."

"Good for him." I hold my hands out and he tosses me the ball. "Whoa," I say, catching it and turning it in my palms. "I haven't held one of these babies in a long time."

"Do you feel powerful?"

"Like a god. Go long."

He blinks at me and smiles. "*Go long?*"

"Yeah. Go. Long." I wind my arm up to throw and wait for him to back up.

He shrugs and takes like four steps backward.

"Seriously?" I say. "Don't insult me."

He lifts his hands in apology and takes a few more steps back. "Far be it from me to insult a god."

"Keep going." I wave him farther and farther away until we're standing a decent distance apart in the lavender field. Then I throw a perfect arc to him.

"Damn, girl." He catches the ball with a smile. "Who taught you how to throw?"

I shrug. "Some hotshot quarterback I knew in high school."

He throws the ball back to me. "He sounds wildly talented—and extremely good-looking."

"Meh." I catch the ball. "He was okay. He was a decent ball-player but an awful artist. The boy couldn't draw a stick figure to save his life." I grin and throw the ball back.

He catches it with one hand. "Stick figures are overrated."

"So are quarterbacks."

He shakes his head with a smile and sends it flying back to me. I catch it.

"Charity's birthday is today," he says.

I wasn't sure if either of us was going to bring that fact up. But now that it's here, out in the open, it's...nice. It doesn't feel sorrowful. Just true.

I throw the ball back to him. "I know. She would be turning twenty."

He catches it. "Yep. And probably be getting herself arrested."

He throws it back. I catch. "Or thrown out of a bar."

I throw. He catches. "Or running away to Vegas to get married."

Throw. Catch. "Or all of the above."

He laughs. "Yeah, probably all of the above."

We stand there, two thousand lavender flowers between us in the setting sun, smiling at the memory of our favorite person, and it doesn't hurt. Not at all.

"Hey, Pix?" Levi holds the ball still and looks at me. "I've missed you."

I smile. "I've missed you too, Leaves."

50

LEVI

Charity's birthday is almost over.

I settle into bed and stare at the ceiling. Two minutes later, my bedroom door opens to Pixie's silhouette.

Without a word, and by the moonlight shining into my room, she makes her way to my bed and crawls in next to me. She tucks her body up against my side and places her head in the crook of my shoulder and her hand on my chest.

My heart feels funny and I don't know what to do, but I know I don't want to let go. So I wrap my arm around her and pull her close, resting my cheek against her head like we're kids again and no tragedy has marred us.

Charity's not here, but Pixie is. And that makes everything okay.

Not perfect, but okay.

I pull a sheet over us and, with my arms around the best piece of the worst thing that ever happened to me, I close my eyes and fall asleep.

51

PIXIE

*L*evi's steady heart pulses against my ear, and I'm completely surrounded by his body heat. His room is dark and quiet as I draw in a slow, deep breath.

God, I've missed him. His strength. His friendship. So much so that I could cry right now. I didn't realize how much I needed this—needed HIM—until right this moment. I nuzzle my face against the soft cotton of his T-shirt where it's safe and warm and smells like the boy who makes up all my memories.

52

LEVI

Three days and hundreds of plays later, I'm sweaty and exhausted and more alive than I've felt in months. God, it feels good to do something I'm good at and have a purpose outside of the inn.

I didn't mean to keep coming to practice, but Coach kept asking and my stupid mouth kept saying yes. So here I am again, after three hours of grueling workouts and running plays, sweating my ass off as we wrap up the day. And I love it.

I bullshit with the guys for a little while before heading home. Another storm is moving in as I drive along. I can tell from the dark purple hue of the clouds and the violent shades of orange in the sunset sky that this one will be big and powerful.

By the time I park, rain is coming down in buckets and the parking lot is a giant puddle of mud. I splash my way to the back door by the kitchen—not the front door since I know Eva hates it when I track in mud—and let myself inside as the purple clouds turn to gray and hide the sunset completely. The outside world is a dark mess of wind and rain as the kitchen lights flicker on and off. I wipe my feet on the mat and head down the back corridor, running smack into Pixie.

Her curves press against my soaking-wet body and mold to me with heat as she looks up through startled eyelashes.

"Sorry," I quickly say, stepping back from her in the tight space. The front of her white T-shirt is completely wet and sticking to her breasts in a way that's making my body ache and want to do bad things.

"No problem." She licks her lips.

More bad things fill my head.

"Practice again?" she asks as she takes in my wet state.

"Yeah." I look over her paint-stained shirt and the smudges of gray on her cheek. "Are you painting?"

"Yeah, a little. Storms make for great painting weather."

I nod. "I remember. You used to say that all the time, always dashing home to paint before the rain let up." I swallow, because maybe that was too revealing of just how much I know and remember about her.

"Oh. Yeah. I did." She licks her lips again.

I need to get the hell away from her before I start licking her lips as well.

I clear my throat and shift past her. "Sorry, again, for running into you." When I'm free and clear of her wet boobs and glistening lips, I hurry upstairs to the bathroom. After showering off the day's workout, I shut myself in my room and stare at the blank page on my computer screen for a long time.

One essay on winning. I can do this.

I stare at the screen. Nothing.

I absently open my in-box and, sure enough, there is a response from my parents. Actually, there are four responses—all group e-mails.

I start to read.

From: Mark Andrews
To: Levi Andrews; Linda Andrews
Subject: RE: College

Levi,

First of all, please be nice to your mother. She was reaching out to you because she cares about you.

Second, our concern for you—while it may be a little late—is sincere. You're our son, and we love you more than we could ever express.

But third, and most important, WE DO NOT BLAME YOU AT ALL for Charity's death. And we never have. Not for a moment. What happened to Charity was a horrible accident, and your mother and I were nothing short of blessed that you weren't killed as well. If we have made you feel guilty, in any way, for Charity's death, then we have failed you.

It was wrong and selfish of us to leave you like we did. You were a young man in college, and I guess I assumed that meant you knew how to heal on your own. But considering I myself didn't know how to heal, that was rather dumb reasoning on my part. And no excuse, whatsoever.

We should have stayed together, as a family. Please forgive me.

Dad

From: Linda Andrews
To: Levi Andrews; Mark Andrews
Subject: RE: College

Levi,

Oh, honey! We don't blame you at all for what happened to Charity. I feel just awful that you thought that for even a second. And I'm so sorry for leaving you like I did.

I just didn't know how to be around you and your father without feeling complete sadness at all the reminders of Charity, and that was wrong of me. I am so sorry. And I can't believe I let this much time go by without seeing or speaking to you. I have failed you in so many ways.

And Sarah! Oh my Lord, I didn't even think about Sarah. That poor thing was just left in the dust by us too. Oh, Mark—how could we have let this happen?

Clearly, I've made some terrible mistakes as a mother, and I don't know how to undo them. Please forgive me for leaving. I'm so sorry. I love you, sweetie. So much.

Mom

From: Mark Andrews
To: Levi Andrews; Linda Andrews
Subject: RE: College

Linda,

Obviously we have some mistakes we need to work out concerning Levi, and Sarah also. Maybe we should talk on the phone? Do you still have my new number? I only check my e-mail on Tuesdays.

Mark

From: Linda Andrews
To: Levi Andrews; Mark Andrews
Subject: RE: College

Mark,

    I agree. A good long phone conversation is overdue. Yes, I have your number still. I'll give you a call later this week.

                          Linda

I sit back and gape at the screen. Well. Okay. My parents are talking—maybe even on the phone. This is good. This is a start.

I bite the inside of my cheek. Leaving me was careless of my parents. But they didn't stop loving me. And who am I to judge them when I abandoned Pixie in the same way?

My life fell apart, a shambles everywhere, and the only thing left standing was Pixie. And then I left her. God, I still can't believe I did that.

With a deep breath, I reply.

From: Levi Andrews
To: Linda Andrews; Mark Andrews
Subject: RE: College

Mom and Dad,

    I think we all might have a lot of guilt and blame we need to let go of. Charity's death was hard for us all. Even though I don't understand your leaving, I forgive you guys. We're just human. And it's not like I've been a model son this past year, but I want to fix that. Maybe we could all talk on the phone one of these days?

Levi

P.S. Sarah is doing okay. She misses you guys.

I click Send and feel something I haven't felt in a long time. Hope.

53

PIXIE

I stare at the tube of red paint as the storm outside rages on. There's something inside me, something untamed and fearless, that wants nothing more than to run out into the night and feel the storm on my skin, the rain in my hair, the thunder in my bones.

Which is exactly why this is perfect painting weather.

I haven't painted with colors since last summer. For no reason other than I just wasn't feeling…colorful. But these past few days, something has been growing inside me. Coming to life. Waking up with demands. And I couldn't ignore it any longer.

So I dusted off the many unopened boxes in my room and tore through them until I found my colored paints. Then I threw on some Florence + the Machine at full volume, and now here I am, standing before this blank canvas with no idea what I want to paint.

I look down at the tube again.

Red. It's such a statement. Passionate. Unavoidable.

I turn the bottle over and squeeze a drop onto my palette. There it is. Red.

Now I just need to dip my brush in it and—oh, what the hell.

I turn my hand over and squirt a handful of paint into my

palm and smear it against the canvas. It looks harsh and unwelcome against the smooth white. Like a blemish. The corner of my mouth turns up as I squirt more red into my hands and start to spread the crimson every which direction until the canvas is no longer a blank square, but a collection of red movement.

Once the red is emptied, I grab a blue bottle and fill my hands with the color of peace and calm, wiping it alongside the red.

Then green. Life. Beginning. Healing.

Then yellow. Happiness.

Purple. Hope.

Colors fill my eyes until I can't imagine anything without them. My heart is on fire, like it's been frozen for so long and has just now started melting into this blaze of … God, *life*.

I pull colors through my hands as lightning flashes and thunder booms. It's madness outside, madness inside. And it's beautiful.

And then I hear Levi's TV turn on.

54

LEVI

I watch TV and try not to think about what the girl next door is wearing as she paints away—which I know she's doing because Florence + the Machine is blasting through the wall, and that is most definitely her painting music.

Three pounds sound on my wall.

"Turn it down!" she yells.

I turn the volume up two notches.

More pounding. "Turn it down!"

"Shh! I can't hear my show over all your pounding!" I shout.

"Aaaagh!"

Victory is mine.

As I go back to my show, the wind howls outside and I frown at my window. I just know my day is going to be full of yard cleanup tomorrow.

The power suddenly goes out and I clench my jaw.

Pixie.

In a storm? Really?

Stomping out of my room, I go down the hall and throw open her door, more amused than angry, but still.

Two things surprise me.

One—the innocent look on Pixie's face in the gray light from the mostly hidden moon outside.

Two—she's wearing nothing.

Well, not nothing exactly. She has on a see-through tank top and a pair of panties that leave little to the imagination. But she may as well be wearing nothing because all I see standing before me is a naked Pixie, covered in paint.

"What the HELL are you doing?" She's pissed, and manages to look a little embarrassed by her outfit, which confuses me. "What makes you think you can just keep barging in here?"

I scoff. "Maybe the same thing that makes you think you can just blow the fuse whenever the hell you please."

"I didn't blow the fuse!"

"Next time, just threaten the fuse thing and I'll turn the goddamn TV down to save myself a trip outside."

She takes a step forward so now she's standing right in front of me. "I didn't. Blow. The fuse."

Lightning flashes into the room, and a loud clap of thunder shakes the window. That's when I realize the storm knocked out the power. Not Pixie.

Well, shit. Now I feel like an idiot.

She stares at me in the foggy light, and her expression slips into one of . . . well, want.

I should leave. Right now. I really should.

But Pixie's eyes are on mine, and she's so damn close to my body that I can't seem to do anything other than stare at her with want and need and desire and every other hell-born pleasure known to man.

But I'm not going to kiss her.

I'm not.

If I kiss her, there's no going back. If I kiss her, I'll touch her. And if I touch her, then I'll forever kill any other guy who tries to touch her and then I'll be royally screwed.

But my head and my heart and my body all want the same thing—and when the hell has that ever happened before?

This is Pixie.

I shouldn't want her. I don't deserve her. I shouldn't... I don't...

55

PIXIE

*L*evi is looking at me with nothing but hunger, and I've never wanted to feed anything so desperately.

My chest is in front of his, breathing. Inhale. Exhale. Life in. Life out.

My hands run with all the colors of the rainbow, dripping onto the floorboards and my bare feet and legs as I stand before him.

Lightning strikes, brightening the room for an instant, flashing against our faces with urgency. I see the hesitation in his eyes, the fight between need and guilt, the fight both he and I have been losing for a year.

I hesitantly move closer.

Closer.

Then I give in to the untamed thing inside my soul and kiss him.

I'm against him with my body, pressed to his mouth with my lips and molded to his skin with my hands. I want him. No, I need him, and he needs me. Not just in desire, but in life and healing. And here we are, under the sound of rain against the window, the fields. Alive.

He kisses me back, and there's nothing between us anymore. Sadness and pain and loss and regret still exist, but they swim around us, unable to break through the wall we built decades ago. With friendship. With love.

His mouth moves against mine as he wraps his hands around my body, holding me steady, setting me free. My lips part and his tongue sweeps inside, pulling hot breaths from my chest as our tongues meet and mend.

I grip his shoulders, trying to climb up his body so I can sink into him. His hands lock on to my waist and his fingers slip under the raised hem of my shirt, pressing into my back. I can feel each pad of his fingers, like small flames branding fingerprints into my hips, my spine, my bare skin.

I lift up on my tiptoes as our kissing becomes desperate and breathy, shoving my hands into his hair and feeling it run through my fingers for the first time. It's intimate, the feel of his hair gliding between my fingers.

His hands run under my shirt and around the sensitive skin of my belly. I whimper into his mouth as every muscle in my body is clenching beneath his touch. I want to arch my back. I want to climb inside him.

His mouth moves to my throat, where he barely sets his lips against my windpipe. Not kissing. Not licking. Just breathing. And God, I'm melting.

My body is wet and wanting, and I want to cry almost as much as I want to howl. I tip my head back and gasp as his tongue slowly burns against the vulnerable skin there.

I cup his face and pull his mouth back to mine so I can kiss and grab and hold every piece of him. His scruffy jaw sits in my palms as I devour him, and I love the sensation of his rough stubble against my soft skin. Burning me. Marking me.

He picks me up and moves us to the bed, where I'm soon

on my back and rolling my hips up to meet him. We pull at each other's clothes and skin and hair until he's only in his jeans and I'm only in my panties. I'm out of breath and wild inside. I feel like an animal and a goddess at the same time, tearing into him with my tongue and my nails and not getting enough. Not nearly enough.

His hand runs up the inside of my thigh to right where I need him, and my eyes flutter. Guttural sounds fall from my mouth, and he growls—he *growls*—in appreciative response. God. I want him to growl more.

I run my paint-covered hands all over his body as his mouth travels to my chest. He pulls his head up and stares down at my scar in the stormy moonlight, and my body tenses.

I'm afraid he's going to change his mind and stop touching me. But instead, he slowly leans back down and presses a soft kiss to the top of the scar.

"I'm so sorry," he whispers. He places another soft kiss just below the first, his lips featherlight as they brush against the red mark. "I'm so sorry you wear this."

I skim my hands up his back and into his hair, stroking the strands as gently as he's kissing my scar and loving that his lips—*Levi's* lips—aren't afraid to touch my brokenness. "I'm not."

He looks up from under his dark lashes, his mouth still against my damaged skin.

"My scar reminds me of my hero," I say.

At first, I think he's going to refute my words. But quick as lightning, his mouth is back on mine, kissing me like he needs me. And I need him right back.

His back is too broad for me to get a good grip on him, but I sink my fingers into his shoulder blades anyway, grasping at his hot, slick skin as he kisses down my jaw and over my chest. He sucks on my nipple, and I'm pretty sure I would scream if I wasn't so busy trying to catch my breath. He suckles and cups my other breast as I arch into him and yank him tighter to me before he moves his mouth down to the sensitive skin of my lower stomach and pulls my panties off.

His hands, his mouth, his everything, work against me, finding wetness, finding the only part of my body that can leave me empty of everything but primal need, and then his mouth is between my legs.

Not touching me, just breathing—which is crazy arousing. Hot, deliberate exhales tickle the sensitive flesh spread out for him, and it's all I can do not to scream and cry and wail in desire. I shove my hands in his hair and grip his head as his tongue slips from his mouth and slowly licks a trail up the crease where my hip meets my thigh and back down to the most southern skin of my belly. And then slowly, so slowly I think I might die, his warm, wet tongue gently strokes the very center of me with three soft caresses.

Holy hell. Sweet Jesus in heaven. Son of a biscuit eater. I'm in heaven.

Figuratively. Literally.

Heaven.

His tongue rolls over me twice more, and I cry out and fall apart and lose my mind under the blinding and brilliant sensation of his mouth. My thighs tremble violently as I arch my back and claw at the sheets. I don't know where I am or what my name is or how to breathe, but who the hell cares about minor details like breathing?

Levi Andrews just undid my whole world. With his tongue.

"Condom," he says breathlessly.

I force my eyes open. "What?" Is someone talking to me? Who DARES to interrupt my bliss?

"Condom," he repeats.

"Oh. Yeah," I say. "Good idea. Uh…" My brain doesn't work. My brain doesn't work. "My purse!" Brain working now. "My purse." I point to where it sits on the floor.

He shimmies off the bed and starts digging through my bag. "Why do you have so many condoms in here?" He pulls one out and rips it open.

"Because my best friend travels like a porn star," I say absently, my muscles flexing with needy bliss.

Did I just call Jenna my best friend?

Levi climbs back on the bed. "Remind me to ask you about that later."

"Absolutely," I say, my body still quaking. "We'll have that conversation right after our conversation about knocking on Pixie's door before entering her bedroom."

He puts the condom on and smiles. By the time he's hovering over me again, I'm pulling at his large body, trying to bring him into me like my vagina is starved and dying. On his elbows above me and with his body up against mine, he stops and stares down at me. Terrified. Nervous.

I shift my hips and whisper, "Please."

"You sure?"

"God, yes. Yes, yes, yes—"

He pushes into me and I howl like a werewolf. Seriously. It's that kind of doglike sound that comes out of my mouth. But I don't care because Levi is inside of me and I feel complete.

He slowly pulls out, eases back in, and I moan impatiently. I don't want slow.

I'm pulling at him, slapping at his back for more, for faster, and he just smiles at me, driving me crazy with slowness and gentleness.

I whisper, "Pleasepleaseplease—"

And then he shoves inside me, deep and full, and starts pumping away just like I need. He rocks out of me, then back in, until I'm once again on the verge of barking at the moon. I'm clawing at his back, breathing out moans and breathing in spearmint and safety and friendship and hope and healing.

Lightning strikes, and the room fills with thunder and blue light.

Yes.

Rain beats down on the window. The lavender field outside.

God, yes.

He groans and I whimper and we move against each other, two shadows merged into one against the flashing storm outside the window. Nothing has ever felt so right as Levi's body inside me, his arms around me, and his mouth against me.

He works me to the brink of heavenly bliss again, and I come apart again, losing my mind, and probably my voice, as he thrusts into me one last time.

Lightning. Thunder. Panting. Racing hearts. Rain.

Love.

———

I wake up in Levi's arms, morning sunlight glowing in from the window and lighting our bodies. I'm draped over his chest, my naked body rising and falling with each of his deep, even breaths. His skin is soft beneath my cheek and warm against my hands.

Everything before this moment seems like limbo, like I forgot who I was. Like without Charity and Levi to anchor me, I was cast into nothingness, all alone. Lost.

But here, in the warmth of Levi's arms, I'm me again. Free. Brave. Flawed. Loved.

I want to cling to him for dear life, afraid that if he lets go, I'll get lost again. I don't want to be lost. I don't want to be anything other than what I am right now.

I look him over. A line of bright blue is smeared across his pecs, and a dash of green paints his jaw. I lift up slightly and gaze down at his body. Bright strokes of red and yellow, blue and purple, mark here and there. Evidence of my paint-stained hands on his skin. I look at my stained hands and then at my own body, finding more vivid colors slashed against my hips and chest and arms.

Green and blue strokes smear across the bedsheets, and a splotch of yellow runs along the shell of his ear. A smile plays on my lips as I trace a green finger across a blue stroke on his collarbone. We're a complete mess. A perfect, colorful, naked mess.

Naked.

Oh God. My scar.

Sure he saw it last night, but this is the light of day. This is undeniable reality.

I start to slip out of the warm bed so I can search for a shirt or scarf or something, but Levi's fingers wrap around my wrist before I can make my escape.

I quickly position my free arm over my chest in an awkward attempt at covering up my damaged skin. Not my boobs, however. Those babies are just hanging out in the open like they're trying to get a tan or something.

"Where are you going?" He opens his sleepy eyes and looks up at me.

My room! The bathroom! A pet store! All better answers than what actually comes out of my mouth.

"Boob tan."

"Boob tan?" He starts to smile, but his eyes drop to my chest and his smile fades. "Pixie," he says softly. "Move your arm."

I make a face.

He slowly pries my arm from my chest, and now my scar is just there. In between us, under the sun and highlighted in blue.

I hold my breath.

He moves his fingers up my arm and traces them gently over my elbow, up along my shoulder, and back down my scar. The touch is so careful and unburdened I could cry.

"You're beautiful," he says, his eyes roving over my naked body. For the first time, no part of me wishes to hide from him. Not my scar, not my body, not my heart, my dreams, my fears. Nothing. I want to be completely seen by him and known by him and loved by him and—

My heart starts to race.

I love him.

Oh my God. I love him.

I mean, I've always loved him. But I just realized I love him in the mushy gushy kind of way. The irrevocable way. The true way. The way that changes you forever.

And I'm suddenly scared out of my mind.

"I have to go," I say, quickly moving off the bed.

I wrap myself in a sheet and look around at the paint stains on the floor and the walls. Crap. We're in my room. It's hard to flee gracefully and without question from your own room.

I twitch my lips. "I mean, *you* have to go."

"What?" He sits up with a furrowed brow.

"You have to go," I repeat, looking just beyond him so I don't meet his eyes. My gaze lands on a red handprint on my headboard and my heart twists.

"Pix, what's wrong—"

"Fine, I'll go!" I throw a hand up and stomp out my door like a true drama queen. I don't look back. I don't blink. I just shut myself in the bathroom across the hall and stare at the blue dots on the wallpaper until everything goes blurry.

Love—real love—that's going all in. That's putting everything at stake. But I can't lose him again. We've barely recovered our friendship, and this—whatever *this* is—could backfire and steal him away from me forever. And what's going to happen when summer ends and school starts and life gets real? Oh God, oh God.

Things need to go back to being normal. Platonic. Friendly. Sexless.

God, did I really have sex with Levi last night?

I did.

Hot sex. Great sex. Real, honest-to-God, clawing-at-the-sheets-and-begging-for-more *sex*. And it was everything it was supposed to be. I wasn't distracted or caught up in my own head. I was a crazy lunatic who couldn't get close enough to Levi's skin and his mouth and his hands, and it was perfect. Powerful, stormy, perfect sex.

But never again. I can't afford to lose Levi, so I can't risk having him.

The blue dots grow even more blurry as my eyes fill completely.

56

LEVI

I tap my knuckles on the bathroom door. "Pix?" I hear her sniffle from within and my stomach drops. "Please let me in."

She opens the door but only halfway, looking up at me through hastily dried eyes as she clutches her bedsheet to her chest. "Leaves, hey," she says, like this is a perfectly normal conversation.

I pause. "Are you okay?"

"Yeah, I'm fine." She sniffles again.

I lean into the bathroom, occupying her space so she can see me, really see me, when I say, "What's wrong? Was it... was it last night?"

"No." She shakes her head. "No. Last night was perfect."

I scan her face, completely at a loss.

She looks at the floor and swallows before looking back up at me. "Remember when we were like eleven and twelve and you taught me how to fish? I thought fishing was disgusting, which it is, but you taught me how to bait a hook and cast a line and wait patiently for a bite? And we fished all afternoon but didn't catch a single thing? But we didn't care because we had fun all day joking about what it would be like to grow up and be famous and drive fancy cars and have butlers?"

I slowly nod.

She swallows again. "That's what I need from you, forever. Friendship."

"You have that."

"Do I?" She shakes her head. "Because I thought I had that when I was eleven, but then I lost you after Charity died, and I . . . I can't lose you again."

"You're not going to lose me."

"But I could."

"You won't."

"But I COULD." She overenunciates the last word with defiance in her eyes.

I lean back. "So what are you saying?"

"I'm saying." She inhales. "I'm saying that we need to be just friends. No complicated sex stuff or relationship stuff. It's too risky. We could lose each other. We could lose everything we've just barely started to repair." Her voice is incredibly steady despite the tear rolling down her face. She swipes it away.

A muscle flexes in my jaw. "You want to be just friends?"

She nods.

"Pix." I lean back in, closer this time. "We stopped being just friends before Charity died."

"Yeah, well." She shrugs with a jerk. "Maybe if we had stayed just friends I wouldn't have been trashed that night and I wouldn't have told Charity to drive drunk and—"

"Bullshit," I snap.

"I'm being serious."

"You're making excuses."

She says, "For what?"

"Hell if I know. You're standing there in a sheet covered in sex and blue paint, trying to tell me that we should be *just friends?*"

"Think about it! What if we jump into something and it all goes to hell, what then? No more friendship. No more us. No more…*anything.*" Her voice cracks. "I can't DO that, Levi. I can't." She shakes her head. "Please don't ask me to risk losing you again."

"You're not going to lose me—"

"Please?" she pleads as another tear falls.

I watch her in silence for a long time, half of me wanting to scream, the other half wanting to surrender completely and disappear forever.

"So you want to go back to being just friends." I nod and take a step back, my jaw still tight. "Like last night never happened."

I see pain flash in her eyes, but it's gone just as fast.

"Yes," she says quietly.

I blink, still baffled. But in the midst of all my bafflement and hurt and silent screaming, there's a part of me that gets what she's afraid of and shares in her fear.

"So can we do that?" she asks, waiting. "Can we be just friends?"

I take another step back and raise my hands in surrender.

57

PIXIE

*I*t was the right decision. It was. Levi and I don't need to add any more drama or complications to our lives anyway.

I take a shaky breath and knock on Jenna's door.

It was the right decision.

She answers with a surprised smile. "Hey. I didn't know you were coming by."

"I'm afraid of lizards," I blurt out.

She stares at me. "Okay..."

"And I hate eighties music. I truly do. I know it's blasphemous to say so, but there it is. I hate Van Halen and Billy Joel and Cyndi Lauper."

"Cyndi Lauper? Really?"

"And I'm afraid of losing people. Like abnormally terrified. And I'm scared out of my mind that you're going to die and it'll be just like Charity all over again and I'll never recover and I just can't—"

"Whoa. Slow down." She holds up a hand. "I'm not going to die, Sarah."

"But you could."

"Well...sure. We could all die." She shrugs. "But that's just reality. Come here." She pulls me into her apartment, drags me to the couch, and forces me to sit down. "Now, what is this really about?"

"Nothing. I'm just scared of you dying."

"So you suddenly decided to knock on my door and confess your distaste for Van Halen? Uh-uh. I don't think so." She squints her eyes. "Does this have something to do with Levi?"

"No."

"Sarah."

I huff. "Yes."

She looks at me sympathetically. "What happened?"

I not-so-briefly fill her in on all of the kissing and sexing and painting and crying of the last twenty-four hours—Jenna wanted every dirty detail and I had no qualms handing each one over to her—and for a moment, she just stares at me with her face twisted into a cross between utter confusion and extreme disappointment.

"So let me get this straight," she says, pressing a finger to her lips. "You had crazy-hot sex with Levi."

"Yes."

"And then you broke up with him."

"Yes."

"Because you love him?"

"Correct."

Jenna blinks. "I think we need to brush up on *good* reasons to break up with a guy."

I sigh, exasperated. "You don't get it."

"Oh, I *totally* get it. You're running away again."

"No, I'm not. I'm making a preventative choice because I'm scared of losing Levi."

"The same way you're scared of losing me?"

"Well . . . yeah."

"Coward."

I mock a look of hurt. "I am not a coward."

"Yeah, you are. Listen," she says. "It's okay to be afraid of lizards. It's really weird, but it's okay."

"They're like tiny, terrifying dinosaurs."

"And it's even okay to be ridiculously afraid of Disney's *Alice in Wonderland*—"

"It is a *really* creepy movie," I say defensively. "There were talking umbrella vultures and mean flower giants and hedgehog croquet balls—"

"But you can't be afraid to *love*." She looks at me seriously. "Love isn't safe and life isn't guaranteed. So yeah, I could die and you could lose Levi and your heart could hurt again, but that's just life. The only alternative—Sarah, look at me—the only alternative is living without fully loving anyone else. And that's not living at all."

I really hate that she's speaking to me like some wise old oracle.

And I really, *really* hate that she's right.

I slump against the couch and exhale. "I know."

She reaches for me with a tattooed arm and pulls me closer, squeezing my shoulder. "Don't be afraid to live, Pixie."

I still.

She cocks an eyebrow. "What? I called you Pixie. What are you going to do about it?"

I open my mouth. No one other than Charity, Ellen, and Levi have ever called me that, and Jenna calling me Pixie just feels . . . well . . .

Right.

It feels absolutely, incredibly, without a doubt right.

"Nothing," I say with a slow smile. "You should definitely call me Pixie."

She smiles back. "I'm glad you feel that way because I wasn't asking your permission."

I nod. We sit in silence.

"Hey, Jenna?" I say.

"Yeah, Pixie?"

"I want to let you in."

She smiles again. "I think you just did."

58

LEVI

*I*t's been a shitty day. In fact, every day since Pixie basically kicked me out of her life has been shitty. So when I hear the back door of the inn squeak and see Ellen come sauntering over to where I'm replacing a broken shutter on one of the inn's back windows, I curse under my breath.

"Hey," she says.

I don't look at her. "Hey."

Her focus snaps to something in the distance. "What in the world...?"

I turn around to see two figures, covered in dirt and sweat, staggering toward the inn's back door—*handcuffed* to each other.

One is a girl with long, muddy, blonde hair. And the other is...

"Daren?" Ellen takes a step forward as they near.

"Uh, hi." He smiles sheepishly and starts to wave with his cuffed hand, causing the girl's wrist to yank up with his.

She whips her arm down and hisses, "Use your other hand, asshole."

"What the *hell*...?" I stare, horrified, at Daren and point at his bound prisoner. "Did you *kidnap* this girl?"

"What?" He makes a face of disgust. "No! Hell, no. You think I *wanted* to be handcuffed to this girl?"

The girl rolls her eyes. "Oh, like I wanted to be leashed to *you*?"

"Will someone please explain what's going on?" Ellen looks around the lavender fields in confusion. "And where you guys came from?"

Daren says, "It's a long story."

"It's a stupid story," the girl corrects.

Daren glares at her. "Are you incapable of shutting up for even a second?"

"Oh, I'm sorry," she snaps back, raising their cuffed wrists. "You'll have to excuse my bad mood. I have a *douche bag* attached to me." She turns to us and holds out her free hand. "I'm Kayla, by the way."

"Ellen." Ellen slowly shakes her hand, glancing between the two of them.

Kayla cuts her eyes back to Daren. "See how I used my *non*-cuffed hand to do that? It's not rocket science."

"Yes, well." Daren smirks. "We've already established that you're an expert on handcuffs."

Kayla glowers at him. "I hate you."

"Ditto." He narrows his eyes at her before turning back to Ellen. "Is Angelo here?"

Ellen hesitates. "Uh, yeah…"

"Excellent. If anyone can get us out of these things, it'll be him. Come on." He pulls Kayla by the cuffs to the back door and inside the inn, while she mutters death threats and curse words at him.

For a moment, Ellen and I just stare at the closed back door.

"I don't like that guy," I say.

Still looking at the door, Ellen slowly nods. "But I think someone does." She sounds amused.

I curl my lip. "What, the prisoner girl?"

Ellen gives me an *oh please* look. "That girl is hardly a prisoner."

"Whatever." I shake my head and go back to fixing the shutter. Ellen watches me.

"So Pixie's leaving in just a few minutes," she says, after an awkward amount of time has passed. "She's driving up to Copper Springs to pick up some stuff from her mom's before heading back down to Phoenix."

Where she'll get on a plane and leave me forever.

"Yeah," I say. I pull the damaged shutter down and set it against the wall before picking up its replacement. "I know."

A gust of wind sweeps past, carrying the scent of rain and the promise of another storm. I don't know why I feel so hollow inside today. I haven't lost Pixie. We're still friends.

Positioning the new shutter, I grasp my hammer and begin to nail it into place.

We're friends.

Ellen eyes me. "Are you going to say good-bye?"

I grab another nail and hammer it in. "Probably not."

She slowly nods and studies the discarded shutter for a moment. "You know, one of these days I'm going to run out of things that need to be fixed around here and you're going to be out of a job."

I stop hammering and look at her. "Is that a threat?"

"No," she says, something unrecognizable in her eyes. "Just the honest truth."

With a brief smile, she turns and walks away.

59

PIXIE

I'm packing. I'm crying. I'm hoping Levi will knock on my
door and say something, *any*thing. I'm packing.

I know he won't do it, just like I know I won't do it.

And I don't even really know why I'm crying, other than I feel
like I'm never going to see Levi again. Which is ridiculous. I'll see
him again.

I press a hand to my chest, where a sharp ache throbs with
each of my heartbeats. Loving someone and not being with them
hurts.

Thunder grumbles in the distance.

I look at the wall that separates my bedroom from Levi's. Did I
make the right decision?

The throbbing in my chest continues and I have to take a deep
breath to keep more tears from falling.

I blink. I swallow. I'm fine.

I look around my room. Boxes everywhere. Paint stains on my
headboard. Canvases of Charity in the window. More boxes.

Something green peeks out from beneath one of the dusty
boxes and I bend to retrieve it. It's the flag from our capture the flag
game last summer. I run the old faded material through my hands
and bite my lip.

Time.

It just goes.

And now I have to go with it.

This is the beginning of my future. Another tear rolls down my face and I swipe at it angrily as I shove the flag into my suitcase.

It's better this way. It really is. It's safer.

I yank off the painting shirt I have on and start to change into a clean tank top, but when I catch my reflection in my bedroom mirror, I pause.

I run a finger along my scar, tracing its jagged pattern with my eyes as the damaged-yet-healed skin meets my fingertips.

It's a best friend and a place to call home. It's a lesson learned and a reminder that life is fragile. It's my first taste of death and a second chance at life.

It's everything I never want to forget. And it's beautiful.

I'm glad I shared it with Levi.

I've made my decision and sure, my heart is broken, but it's the good kind of broken. The kind that leaves you branded, so you never forget, and heals over time, so you can see just how far you've come.

It's the best kind of broken.

I touch my scar again.

Like me.

60

LEVI

I stare at my computer screen as the sky outside darkens with the encroaching storm.

Pixie left twenty minutes ago. I know this only because I heard the wheels of her suitcase squeaking past my door. I didn't say good-bye.

A friend would have said good-bye.

She's off to New York, where she'll have a new life and new opportunities, and I'm sitting here in front of a blank computer screen with nothing to say.

This isn't how I thought things would go. This isn't how I wanted things to go. Even though I haven't technically lost anything, I feel incredibly defeated.

But the game isn't over yet.

I straighten my shoulders and crack my knuckles. One essay on winning. I can do this. I start to type.

As a football player, I know all about the principles of winning
and the strategies—

I delete and start over.

The great football coach, Vince Lombardi, once said, "We didn't lose the game; we just ran out of time." I've always appreciated this attitude because—

Delete.

I bite the inside of my cheek for a moment, staring at the wall as I think through what I want to write.

The new drywall over the hole I patched up hasn't been painted yet, so it remains a dark gray splotch against the otherwise beige wall. The hole seems like forever ago.

I look back at the screen and start to type. Slowly at first, then gaining momentum as I carry on. Forty minutes later, I stop typing, scan the document, and start rereading what I've put down so far.

HOW TO WIN

Winning is an effect of trying. You have to want it badly enough to go through pain, discipline, and failure to find it. To confront it. To claim it. But most of all, you have to fight for it. Everything else—anything else—is absolute surrender.

My eyes snap to the dark patch on my wall again as my heart grows loud and heavy in my ears. Without another thought, I click Send on my half-assed essay, grab my keys, and race out the door.

61

PIXIE

*T*he sky grows darker as I head south, the storm clouds closing in on the day and blanketing the earth below in a muted gray. After leaving Copper Springs, I decided to take Canary Road down toward Phoenix instead of the freeway. I haven't been on this road since the night of the accident. It looks the same.

It feels different.

I hear a sharp crack of thunder and see a flash of hot white lightning cut down through the purple clouds, touching the horizon not far from the road. Less than a minute passes before thick drops of rain begin to splash against the windshield.

Storms are supposed to be terrifying things, reckless and unpredictable, violent and wild, but they energize me. Remind me of life and love and the brink of happiness. The urgency of breathing in, the wonderment of jumping out with your eyes closed.

I think back to the stormy day in the little fort with Levi. The rain. The kiss. The love...

I quickly push the memory away.

The old back road winds through the forestland, barely visible now through the downpour and darkening day. The monsoon clouds split open and a sliver of sunlight shines through the torrent onto the road in front of me, an oddly bright ray of hope against the violent rain and thunder. The patch of light illuminates a large object blocking the road. It's coming up fast. Too close, too large, to ignore—and it's right beside the ridge burn, the exact same spot where Charity died.

I slow down as I near. My heart flies into my throat when I realize it's Levi's truck, blocking the storm-ridden road.

And in front of the truck, under the gray deluge, is Leaves.

Blue eyes, waiting for me.

62

LEVI

*S*omehow I knew I'd find Pixie here. Not on the freeway. Not on the commonly used back roads. But on Canary Road.

She pulls over to the side, and I'm at her door before she comes to a full stop. I yank it open and stare down into wide green eyes.

"No," I say, loud enough to be heard over the roaring wind and rain.

She blinks. "No?"

"No, we can't be just friends." Rain drips down my face as my heart hammers against my rib cage. "Because we're more than just friends, and we always have been. And I'm not talking about sex, Pix. I'm talking about trust and comfort. I'm talking about *home*." Lightning strikes nearby and the wind picks up. I raise my voice. "You are not my friend, Pixie. You are a piece of my heart and a part of who I want to be."

She gets out of the car and stands in the rain. "But, Leaves—"

"I love you," I yell, thunder echoing my words, rain drenching my clothes. "I love you when you're Pixie and when you're Sarah and when you're messy and when you drive me crazy and when you scare the hell out of me. *I love you*, Pixie. And I know you're scared." I step closer so I no longer have to shout, and cup her wet face. I look into her eyes. "But you have nothing to be afraid of. I will never leave you again. Never."

Hot tears run from her eyes, mixing with the cool rain as I run my thumb over her cheek. "So you can move to New York or fly across the world, but I want to be there too. Wherever you are. By your side. Always," I say. "Because I'm yours. Even when you don't want me, I'm yours."

She puts her hands on my cheeks and halts my speech, looking into my eyes as rain beats down on us. Then she crushes her lips to mine.

I kiss her deeply, still cupping her wet face as I pull her close to me, not wanting to let go, not wanting another minute in this life of mine to pass without her here, with me.

"God, I love you," she says in between kisses, and the words fill me like nothing ever has before. She smiles against my mouth. "By the way? I'm not going to New York," she says. "I never was."

I pull back slightly and scan her face, my heart pounding. "But you left."

She nods. "I went home to get a box of my stuff from my mom's, but I was heading down to Phoenix to move back into the dorms with Jenna so I can return to ASU this fall. I declined NYU's acceptance a few weeks ago."

"But...why?"

"Because I realized that this is my home. Arizona. Ellen." She trails her eyes along the lines of my face. "*You*." She looks up at me. "I didn't want to leave. Even if I didn't have you, I wanted to be where you were. Because I'm yours." A playful smile pulls at her lips. "Even if you don't want me..."

I slowly smile. "Oh...I want you."

"Yeah?" she says, over a roll of thunder.

"Oh yeah."

Then I'm kissing her all over again. Pixie—beautiful, wild Pixie—is mine. I'm more alive than I've ever been.

63

PIXIE

*R*ain pours down from the heavy clouds above, washing over us as Levi pulls me into his arms.

Here, on this wicked road where so much was lost and even more was found, we kiss to the sound of rain. Falling on the scarred earth. Falling on this place of tragedy. Washing away all the painful things and drenching the beautiful things left standing.

And lightning strikes.

EPILOGUE

I can't believe I let you paint on me, Pixie." Jenna rubs her cheek where I've painted a sun devil in maroon and gold. "I feel like my skin is dying."

"I think it looks cute," Ellen says, smiling.

The three of us are seated in Sun Devil Stadium, high up in the stands overlooking the brightly lit football field below and waiting for the game to begin. I'm wearing one of Levi's old jerseys and have my own sun devil painted on my cheek.

"Cute and sticky," Jenna says.

"It's called school spirit," I say as a few crazy blonde curls fall into my face. "We're here to support Levi and Zack."

"Um, *hello*? We're already giving Zack plenty of support." Jenna gestures to Marvin, who's chewing on my shoelace. "I don't know why you even brought his goat up here."

Ellen wrinkles her nose. "Me neither."

I shrug. "You know Marvin is a yeller. I couldn't leave him in the parking lot. Besides, I promised Zack I'd keep a close eye on him."

Ellen frowns. "I thought Zack was only supposed to have his little goat pet until the end of summer. It's November."

I scoff. "Well, the girl who talked him into goat-sitting for the summer went off to Argentina and decided to vacation there, permanently. So Zack is now a goat daddy."

"Goat daddy. Ew," Jenna says. "The images running through my head right now are very disturbing." She gasps. "Marvin! Get away from my boots or I swear to all the goat daddy gods—"

"Pixie!" says a cheery voice.

I turn to see Linda Andrews squeezing her way through the crowd to come sit with us. Mark is right behind her. They call me Pixie now, just like pretty much everyone else in my life. I love it.

"Hi, guys." I smile and give them both long hugs. I love how Linda Andrews smells. And I love that she and Mark moved back to Copper Springs two months ago. I get to see them every other weekend when Levi and I go back home.

Their marriage still needs a lot of work, according to them, but they're living under the same roof and participating in Levi's—and my—life as much as possible. So that's progress.

"I see you got roped into goat duty," Mark says, scratching Marvin behind the ears. Mark complains about Marvin, but I think he secretly likes him.

"You and Levi are coming home for Thanksgiving, right, dear?" Linda asks with bright eyes. She loves holidays, and she's been desperate to get a family holiday thrown together since she and Mark moved back to Arizona.

I smile. "I wouldn't miss it for the world."

"And you too, Ellen and Jenna," she says, looking across the bench at the two of them. "The more the merrier."

Jenna yanks her purse out of Marvin's reach and grits her teeth. "I wish I could, but I'll be busy slaughtering a goat."

Ellen turns to Linda. "I'd love to come."

Mark stands up and starts cheering as the players run out to the field. The rest of us follow suit and holler along with him.

The game begins and we sit down, all on the edge of our seats. I find Levi's number and follow him with my eyes. Dean Maxwell readmitted him to ASU shortly after receiving Levi's essay, which worked out perfectly since I started the art program at ASU this fall.

For the past few months, Levi's been training like crazy for football and I've been spending more time painting, in color. And of course we've been pretty much inseparable—which is exactly how it always should have been.

He's my best friend, and I'm his.

Levi sends a perfect throw down the field, and I cheer. I love watching him play. And I love cheering him on. And I love the way he always searches the crowd for me and smiles when he finds me. Like right now.

I watch his eyes scan the fans…up and down stadium seats… searching…

He finds me and a large grin stretches out his face. He always looks so relieved to see me in the stands, watching him. I don't know what he's worried about. I'm not going anywhere.

Because I'm his.

And he has me.

Levi's eyes rove over the rest of our clan, and his face lights up. On the far end is Mark, smiling at his son with pride. Then Linda, who always gets teary eyed when she watches Levi play. Then me, with my sun devil face paint and giant jersey that says ANDREWS in big bold letters. At my feet is Marvin, who is once again chewing on my shoe. I tug my foot away and Marvin goat-cries—loudly—but the crowd drowns out the sound. Next to me is Ellen, who has her arm linked through mine. And last is Jenna, with her high-heeled boots and her rock-star makeup, always keeping me in line and believing in our friendship.

I see the joy in Levi's eyes as he looks up at us and I share the feeling.

This is life. This is what we have. We can mourn over the broken pieces or we can cling to what's left.

And we're clinging like hell.

BONUS DELETED SCENE

Dear Reader,

Thank you so much for reading *Best Kind of Broken*! I can't tell you how thrilled I am to get to see this novel in bookstores. I wrote it nearly four years ago, so it's incredible to finally be handing it over to you, my beautiful readers!

I originally wrote *Best Kind of Broken* as a 30,000-word novella, but my amazing agent, Suzie Townsend, encouraged me to develop it into a full-length novel, and wow! I love it a hundred times more now than I ever did before.

My original *plan* was to write an opposites-attract romantic comedy about two college kids who fall in love while working at a retirement community over the summer. What I ended up with was a romantic dramedy about two childhood friends, torn apart by tragedy, who learn to love—and to heal—each other and themselves while working at a cozy little Arizona inn. Crazy how some things just don't go according to "plan" at all, right?

Crazy wonderful!

Because after three long years of sitting on Levi and Pixie's sweet little story, I finally get to see it in print! And YOU fabulous readers get to read an extra deleted scene!

In chapter seventeen, Pixie remembers Charity making catcalls at the football team and Levi teaching her how to throw a football. It's a brief memory, no more than a few paragraphs, but it originally had much more content—and was written from Levi's point of view.

This deleted scene is Levi's recollection of those same events, but with behind-the-scenes stuff Pixie didn't know about. It gives you a glimpse into what it was like for Levi trying to protect Charity and Pixie from all the scumbag boys in school. Guys constantly taunted him about his attractive sister and her beautiful best friend, and Levi had to ride a fine line between possessiveness and protectiveness to keep the bad boys away—and Charity and Pixie didn't even have a clue.

Thank you, once again, for reading *Best Kind of Broken*. This is my dream come true and you're the most important part of it. I LOVE YOUR GUTS!

Happy reading!

LEVI

$\mathcal{I}$ usually enjoyed football practice after school. But on the days when Charity and Pixie would sit in the stands and watch, I hated it.

They had to stay because I was their ride home, but that didn't mean they had to sit in the goddamn bleachers the entire practice. I suggested, on several occasions, that they occupy their after-school hours elsewhere. Like the library. Or the girls' bathroom. Just any place void of sexually charged males.

But Charity was stubborn and dragged Pixie up those bleachers every single day. It wouldn't have been a problem for me if every guy on the team hadn't been such a pervert. Especially Kenton.

Josh Kenton was a complete jackass and so full of shit I could smell him a mile away. He was a self-proclaimed V-card collector, which I thought was kind of twisted. What kind of guy gets off on seducing virgins? A jackass, that's who. I never understood why so many girls let him weasel his way into their pants. But he would say or do just about anything to convince a girl he was a good guy. And I mean anything.

The asshole actually proposed to a girl once, just to get her to have sex with him—which she did. In the backseat of his car. In the parking lot of a Wendy's. She was just as much to blame as him, though, since he'd only taken her on two "dates," and the "engage-ment" ring he gave her was one of those plastic things you get out of the quarter machines at the grocery store, but still. He proposed to her, promised to marry her and have kids with her, and then took her virginity and never spoke to her again. So he was a total dirtbag.

But I never really cared one way or the other about Kenton and his douche-bag ways—until Charity and Pixie started hanging out at football practice, and Kenton turned his V-card collecting atten-tion their way.

I felt responsible for Charity and Pixie; for keeping them safe; for protecting them from loser guys and the rest of the world in general. It started in junior high, when every friend of mine sud-denly realized that Charity was a *girl*. And not just any girl, a pretty girl. They would drool over her and stare too long in the hallways. It was harmless, really, but I knew what guys thought about and I hated the idea of my sister starring in any of their twisted fantasies. So I made it clear that she was off-limits and kept an eye on my out to make sure she stayed that way.

But Pixie was a different story.

She wasn't my sister so I didn't have a reason to warn my friends off, or a way to keep them from telling me what they'd like to do with her. It was hell. It was a horrible, soul-raking hell and, for the most part, I had no choice but to keep my mouth shut.

But then high school came around and Charity and Pixie turned into young women. And I experienced a whole new level of hell—one wrought with rage and jealousy that I hadn't known existed. I could no longer fend off the dogs with just a warning glare or knock to the gut. I had to endure the locker room jokes and nonstop razzing.

Most of the guys at school respected me enough not to cross any lines when it came to Charity and Pix. But not Kenton. He liked how much it irked me to hear him talk about them.

It started with crude comments here and there, just busting my balls because he could, but it quickly morphed into a sick goading.

And then one day at practice, Charity started making catcalls from the bleachers and Kenton took that as an open invitation to drive me to the edge of insanity.

Charity was always a flirt, making my desperate desire to protect her that much more difficult, but catcalls at my football team? I wanted to throttle her.

The first time she did it, I simply ignored her. Her lewd cooing echoed down the stands and onto the field where my teammates and I lined up for practice, and everyone turned their eyes to her—except me.

Kenton's lips curled into a crooked smile. "Sounds like little sis wants it pretty bad." He sucked in through his teeth. "I wouldn't mind having a go at that sweet ass."

I shot my eyes to him, fully aware that everyone else on the team was watching my reaction. It's a delicate thing, reacting to provocation. If you overreact, you give the provoker power and make yourself look weak. If you underreact, you give the impression that the target of their provocation isn't important and therefore fair game. I glowered at Kenton and kept my gaze locked on his until he finally looked away.

We ran a few plays before it happened again.

The second time Charity whistled, I shot *her* a warning glare and made sure my eyes traveled over to Pixie as well. Charity was wild and impossible to control, but Pixie was reasonable. I knew she would understand that catcalling my teammates was a sure way to piss me off.

Kenton *tsk*ed under his breath. "Damn, Andrews. She sounds horny as hell. Someone should probably go up there and give her what she wants. Hard."

I whipped my eyes to him.

"Hard and rough," he jeered, making a grunting noise to drive his point home.

I growled. "Shut up, Kenton."

We lined up for another play and, being the quarterback, I waited for the ball to be hiked to me. Kenton's eyes shone with amusement and taunting amusement as they locked on mine.

"On second thought," he said loud enough for the nearby players to hear, "I hear your little sis isn't a virgin anymore, so I probably shouldn't waste my time. The blonde one though…" His eyes slid up to the stands where Pixie sat smiling with her golden curls cascading around her face. "Oh yeah. She's definitely pure. And she looks like she'd be a fun one to taint." He made a disgusting noise of appreciation, and something inside my chest crackled.

Kenton talking about Charity pissed me off in an annoying way. But hearing him talk about Pixie infuriated me in a way that woke something beastly inside me.

I called the play and the ball snapped back just as Charity let out another catcall. I caught the football in a rage and immediately turned around and threw it right for the stands.

I aimed at a spot just beyond Charity and Pixie, knowing the ball wouldn't hit either of them. It flew through the air and nailed my target, scaring the shit out of the girls but giving me a momentary sense of satisfaction. They looked at me in horror, but I didn't give a damn. Charity needed to shut up.

Coach yelled and called me in, yanking me by the helmet as he shouted out his disapproval. Spit flew off his words and into my face but I didn't hear a thing he said. My eyes were too busy following Kenton as he gave me a smug smile.

Thrusting me back, Coach ordered me to switch positions with another teammate before having us line up again. I glanced at the stands.

Pixie had her head hung a bit, looking at me in half anger and half regret while Charity sat fuming beside her. She had received the message, loud and clear, and was now glaring at me with hate and embarrassment. Good. I didn't care if she hated me forever. I couldn't have guys like Kenton thinking she was something she wasn't.

With my new scrimmage position, I now faced off directly across from Kenton.

He slid his eyes back to Pixie. "I like blondes, you know. They're sluttier than the others." He grinned at her through his helmet. "I think she'll be my next V-card. I bet she feels really good. Nice and tight and hot."

A low growl burned in my chest as the hike count went out.

His eyes came to mine and an evil smile curled up his mouth. "I bet she'd moan and beg for more. I bet she'd whimper as I shoved into her—"

The ball snapped and I rammed my body into his shoulder with all the force I had, knocking him to the ground with all the rage inside me and pinning him there with both my weight and my eyes.

With a low voice I said, "Stay the fuck away from Pixie." Then I pulled myself up and stretched my neck as I walked away.

"Andrews!" Coach screamed. "What the hell was that? You just dislocated Kenton's shoulder!"

I lifted my chin but didn't look back. "Good."

The rest of practice was pretty tense. Kenton had to go see the sports medicine guy and Coach made me sit on the bench to "cool off" for forty-five minutes, but I didn't feel bad at all. Because Charity and Pixie were safely in the stands and no one was making catcalls or telling me how they were going to make Pixie whimper.

After practice ended, I had every intention of marching up to the girls and chewing Charity out. But when I saw them at the far end of the field, throwing the ball I'd tossed at them earlier, all my anger melted away. They were both horrible throwers and even worse at catching. But they were having a blast, laughing as they played.

I inhaled deeply as I watched. Loving someone is terrifying. You can't always protect them or be there. You can only try your hardest to show them how valuable they are and hope for the best.

Charity missed a catch and the football bounced over to my feet. I glanced down.

Shaking my head, I looked up at Charity. "I'm ashamed to call you family."

She grinned. "Because I was whistling at your friends' cute butts?"

I felt a flame of rage tease the back of my mind and quickly snuffed it out as I picked up the ball.

"That too." I nodded. "But ducking every time a football comes at you? That's unacceptable. It's not going to bite you. And *you*." I pointed at Pixie. "Why are you using two hands? You're throwing like a moron." She smiled and I had to move my eyes away to keep from smiling back. "Come here, both of you." They walked over to me. "This"—I pointedly looked at Charity, then at Pixie—"is how you throw a football." Stepping a few steps back, I pulled my arm back and tossed the football in a perfect arc to Charity.

She flinched and jumped out of the way as the ball hit the grass. I sighed. "Are you kidding me?"

"Oh come on, Leaves." She laughed. "You can't really blame me. I don't want to get hurt—and that thing is all pointy and dangerous."

I raised my eyebrows. "Dangerou—ugh. Never mind. Pixie." I looked at her. "Your turn."

Her green eyes sparkled playfully. "You know I'm just going to wimp out the same way Charity did."

"I did not wimp out." Charity crossed her arms and muttered, "Traitor."

I smiled at Pixie. "No you won't. You're tough. And you know I would never let the ball hurt you."

Her expression remained playful but something in her eyes deepened. She stepped back. "Okay. Go for it."

I threw the ball to her as softly as possible. She didn't catch it, but she also didn't shy away from it. It bounced off her reaching hands and rolled to the ground.

"Good job." I said.

"Good job?" She picked up the ball and shook her head. "I totally missed it."

I shrugged. "At least you tried."

Our eyes locked and her face flashed with pride. She smiled like my approval meant the world to her, and in that moment, I knew I'd dislocate a thousand more shoulders if it meant keeping her safe. From anything.

Kayla Turner has lost everything. So when her late father leaves her an inheritance, she breathes a sigh of relief—until she learns the inheritance comes with strings...in the form of handsome playboy Daren Ackwood.

Sometimes when perfect falls apart, a little trouble fixes everything...

Please see the next page for a preview of

Perfect Kind of Trouble.

I

KAYLA

On the other side of the casket, a middle-aged woman wearing a navy blue dress glares at me.

The man in the wooden box has only been dead for three days and this woman already has me pegged as the slutty mistress he kept on the side. I'm probably an ex-stripper with a coke problem as well, based on the way she's sizing me up. But this isn't my first rodeo—or my first funeral—and deadly looks like the one Navy Nancy is angling at me are nothing new, unfortunately.

Now feeling a little self-conscious, I slowly slide my black sunglasses on and tip my head down, concentrating on the casket in front of me as the preacher/priest/certified-online minister drones on about peace and eternity.

It's a nice casket, made of polished cherrywood with decorative iron handles and rounded edges. I should care more than I do about the deceased man within, but all I can think about is how that casket probably cost more than any car I've ever been in, and how the man inside is probably tucked against velvet walls lined with Egyptian cotton.

And now I'm angry. Great.

I promised myself I wouldn't be angry today. Bitter? Sure. That was a given. But not angry.

Taking a deep breath, I raise my head and try to avert my attention. Behind my dark shades, I glance around the cemetery. More people showed up than I had expected, most of them looking like they're sweet and respectable. I wonder how well they knew James Turner. Were they friends of his? Coworkers? Lovers? Folks around here probably show up at funerals regardless of their relationship with the deceased. That's the thing about small towns; everyone cares about everyone else—or at least acts like they do.

"James was a good man," the minister says, "who lived a solid life and has now gone on to a better place…"

A roll of thunder sounds in the distance and I turn my eyes to the heavy gray clouds above. The weatherman said it's supposed to rain tonight. They'll bury James, cover his casket with dirt, and rain will fall and seal him into the earth. What an ideal passing.

Screw him.

A woman beside the minister begins to sing "Amazing Grace" as the pallbearers lower him into the grave. Across the way, a teenage boy openly gawks at me, his eyes gliding up and down my body like I'm standing here naked instead of fully clothed. I'm wearing a knee-length, long-sleeved, turtlenecked gray dress, in *July* no less. I'm ridiculously covered, not that Navy Nancy and Gawking Gary care.

When the boy catches me watching him, he quickly looks away and his face burns bright red. I turn away as well and play with the bracelet on my wrist as I focus my attention on the back of the crowd.

A huddle of women dab at their eyes with handkerchiefs. Beside them, a young family stands quietly with their hands clasped together. Nearby, an older couple mouths the words to "Amazing Grace" as the singer starts on the third verse. Looking around, I realize everyone else is singing along as well. *Of course* the people of Copper Springs would know the third verse of "Amazing Grace."

I really need to get out of here. I don't belong in this tiny town. I never have. One last obligation tomorrow then I'm gone.

In the far back of the congregation, a guy moves out from under a large oak tree and I tilt my head. He looks vaguely familiar but I can't quite place him.

He's average height, with dark brown hair, and a dark purple button-down shirt covers his broad shoulders. The long sleeves of his shirt are rolled up to his elbows and he's got on a pair of dark jeans to match the dark sunglasses that cover his eyes. Dark, dark, dark.

He's attractive. Dangerously attractive. The kind of attractive that can suck you into a sweet haze and undo you completely before you even know you've surrendered. I know I've seen him before but for the life of me I can't remember where, which is probably a good thing.

The singer wraps up the fourth verse of "Amazingly Depressing Grace," and a long silence follows before the minister clears his throat. He glances at me and I subtly nod. With a few last words about what a *wonderful* man James Turner was, he concludes the funeral and I let out a quiet breath of relief.

The end.

People disperse, most of them heading to their cars while the rest pass by the lowered casket and throw a handful of dirt or a flower onto the shiny cherrywood top. I step to the side, sunglasses strictly in place, and watch the mourners. Navy Nancy glares at me again and I look away. Wow. She really must think I'm some sort of James Turner hussy.

As offended as I am, I know she's probably just hurting. She was the first person to arrive at the funeral today and she teared up several times during the ceremony so I'm assuming she and James were pretty close. And if judging me makes her feel better on this sad day, then I'll let her hate me all she wants. I watch her leave the cemetery with a small group of other mourners. It's not like I'll ever see her again, anyway.

The guy in the purple shirt steps up to the grave and drops a handful of red dirt on the casket. The red stands out against the brown dirt beneath it and I wonder what its significance is. Then I wonder about the guy in purple. He doesn't seem to be here with anyone else, which is only strange because of how good-looking he is. Hot guys don't usually travel places without an equally hot girl on their arm. But this guy is definitely alone.

He strides to the parking lot and climbs into a black sports car, and all my wondering comes to an abrupt halt. I no longer care about who he is, or how he knew James, or why he looks familiar. Spoiled rich boys are the last thing I care about.

When everyone has left the area except the funeral home people, I carefully walk up to the casket. The heels of my black pumps slowly sink into the soft grass as I stare down at the last I'll ever see of James Turner. I try to muster up some sort of sadness, but all I come up with is more anger.

With a long inhale, I toss a soft white rose petal onto the brown and red dirt, and quietly say, "Rest in peace, Daddy."

2

DAREN

*S*ome people don't name their vehicles. Most people, probably. But there's something about a black Porsche that just makes you want to call it...Monique.

I climb inside my sports car, close the door, and look through the windshield at the dark clouds. Looks like Monique might need a bath tomorrow. My eyes fall back to the cemetery and my chest tightens. I still can't believe Old Man Turner is gone.

When I was thirteen, my life took a sharp turn to the shitty side of the street and Turner offered me a job mowing his lawn for fifteen dollars a week. A year went by before he asked me to start taking care of his garden as well, then gave me a raise. Shortly after, I was taking care of his entire yard and did so until last year when he requested that I focus my energy on my "real" jobs.

I didn't know he had cancer at the time. Hell, I didn't even know he was sick until he passed away. We lost touch for only a few months, but apparently, during that time Turner fought a short and intense battle with cancer and lost.

And I didn't even have a clue until last week.

My gut coils as I think about the day I found out—and all the days after—and I let out a heavy exhale. This past week has not been my finest. And now I'm at the funeral of the only man I ever really considered a father. I didn't even get a chance to tell him good-bye.

I inhale, slow and steady, and I crack my knuckles. It's just been a shitty few years, all around.

Through the windshield, my eyes catch on a gray dress walking away from the casket with hips swinging and blonde hair swishing. I almost didn't recognize Kayla Turner behind those black sunglasses and that cold look she had on. But looking at her now, there's no mistaking.

She used to visit her dad in the summer, so every once in a while I'd catch glimpses of her inside the house while I was out mowing the lawn. And there are some faces you just don't forget.

Back then, she was all elbows and knees and freckles. But damn if Kayla Turner didn't grow up to be a total knockout. There wasn't a breathing soul in the cemetery today that didn't openly gape at her. I thought the kid in the front row was going to choke on his own drool, the way he was drinking her in.

I'm surprised she bothered to show up. She stopped coming around a few years ago and I saw how it tore Old Man Turner up. He missed her fiercely, but that didn't bring her back.

It's nice of her to finally visit again. Too bad she waited until her father's funeral to grace him with her presence.

With a clenched jaw, I start the engine, back out of my spot, and pull out of the parking lot. Monique purrs as I drive away from the cemetery and I want to purr right along with her. Cruising down the road eases the pressure in my chest and I feel like I can breathe again. I put the convertible top down and suck in a lungful of fresh air. Much better.

A distant roll of thunder echoes around. I pass a large gated community and a sour taste slips down my throat. Westlake Estates. The place I lived when life was good.

Well, not good exactly. But easier.

Turning onto the road that leads out of town, I head for work. I have two part-time jobs: one at the cell phone store in Copper Springs and one as a stock boy at the Willow Inn Bed & Breakfast outside of town. My job at Willow Inn is the only one I actually like, though.

Willow Inn is fifty miles south of town, in the middle of nowhere off the freeway, but I make the drive every week because of my awesome boss. Ellen owns and operates the quaint little inn and, in her spare time, she's a guardian angel.

Glancing at the time, I realize I have to be at Willow Inn in an hour and it takes at least that long to get there. Shit. And Monique is low on gas. Double shit.

With a muttered curse, I pull into the nearest gas station—a run-down fill-up place that looks closed except for the blinking neon sign that reads O_EN—and pull up next to a grime-coated gas pump before turning off the engine.

Getting out, I count the money in my pocket with a groan before shoving it back inside. As I start to fill Monique up, my phone beeps and I glance down to see another missed call from Eddie.

Eddie Perkins is the closest thing Copper Springs has to a professional lawyer, and lately he's been the bane of my existence. He's left me eight voice mails in the past week, none of which I've bothered listening to because I'm sure they're all about my dad. But ignoring him doesn't seem to be working.

Stepping away from the car, I listen to the most recent voice mail.

"Hello, Daren. It's Eddie again. I'm not sure if you've received my

previous messages but I've been trying to reach you regarding James Turner. As I'm sure you know, he's passed away. A reading of his will is scheduled for tomorrow at 11:00 a.m. at my office, and Mr. Turner's last wishes specifically request that you be present. Hopefully, I'll see you there. If not, still give me a call so we can discuss . . . the other thing."

The message ends and I stare at my phone. Why in the world would Turner want me at the reading of his will?

Unless . . .

A thought hits me and it's almost too ridiculous to grasp.

Could this be about the baseball cards? Would Turner have remembered something from so long ago?

A small smile tugs at my lips.

Yes. He absolutely would have. That's just the kind of guy he was.

When I was thirteen, my dad gave me a set of collectable baseball cards for Christmas. I remember that Christmas clearly. It was the same Christmas that our housekeeper, Marcella, gave me a copy of the book *Holes*. It's about a boy who digs seemingly pointless holes as a punishment for something he didn't even do wrong. I was obsessed with the book; I must have read it ten times, and talked about it every day.

My mother and father barely paid attention to my interests. I doubt they ever even knew I'd read a single book, let alone one in particular over and over. But Marcella knew. She always made a point to care about the things I cared about. "You are my favorite boy, *mijo*," she would say.

She always called me *mijo*.

Son.

That Christmas, she'd wrapped the book in a green box with a red ribbon. I remember because that was the same box I decided to keep my collectable baseball cards in.

I brought the box to Turner's house one day to show off my new cards and proudly informed him that I had looked up the value of each one and knew I could sell the lot for at least a hundred dollars. Money was important to me back then. Money was all that mattered. My dad taught me that.

But later that day while I was mowing his lawn, Turner took my box of cards because, according to him, I was "too spoiled to appreciate them."

He was right, of course, but at the time I didn't care. I was furious, convinced he was going to sell the cards himself so he could have the money. But because I was just as spoiled as he'd claimed, I only stayed mad until my father bought me more baseball cards a few days later.

That's how things worked in my family: My parents bought me whatever I wanted, whenever I wanted, as long as I stayed out of their hair. I was an only child and I'm pretty sure I was a mistake. If my parents had *planned* to have me I'm sure they would have put a little more effort into... well, me. But I was an accident and, therefore, an inconvenience. An inconvenience easily soothed with a few new toys.

When I announced to Turner that I no longer cared about my stolen box of baseball cards, he laughed and said, "Someday you might." Then he promised that, someday, he'd return them to me.

I stare at my cell phone where the voice mail screen blinks back at me. Maybe this is Turner's way of coming through on that promise, after death.

The pressure starts to wind its way around my chest again,

thick and tight, and I feel the air seep from my lungs. I can't believe he's gone. Really gone.

A clanging noise startles my thoughts and I whip around to see a tow truck backed up to Monique and hauling her onto its bed. My eyes widen in horror.

"Hey!" I shout at the overweight truck driver, who's got a toothpick in his mouth and a handlebar mustache. "What are you doing?"

He barely glances at me. "Taking her in. Repo."

"Repo?" I start to panic. "No, no. There must be some mistake. A year's worth of payments were made on that car. I still have until next month."

He hands me a crumpled statement stained with greasy fingerprints and an unidentifiable smudge of brown. "Not according to the bank."

I quickly scan the paper. "Shit." I was sure those payments were good through August. I rub a hand over my mouth and try to clear my head. "Listen," I say, trying to stay calm as I appeal to the driver. "We can work this out. What do I need to do to get you to unhook my innocent car?"

He looks bored. "You got four months of payments on you?"

"Uh, no. But I have..." I pull out the contents of my pocket. "Forty-two dollars, a broken watch, and some red dirt."

A few grains of the dirt slip through my fingers and I think about all the weekends I spent taking care of Turner's yard. The lawn was healthy and the garden was abundant, but Turner's favorite part of the yard was the rose garden. I could tell that he was especially fond of his white roses, so I cared for those thorny flowers like they were helpless babies, and Turner wasn't shy about praising me for it. Every Saturday, I'd rake through the rare red topsoil Turner planted around his precious roses, making sure the bushes could breathe and grow. I pricked my fingers more times than I can count, but those roses never withered, and for that I was always proud. I think Old Man Turner was proud of my work too.

The tow truck guy shrugs. "No cash, no car. Sorry." He starts to lift Monique off the ground and I swear it's like watching someone kidnap a loved one.

"Wait—wait!" I hold up a hand. "I can get it. I can get you the money. I just—I just need a little time."

"Talk to the bank."

I quickly shake my head. "No, you see. I can't talk to the bank because the bank hates me—"

"Gee, I wonder why." He doesn't look at me.

"But I can get the money!" I gesture to Monique. "Just put my baby back down and you and I can go get a beer and talk this whole thing out." I flash a smile. "What do you say?"

He scoffs. "You pretty boys are all the same. Used to getting whatever you want with Daddy's money and pitching fits when someone takes your toys away." He shakes his head and climbs back into the tow truck. "See ya."

"But that's my ride!" I yell, throwing my arms up. "How am I supposed to get home?"

He starts the engine and flicks the toothpick to the other side of his mouth. "You should've thought of all that before you stopped making payments." Then he pulls out of the gas station with sweet Monique as his captive and I watch the last piece of my *other* life slowly disappear.

Motherfu—

"Sir?"

I spin around to see a scrawny gas attendant wiping his hands on a rag.

"What," I snap, frustrated at everything that's gone wrong in my existence.

"You gotta pay for that," he says.

I make a face. "For what?"

He nods at the pump. "For the gas."

"The ga—" I see the gas nozzle dangling from where poor Monique was ripped away and I want to scream. "Oh, come on, man! My car was basically just hijacked! I wasn't paying attention to how much *gas* I was using."

He shrugs. "Don't matter. Gas is gas. That'll be eighty-seven dollars."

"Eighty-se—" I clench my jaw. "I don't have eighty-seven dollars."

He scratches the back of his head. "Well I can't let you leave until you pay."

I scrub a hand down my face, trying to contain the many curse words that want to vault from my mouth. With a very calm and controlled voice I say, "Then do you have a manager I can speak to about settling this issue?"

He tips his head toward the small gas station store. "My sister."

Through the store's front window, I see a young woman with curly red hair at the register and a smile stretches across my face.

"Perfect," I say.

As I head for the entrance, a few drops of rain fall to the ground, plopping on the dirty concrete by my shoes. I look up at the dark clouds, fat with the oncoming storm and frown. I really don't want to walk home in the rain.

A string of gaudy bells slaps against the station door and chimes as I enter the store, and the sister looks up from a crossword puzzle. Her name tag reads WENDY. I file that information away.

Roving her eyes over me, her face immediately softens. "Why, hello there," she says in a voice I know is lower than her natural one. "Can I help you?"

I give her my very best helpless-boy grin and sigh dramatically. "I certainly hope so, Wendy."

Her eyes brighten at the sound of her name on my lips. Girls love it when you say their name. They melt over it. It's like a secret password that instantly grants you their trust.

She leans forward with a smitten grin and I know I've already charmed my way out of an eighty-seven-dollar gas bill. And maybe even found a ride home.

"Me too," she says eagerly.

I smile.

Sometimes it pays to be me.

Jenna Lacombe needs control—whether it's in the streets, or between the sheets. But the infuriatingly sexy Jack Oliver is starting to strip away her defenses. When Jack's secrets put them both in harm's way, Jenna must figure out how far she's willing to let love in...and how much she already has.

Please see the next page for a preview of

Right Kind of Wrong.

I

JENNA

*L*ook at you. Being all in love like a grown-up. I'm so proud," I say, smiling at my best friend, Pixie, as we carry boxes into our joint dorm room. "And Levi," I add, turning to address Pixie's hot new piece of arm candy, "you're welcome."

He sets a box down. "Am I now?"

I nod. "If it weren't for me telling Pixie to suck up her fears and just let herself love you, you'd still be a miserable handyman."

"I am still a handyman."

"Ah, but you're no longer a *miserable* one." I grin. "Thanks to me."

He pulls Pixie into his arms and kisses her temple. "Then I guess I should thank you."

As they start kissing, my phone rings and I'm relieved for an excuse to leave them to all their lovebirding.

I slip out into the hall and close the door before answering my cell.

"Hello?"

"Hi, Jenna." The sound of my mom's voice makes me smile. "How's my baby?"

"I'm good," I say. "Pixie and I are almost all moved in. She came down here with her boyfriend tonight so we were able to get mostly unpacked. I just have a few more boxes left at the apartment, but I'm going to pick those up later. How are you?"

She pauses. "Well *I'm* okay."

It's the way she emphasizes the "I'm" that tells me exactly what this phone call is about.

"Grandma?" I sigh in exasperation. "Again?"

"I'm afraid so. She says she can feel the end coming close."

I sigh. "Mom. She's been saying she's dying for ten years and she's never even had a cough."

"I know, but she seems serious this time," Mom says.

Every few years or so, my grandmother announces to the family that she's going to kick the bucket at any given moment. The first two times it happened, I immediately flew back to New Orleans—where she lives with my mother and younger sisters in the house I grew up in—to be by her side, only to find Granny alive and well without so much as a sniffle. The last time it happened, I took a few days to get organized before flying back to New Orleans, where I found my "dying" grandmother singing karaoke at a local bar.

So as you can imagine, I'm not falling for her silly shenanigans this time.

"No way," I say. "I'm not spending my hard-earned money to fly out there again just so Grandma can get on my case about love and fate while belting out a verse of 'Black Velvet.' Tell her that I'll come visit when she has a doctor's note stating that she's at death's door."

"Oh, Jenna. Don't be so dramatic. I swear you're just as bad as your grandmother."

"I know," I say, in mock frustration. "And it's getting hard to compete for the title of Family Drama Queen with Granny declaring her impending death every two years. Could you tell her to just give it up already and let me be the shining star?"

I can hear the disapproval in my mother's voice. "That's not funny, Jenna."

"Sure it is." I smile. "And Grandma would agree."

"Please be serious about this," she says.

"I'll be serious about Grandma's death when she gets serious about dying," I quip.

A weary sigh feathers through the line. "Jenna, please."

"Why do we keep pandering to her, anyway? The only reason she keeps crying death is because she knows we'll all come running to her karaoke-singing side to hold her hand as she passes—which she never does. Why do we keep playing her game?"

"Because she's very superstitious and believes dying without the blessing of her family members is bad luck for the afterlife. You know that."

Now it's my turn to sigh.

I do know that. All too well. Since I was a child, the deep roots of Grandma's superstitions have wrapped their gnarled fingers around my family's every move. If her voodoo notions weren't so eerily accurate and, well, creepy, maybe we'd be able to ignore the old woman's ways.

But unfortunately, Grams has a tendency to correctly predict future events and know exactly what someone's intentions or motivations are just by shaking their hand. It's downright spooky. And I swear the old woman uses our fear of her psychic powers as a tool of manipulation.

Case in point? Her recurring death threats.

"Yeah, yeah," I murmur. "She deserves a pleasant send-off. I know."

I hear my mother inhale through her nose. "She does. But even if that weren't the case, your grandmother isn't feeling well and she'd like to see you. Again." When I don't say anything she adds, "And wouldn't you feel horrible if she was right this time and you missed your chance to say good-bye?"

The guilt card. A nasty tool all mothers use on their children.

"Fine," I say. "But I'm not shelling out the cash to fly there. I'll drive this time."

"All the way from Tempe to New Orleans?"

"Yes. And I will save big money doing it," I say. "I'll get my shifts covered at work and leave in the morning."

"Excellent. Your grandmother will be so happy."

I scoff. "Happy enough for karaoke, no doubt."

She clears her throat. "I'll see you here in a few days then. Love you."

"Love you too." I hang up the phone and head back into the dorm room to find Levi and Pixie making out against the wall.

"God. Seriously, you two?" I make a face. "I know you just got together in the middle of the road a few hours ago, but come on! There are other people here."

Levi doesn't seem to notice me as he continues kissing Pixie's face off, and Pixie takes her sweet time pulling back from her lover-boy before acknowledging my presence.

She shoots me a hazy smile and nods at my phone. "Who was that?"

"My mom." I exhale. "Grandma claims she's dying."

"Again?" She bites her lip.

I nod. "So I'm going to drive out there this week and try to be home before school starts."

She pulls away from Levi, just slightly, but it's enough for him to stop smelling her hair—which I swear he was just doing. They're so in love it's almost gross.

"By yourself?" Pixie's green eyes widen.

Pixie and I met last year, at the start of our freshman year at Arizona State University when we were assigned the same dorm and became roommates. When school let out for the summer and Pixie and I could no longer live in the dorms, we split up. She moved to her aunt's inn up north—where she fell in love with Levi—while I moved into a local apartment with three of my cousins. It was a good setup, for the summer, but I'm happy to be moving back in with my bestie.

She and I are both art students—she's a painter and I'm a sculptor—so we have a ton in common and get along perfectly. She's the closest friend I've ever had, so I try my hardest to take the concern on her face seriously.

"Yep." I put my phone away. "By myself."

Levi reluctantly steps away from his girlfriend and busies himself by unpacking some of Pixie's things.

She frowns. "That doesn't sound like fun. Or very safe."

Levi glances at me. It's one of those big-brother protective glances and I have to bite back a smile. Aw...look at this guy. He barely knows me, but he's still worried about my safety. For the hundredth time, I silently rejoice that he and Pixie got together. She deserves a good guy who looks out for both her and her friends. A guy like that would drive me crazy. But he's perfect for Pixie.

"I'll be fine," I say to both Pixie's big eyes and Levi's concerned glance as I wave them off and grab my purse. "But I have to stop by work and then my cousins' apartment for the last of my boxes. I'll be gone a while, so you two can get back to smooching against the wall or whatever." I wink at Pixie. "See ya."

"See ya," she says with a concerned smile as I exit the room.

Jumping in my car, I quickly head to the Thirsty Coyote, where I work as a bartender. It's a decent job for a college student. Good hours. Good money. And it suits me. Pouring drinks isn't my dream job or anything, but it gets me one step closer to finishing school and opening my own art gallery—which *is* my dream job.

I let myself inside and head to the back. It's just past dinnertime so the place is packed and I have to squeeze through the crowd just to reach the bar. When I get there, I lean in and call out to my coworker.

"Cody!"

He turns around and smiles at me. "What's happening, Jenna? Thought you had the night off."

"I do. But I need to get some shifts covered this week so I thought I'd come in and sweet-talk my favorite bartender..." I bat my lashes, knowing full well Cody isn't attracted to me at all. But he's still a sucker for making money, and more bar shifts means more money.

He grins. "I'm listening..."

I whip out my schedule and show him all the days I'd need him to cover. He agrees like the superhero that he is and heads to the back to make it official in the schedule log.

I wait at the counter, thinking about how long my drive to New Orleans will take if I leave tomorrow. Probably at least twenty hours. Ugh. Pixie was right. It really isn't going to be any fun.

My eyes drift over the crowd and fall on a tall figure in the corner. Gunmetal-gray eyes. Tousled black hair. Tattooed arms and broad shoulders. My body immediately goes on alert.

Jack Oliver.

It's not surprising he's here. He comes to the bar all the time, but usually he's with his friends and in a good mood. Right now, though, he's talking on the phone and seems very upset. His gray eyes are narrow slits and his jaw is clenched. But I'm not going to lie. Angry looks good on him.

At over six feet tall, with his broad shoulders and endless tattoos, Jack looks intimidating. But really he's a big softie. I hardly ever see him in a mood other than happy. So this angry version of Jack is a new experience for me. A very hot experience.

He catches me looking at him and tips his chin. His anger dissipates for a brief second as a lopsided smile hitches up the corner of his mouth, but then he turns his attention back to his phone and clenches his fist before ending the call.

In-ter-est-ing.

He shoves his phone into his back pocket and heads my way.

"What's up?" I say. "You seem upset."

He shrugs. "Nothing. Just family shit."

I snort. "God. Yes. I have plenty of that."

He nods and our eyes lock and hold.

One beat.

Two.

I hate this part of our friendship; the part that reminds me of what happened between us last year when we got drunk and carried away one very steamy night. The memory shouldn't still turn me on like it does. But Jack and those gray eyes of his—eyes rimmed with pale green and flecked with dark flints, looking almost silver at times—are hard not to respond to.

We never talk about it, which is better, but in moments like this, when his eyes are on mine with such command, I can almost feel his hands back on my body. Fingertips running the length of my skin. Palms brushing my curves—

"Here you go." Cody returns with the schedule book for me to sign and I silently bless the interruption.

No good comes from me reminiscing about Jack's hands. Or any of his other body parts.

"I switched our shifts and marked you down as *on vacation*," Cody says.

"Thanks," I say, taking the book and initialing by my traded shifts.

"Hey, Jack." Cody nods at him. "What can I get you to drink?"

"Just a beer," Jack says, sitting in the barstool next to me. He's so close I can smell his shampoo. It's a wooded scent, like sawdust and pine, and it plays at my memories in a way that makes my heart pound.

He looks at me. "So where are you going on vacation?" His warm breath skitters over my shoulder and sends a jolt of hot want through my veins.

Damn him.

On second thought, damn *me* for being such a swooner.

I'm not usually like this. I swear it. Guys are the last thing I give priority to in my life. It goes: chocolate, tattoos, a hundred other things…and then men. Because a woman doesn't need a man to have a full life. And I'm living proof of that.

I keep my eyes on the book. "New Orleans to visit my grandma."

He nods. "Is she dying again?"

Even my friends know how ridiculous my grandmother's yearly death threats are.

"Yep." I pop the *p*. "The drama queen just won't hand the spotlight over gracefully."

He smirks. "Like you'd wait to be handed anything."

Jack and I met two years ago, when I first started working at the Thirsty Coyote and Jack was my trainer, but we became friends almost immediately and now he knows me well enough to know that I'm not very patient, and if I want something I usually just take it.

Cody sets Jack's beer down and asks me, "Are you flying out tonight?"

"Nah." I finish signing the book and hand it back to him. "I'm driving there so I'll leave in the morning."

Jack swings his head to me and a slight wrinkle forms between his eyes. "You're driving all the way to Louisiana?"

Jack and I are both from Louisiana. I'm from New Orleans and he's from a small town just north of there, called Little Vail. The fact that we grew up so close to one another, yet met on the other side of the country at this bar in Arizona, was one of the first things we bonded over. That, and tequila.

"Yeah. Pfft. I'm not spending hundreds of dollars on a last-minute plane ticket. Grandma needs to give me at least a month's warning next time she decides to keel over."

Jack takes a swig of his beer, but continues looking straight at me, displeased.

"What?" I snap.

He shrugs. "That's just a long trip to make on your own."

"Yeah, well. Good thing I don't mind driving." I look at Cody. "Thanks for covering for me. I owe you. Later, Jack." I turn to leave just as a drunk guy stumbles into me, knocking me back into Jack's chest.

Jack's hands instantly go to my hips, and my hips instantly want to yank his hands down my pants. My hips can't be trusted.

"Watch it," I say to the drunk guy, giving him a little shove forward so I have room to pull away from Jack.

Jack's fingers slowly slide off my hips, trailing down just before ending contact with my body, and my eyelids lower in want.

Clearly, I need to have sex. Not with Jack—that would be a disaster. But with someone. Soon. So I can sex Jack out of my system. Again.

I've been trying to sex away Jack a lot lately.

I blink up and find Jack's eyes watching mine. He saw my moment of weakness; that split second of desire. Dammit.

"Be careful, Jenn," he says in a low voice, and his words trickle down my skin.

Jack's the only person I've ever let call me "Jenn." Why? I have no idea. I blame his voice, all sexy and deep and brushing along the sensitive places of my ears.

Damn him, damn him, damn him.

"Right." I step back and act casual. "So I'm going to go. I'll see you when I get back. Later."

I spin around and weave through the crowd with a huff, feeling Jack's eyes on me the whole time.

2

JACK

*T*here are only two things I don't ever speak of. My crazy family and my history with Jenna. And both just fell in my lap.

I watch Jenna work her way to the front door and can't help the unease slipping through my veins. I don't like the idea of her going on such a long road trip by herself. She's independent and smart and I know she can take care of herself, but that doesn't lessen my concern any.

Her long dark hair is pulled back into a high ponytail revealing her golden eyes and high cheekbones. Her half-Creole heritage has kissed her skin with a permanent bronze, which only adds to her unique beauty as her shoulders, bare in the strapless shirt she's wearing, show off the numerous tattoos running the length of her arms. The intricate designs disappear beneath her clothes, where I know they continue to travel across other parts of her curvy body. She's beautiful and wild, and drives me absolutely crazy.

Her hips swing as she moves out the door and my gut tightens. If anything were to ever happen to her, if someone ever tried to hurt her, I . . . well I can't even think about it. Which is why I can't think about Jenna all alone in a car on a series of desolate freeways for three days.

I don't like it. I don't like it at all.

My friend Ethan plops down in the barstool next to me, reeking of cologne. "Hey, man."

"Hey," I say.

I've gone through a series of roommates this past year, but Ethan has been my favorite, so far, or at least the easiest to tolerate. He and I have been friends since I first moved to Arizona and, as very opposite as the two of us are, we get along pretty well.

"Was that Jenna I just saw leaving?" He nods at the door.

"Yep."

Ethan smirks. "What did you do to piss her off this time?"

I grin. I do have a way of getting under Jenna's skin. I can't help it. If she would just be a grown-up and address what happened between us last year then maybe I'd back down. But instead she acts like nothing ever went down and dammit, that's just insulting. Because she's not just some girl I hooked up with a while back. She's Jenna, for God's sake.

But she wants to pretend like we're nothing more than friends, so I go along with it. And occasionally I piss her off—because it's *something*. It's some sign that I matter more than she lets on.

"Surprisingly enough," I say, "I didn't do anything. This time."

Ethan shakes his head. "I don't know why you poke at her the way you do."

"Because it's funny." I shrug. "And it's not like she doesn't piss me off just as much, like when she goes off and sleeps with dickhead guys." I shift my beer mug around in a slow circle, one inch at a time. "When she knows she can do better."

"Yeeeah." Ethan purses his lips. "You care way too much about who Jenna sleeps with. That's not healthy, man."

I stifle a groan. "I know."

Ethan orders a drink from Cody while I stare into my beer. I really shouldn't care who Jenna sleeps with, especially since I'm no angel myself. But damn. I can't help it. I don't like her sharing her body with anyone else.

My phone rings again. I look at the caller ID and groan.

I've been fielding phone calls from my family members for a week now and it's grating on my nerves. Earlier, I was on the phone with my frantic mother, who was babbling about how concerned she is for my youngest brother, Drew. He's twenty and should be able to take care of himself by now, but apparently he's been acting shady lately and his behavior has my family on edge. Now Mom's flipping out and I'm running out of reassuring words.

I thought our last phone call would tide her over for a while, but now my other brother, Samson, is calling. Again.

Not a good sign.

I grudgingly take the call and snap, "What?"

"Easy, bro," says Samson. "I'm just the messenger."

"Yeah, well I'm getting sick of all your *messages*."

"What would you rather I do? Not call you? Let Drew go down on his own?"

I let out a frustrated sigh. "No."

"That's what I thought. Drew's in deep trouble this time, I can feel it. And Mom's losing her shit. I need you out here."

A year older than Drew and a year younger than me, Samson is the middle child, and the most laid-back. It takes a lot to stress him out, so the fact that he's been at my ear these past few days is a red flag in and of itself.

But as the oldest brother—and the only real male authority in my family—it's my job to keep everyone calm, cool, and collected. A task that's growing more difficult by the phone call.

"Not happening." I shake my head even though he can't see me. "I left for a reason, Samson. I'm not coming back."

His voice is strained like he's gritting his teeth. "And just what the hell am I supposed to do without you? You know I don't have the pull or the power that you do."

I run a hand through my hair. "Have Drew give me a call. I'll straighten him out."

"That's just the thing, man. Drew's missing."

My heart stops for a moment. "Mom didn't mention that."

"That's because she's in denial and refuses to accept that her baby boy is caught up in a mess. She thinks he's out roaming, but you and I know better."

Fuck.

I rub a hand over my mouth, trying not to panic. Or growl. This is exactly the shit I was trying to stay away from when I moved away from Little Vail, Louisiana, and toward Tempe, Arizona. And now here I am, getting dragged right back into it.

"Fine," I say, my decision made. "I'll come out there this week. Tell Mom to calm down, would you? Her freaking out will only make things worse."

"Got it. I'll see you later then."

"Yeah." I hang up and run a finger over my cold mug.

Drew is missing.

I knew something like this would happen, eventually. You can't play around with drug dealers and not get jacked down the road.

"You all right, dude?" Ethan asks as Cody sets his drink down.

"What? Yeah." I rub my mouth again. "I'm fine. Just family shit."

He takes a drink. "How come you never talk about your family?"

I stretch my neck. "Because there's nothing to say."

Actually there's a ton to say, but no one would want to hear it. And frankly, I like the life I've made for myself out here in Arizona. No baggage to weigh me down. No expectations lingering around me.

I pull up airfares on my phone and scroll through the prices with a grimace. Damn, it's expensive to fly. My eyes snap up as a thought hits me. Jenna's heading to New Orleans and I need to go to Little Vail, which is only two hours north and right on her way.

A slow smile spread across my face.

I might just have to tag along on Jenna's road trip.